Reboot:
A Cosmic Horror

D E McCluskey

D E McCluskey

Reboot: A Cosmic Horror
Copyright © 2022 by D E McCluskey

ISBN 978-1-914381-36-2

Dammaged Productions

www.dammaged.com

Reboot: A Cosmic Horror

For Everyone I worked with in NUVIA
(well, when I say work ...)
Peteo, Geoffo, Bongo, Smigger, Mikey-Moo, Marylin Munroe
Kevvo, Rafio, Jim, Matt, Dave Coss, Liam, Rodders,
The Moss Meister, Charlotte's Webb, Mr Bell,
Danno, Stu, Nibbler, Christoff,
Jay, Nick, Jonno, Phil, and, of course, Shazbatz

TRIGGER WARNINGS:

If any of these trigger you then DON'T READ THIS BOOK

Death, sexual assault, necrophilia, spousal abuse, work based sexual harassment, mutilation, augmentation, gore, banter, inappropriate thoughts, horror, crass humour, creepiness, atmospheric situations.

D E McCluskey

Prologue.

THE HUM OF the air conditioning unit buzzed away like an annoying insect as the small wall-mounted machine churned out its lifesaving, freezing-cold air. On afternoons like this, the frost of the server room was a welcome refuge, an oasis of cold in the stifling heat of the office.

At this time in the evening, the units had automatically turned themselves down to ten degrees Celsius, as the day had been particularly warm. It had been another in the run of unseasonably warm weather the country had been blessed with recently.

The servers were still whizzing away, working to full capacity. The whirring of the fans and the blinking of the lights in the darkened room would offer a much-needed comfort to Carl as his shaking hands keyed the code that would unlock the door. He was excited and expectant for the refreshing wall of freezing cold that would hit him the moment the door opened.

His damp shirt stiffened as the wave caressed him. It caused delicious goosebumps to rise all over his body. He took a moment, closing his eyes and savouring the embrace. He ran his fingers through his damp hair, amazed at just how sweaty he was.

'Shit, that's a beautiful thing,' he whispered to no one. *If only Carrie was here to enjoy this with me,* he thought with a grin, his eyes flicking from side to side. They were scanning the corridor, hoping to see Carrie, the girl from the marketing department. She had been his not-so-secret obsession for the ten years he'd worked this job.

She was beautiful, and as she'd gotten older, he thought she'd gotten even sexier. The smile she gave him every time he came around to fix whatever problem she was having, made his day, it had become a little shining light, something to look forward to, in a lifetime of dull, repetitive, boring nonsense.

A smile spread across his face at the thought of this ice-blast biting into her warm, damp skin, caressing her through the thin fabric of her blouse. 'Oh, the delights I'd see,' he whispered before realising he was daydreaming and talking to himself, out loud. He also realised he'd been enjoying his daydream a little *too* much, and now had to adjust himself below his belt.

The last thing he needed was to be found in the corridor with a daydream erection!

Anyway, Server Room One was no place to bring Carrie, not yet anyway. In fact, after the last few days, Server Room One was no place to bring anyone, other than what he thought of as *authorised personnel*.

He'd changed the code on the door so none of his co-workers could get in without his knowledge. Anything that needed to be worked on could either be done remotely or Carl himself would volunteer to do it. It was his domain now, and, of course, that of the voice who was talking to him from inside the network.

As he stepped inside he released a long breath, marvelling at the frost pluming before him. He remembered when he was a kid, he used to pretend he was smoking cigarettes when that happened. This silly memory took him away from what he was here to do, for a few blessed moments, before it came crashing back to him.

As the heavy door slammed into place behind him, another wave hit. This was different from the ice-blast, very different, but it had become something of the norm over the last few days.

It was a smell.

More of a stench, really.

It was a strange aroma, one he never thought he would be able to get used to, but one that was now becoming the norm for him, maybe even pleasant. He'd come to associate it with the smooth running of the server racks that facilitated his work. But no matter how he thought of it, no matter how much he romanticised it, he knew what it was.

It was the thick, cloying, coppery reek of coagulating blood.

There was also a hint of faeces and an after-whiff of urine. This was the worst part of what he had come to think of as his mission … *or is it a hobby?* he thought.

He was here now to empty the buckets he'd fitted under the metal floor. This was a job he couldn't do during the rush of the working day, and he didn't mind staying behind for another hour or so after everyone had gone to do it, mainly because it all went onto his time sheet anyway. *Not only am I serving The Master, but I'm earning a nice bit of overtime too,* he thought as he eased up the metal tile from the floor.

He reeled back from the waft that hit him then; it was much worse than the initial blast that hit when the door closed. The buckets were full. He shook his head as he regarded them. He'd never realised just how much waste a body would release as it hung on a server rack.

He pushed the hanging cadavers to one side and lifted the heavy bucket, careful not to spill any of it over himself. He often drove to work, but today he'd taken the train, and he had a return ticket. The last thing he wanted was to be the *stinky man* on the train, the one no one wanted to sit next to, the one they would actively stand in another carriage to avoid sitting in the empty seat next to him.

He opened the server room door and popped his head out. He looked both ways, happy there was no one around to see him perform this duty. He propped the door with a fire extinguisher—knowing that if the health and safety guys came around and found it there, he would be in big trouble—then dragged the bucket of human waste from the room. Silently, he thanked the building designers for putting the men's toilets next to the server room as he flushed the waste down the toilets.

When his work was done, he made it back with the empty bucket and replaced it. He stood back for a moment, folding his arms. A nervous smile broke on his face as he regarded his handiwork.

There were four of them at present, all hanging in parallel inside the large cabinet. Bloody cat-six ethernet cables ran from eye socket to eye socket, entering the main data server before terminating in the external router. He chuffed as he thought about what he was doing. The network had never been so reliable in his whole ten years of service to this company. With another grin, he pressed a few keys, bringing a monitor screen to life. He bit his lower lip as he regarded the message blinking away. It was simple white text on a black background.

TURN THEM OFF, THEN TURN THEM ON AGAIN!

Reboot: A Cosmic Horror

1.

A Few days earlier.

SIX FORTY-THREE a.m.

Carl Riggs was lying on his side in the king-sized bed. His pinkish eyes were wide open as he watched Amy sleep. She was a mouth breather. It annoyed him immensely, but over the years, he' kind of gotten used to the guttural growl purring from the back of her throat every time she exhaled. The small line of dried drool that snaked its way from the corner of her mouth and down her cheek fascinated him. His eyes followed it as it clung to her jawline before plunging towards the darkness of her neckline.

This wasn't what anyone could call entertainment, not in any shape or fashion, but he knew it would be the best part of his whole morning, maybe even his whole day.

He closed his eyes and exhaled from his nose. The thought of what the day had in store for him was enough to bring tears to his eyes, not in a sweet, nostalgic way but in a way that highlighted the desperate loss of the dreams of a bright young man, an existential dread kind of way. He lay motionless, dreading the alarm crying out at him like a hungry siren lulling him one step closer to his inevitable death; feeling the weight of every single second pass, each one dragging him closer to the inevitable moment when he had to haul his sorry arse out of the warmth of bed, get into a lukewarm shower, and dress himself ready for another gruelling, soul suckingly dull day ahead.

Eventually, inevitably, the alarm shrieked, calling to him, snapping him from the daydream of being in a car, driving past his place of work while offering the building his middle finger, before looping back onto the motorway, arriving home, and never ever doing that hideous journey again.

He took a deep breath as he forced himself up; there was the repetition of the sigh of resignation, the same one he did every weekday. *That's all it is, a fucking dream,* he thought as he swung his feet out of the bed. *I'm stuck in that shitty rat maze forever.*

As it was summer, the heating was not programmed to come on, but there was a slight chill in the air. He shivered as he shuffled like a warm, not quite dead zombie along the landing before closing the bathroom door behind him. He turned on the shower and urinated letting the water run, warming up the room.

After a few moments of staring—emotionless and expressionless—into the mirror as it fogged up, he stripped off his pyjamas and climbed beneath the cascading water, allowing its warmth to envelop him.

~~~

Fifteen minutes later, he was dressed and downstairs making coffee, his first of *many, many* cups of the day.

He was sitting on his sofa, watching the news on the TV.

All of it was bad. There had been terrorist attacks, knife crime was up, interest rates were up, the cost of living was crippling ninety percent of the population, but it was OK because some Princess or other had been seen out in a dress from a high-street chain.

Jesus Christ, I can't catch a break. This thought was totally without humour as he swallowed the last of his cooling coffee and watched the weather report. This was the highlight of the morning. The weathergirl was gorgeous, and her smile always made him feel a little funny in his stomach. It was like she was smiling to him, and him alone. The clock in the corner of the screen informed him it was fifteen minutes to eight and time he hauled his sorry, lazy arse out of the house and down the road to the train station.

He rolled his eyes to the back of his head and sighed again; this time, a small growl escaped him as he gripped the armrests of his chair, stretched, and pulled himself up.

'I'm off, love,' he shouted up the stairs.

There was no reply.

Shaking his head, he left the house, walking the five-hundred yards or so, to the station at the bottom of his road.

The commute to work was twenty-five minutes on a good day but could be anything up to an hour and a half on a bad one, depending on who was on strike that particular week.

Let's just see what kind of day the universe sees fit to give me today, he thought as the train pulled into the station.

With eyes that just wanted to close and block out every single thing about this morning, he regarded the mass of arms and legs, the fat, sweaty, stinking bodies pushing together, sharing a cramped, confined space, undulating, and writhing in the dance of death that was the Monday morning commute. A heavy air of merged breath and the stink of wet dog assaulted him as the doors to the overcrowded carriage slid open.

He could feel Satan grinning as he entered into this Hell of his own volition.

Today was not shaping up to be a good day.

~~~~

'Morning, ladies,' Carl beamed as he entered the double doors of the office, as if he owned the place. Tunbridge Solutions Ltd was a global project management engineering company that occupied many floors of one of the largest buildings in the centre of the city. He'd worked here for either just over, or just under ten years—he could never remember, as all the years merged into one timeless reoccurring nightmare. It was a well-paid job, but some people, his wife included, thought he could have worked his way higher up the company structure by now. What they didn't know was, he had absolutely no intentions of furthering his career. He'd seen what that had done to perfectly good people, turning them into real life monsters, tyrants, and egotistical pricks.

He knew deep down he was none of those things and had never aspired to become one.

'Oh, here he is,' Margaret laughed as he thrust open both doors, striding in and heralding his entrance.

'Lord muck himself,' Cheryl replied as he sauntered over and leaned on the large white desk that welcomed visitors into the company.

'Five, four, three ...' Margaret began her count down.

'I fucking *hate* this job,' Carl stated with a grin.

'Wow, you didn't even get to the full five seconds today,' Cheryl laughed.

His own grin was filled with mischief, flirtation, and promise. 'Well, there's no point beating around the bush, is there?' He continued. 'Anyway, I've got to go. I'm going to have to at least pretend to do some work today.' As he walked away, he heard the two women laughing behind him.

At least I can make other people laugh through my misery, he thought, strutting down the corridor on his way to the IT department.

'Carl ...'

He ignored the beckoning voice and continued to walk.

'Carl ...'

The voice was nothing if not persistent. He closed his eyes and turned around, knowing *exactly* who it would be calling him.

Alan Bryce.

He tried to smile as he clenched his fists, digging his nails into his palms, almost hard enough to bleed. Bryce was the office *pain in the arse*. He was a computer nerd but only in his spare time. He was employed with the company as a lead engineering specialist.

'Alan, how are you, mate?' he asked, doing his utmost to sound cheery.

'Not really good, no,' Alan said, adjusting his spectacles back up his nose. 'I was trying to upload a three-thousand-part drawing onto Data Server Three, you know, the one that's *supposed* to be the designated server for Scotland. Well, it took me'—he looked at his watch as if for clarification— 'roughly forty-five seconds just for the drive to appear on my screen. Is there something wrong with the network? I've rang the department a few times, but no one seems to be answering.'

That's because they all know your number and decided to fuck you off, Carl thought, smiling inwardly.

'This is going to cause us no end of issues when we're passing drawings back and forth. The client won't appreciate any delays.'

'Alan ... what car do you drive?' Carl asked.

Alan looked at him as if he had just asked him what his mother's favourite sexual position was. 'What? What's that got to do with—'

'What car?' Carl asked again.

'A Volvo. Why?'

'If you got into your Volvo in the morning and turned the ignition and the car didn't start first time, would you; a: turn the ignition again and see if it works then, or b: call the home rescue service and get them to turn up at your house to turn the ignition for you?'

'I don't understand what you're saying,' Alan replied, fixing his glasses again.

'It means, just because the network isn't running as fast as you want it to, you don't need to run straight to the IT department complaining about it. Try it again …' *for fuck's sake,* he added in his head. 'Odds on it'll work properly the next time. Now, if you'll excuse me, I need to get to my desk.'

As he walked off, shaking his head, he left Alan scratching at his cheek before turning away and sitting back at his desk.

Carl rolled his eyes and mouthed something unintelligible, and thankfully silent.

~~~~

'Morning, losers!'

'Riga-mortis, you miserable old bastard, nice of you to join us.'

Carl raised his middle fingers towards the back of his colleague's head. The man's face, as it was every single moment of every single day, was buried so deep into his triple monitor set up that he didn't notice. The legion of white stormtroopers adorning his colleague's desk, each holding black laser-rifles, and each of their heads bobbing on springs, glared at him accusingly via their dark eyes.

He looked at his watch; it was nine-oh-eight. He shook his head and sat down.

There was a steaming hot cup of coffee next to his keyboard; he looked at it and smiled. 'Thanks, Tasha,' he said, waggling his mouse, bringing his computer to life. He was greeted with a picture of a spaceship travelling the vast distance between two planets. Every single morning, he wished he was on that ship.

'Well, I figured you were going to need it.' A petite girl with long, straight black hair popped her head over her monitors and smiled at him, the smile was shy and sheepish. 'Big Rod's looking for you,' she offered, speaking in a way that made it sound like the end of the world.

Carl rolled his eyes, he'd lost count how many times he'd done this just this morning, as his fingers danced over his keyboard, logging himself into the network. 'Does anyone have a fast-forward button so I can just get this day over with already?' he sighed. 'Oh, and can't any of you bastards answer Alan Bryce's phone calls? He just collared me on the way in.'

'Fuck that,' Dean replied with his head still buried in his monitors, running some programme or other. 'I'm not talking to that dickhead so early in the morning. Besides, its networks he wants to speak to, not us.'

Carl shook his head and opened his email.

The first one was from Rod Rhoads, or *Big Rod* as he was known. The manager of the whole IT department. The subject line read: 'Come and see me in my office WHEN you get in.'

Carl clenched his hands together as his body felt like it was deflating. He picked up the coffee and took a swig.

He almost spat it back out over his computer set up. Why he didn't think before drinking it, he didn't know.

There was sugar in it; there was always sugar in it.

He hated sugar in his coffee.

'Tasha, how long have we worked together?' he asked without looking up from his screens.

Tasha popped her head back over her monitors, her brow was ruffled. 'I've been here nearly two years, why?'

'In those two years, you've made me coffee almost every single morning, right?'

She thought about it for a moment. 'Yes,' she replied, a nervous smile creeping over face, not quite reaching her timid, dark eyes.

'And it's appreciated, it really is. But would it surprise you if I told you something again, something I've told you…' he paused to shake his head and look wistfully towards the ceiling. '…a million times before?'

Tasha's mouth pulled down at the edges. 'Nope,' she replied with more than just a hint of confusion.

'*I don't take fucking sugar in my coffee*,' he said slowly, raising his cup into the air.

'Noted,' she mumbled before slinking back behind her screens.

Carl immediately felt bad, his stomach knotted, and he wanted to apologise for his outburst. She had only been trying to help, to be nice, and he had just thrown it back in her face. He thought about standing up and thanking her for the coffee, and maybe even drinking the sickly sweet liquid, but that wasn't how things were done in the IT department. There had to be battle; otherwise, everyone would see him as weak, and they would do everything in their power to exploit it. *One does not simply walk into an apology,* he thought, appreciating the clichéd quote from Lord of the Rings. *Jesus, I really am an IT nerd,* he thought, this time without the chuckle. But he was right; any insult, any argument, any joke that was played, it was an unwritten rule: there were no apologies.

He stood, grabbed his cup, and headed towards the small kitchen that facilitated almost a third of the three hundred or so employees on this floor. Normally, it was an area he tried to avoid until at least ten fifteen. It was usually empty at ten fifteen.

He seethed as he poured the warm coffee down the sink. When he got to the end, the liquid was thick and viscus. *How many sugars did she put in this?* he asked himself, thinking of how hard he was going to have to scrub his cup—otherwise, the residue of the syrupy sugar would affect the taste of his lifesaving brews for the rest of the day, perhaps even longer.

'There you are,' came a voice he really didn't want to hear.

'Tony,' Carl smiled, trying his best not to make eye contact with the office bore, hoping he could slip by him, pretending he'd finished in the kitchen and was on his way back to his desk.

As today was Monday and the stars were not aligning for him, had no such luck.

'So, I got that new car I was telling you about the other day. You know, the one I've been looking at, for ages.'

Carl smiled and nodded. He had no idea what Tony was referring to; the guy would drone on and on for hours about mind-numbing gibberish. Without making eye contact, he turned away, spooning instant coffee into his newly washed cup, hoping the man, who was now shadowing him, invading his personal space, might bore himself into nonexistence.

Today was *not* his lucky day.

'Yeah, well, I wanted it in the original metallic grey, but I had to settle for metallic blue. It's not the original colour, but you know, beggars can't be choosers,' he continued in his nasally whine.

Carl had already turned off.

'It's a bit of a *dooer-upper*, but I'm sure I'll find the time to work on it over the weekends.'

Carl knew the poor guy would find the time over the weekends, as his kids had all grown up and left, and his wife was far too busy eating herself into an early grave, to care what he was up to. He would have plenty of time. 'That's great, man. Listen, I can't really talk right now. I've got a meeting with Rod scheduled for half nine. I got to prep for it. Show me those photos later, eh?' He winced as he said this, understanding that was exactly what would now happen.

Tony looked up at him from his mobile phone, where he was already pulling up the pictures. This was how Carl knew Tony's wife was fat; he showed him photos of absolutely everything in his life, from his kids to his stereo set up, to his Lego collection. Carl had never been interested in any of it.

'No worries,' Tony said, putting his phone away. 'I'll catch you at lunch.'

No, you fucking won't.

As the man left the kitchen, Carl fetched the milk out of the fridge. He seethed again as Eddie, the football bore, entered.

He was getting them all today.

'Caaaarlos,' the man growled. 'Did you catch the game last ...'

Carl dropped his head and stormed out of the kitchen, still stirring his coffee. He could feel Eddie's eyes following him as he went.

'Obviously not,' he heard him mutter.

'For fuck's sake,' he sighed, flopping back into his chair.

'Carl,' *Big* Rod Rhoads popped his head around the door to his office. 'A word?'

All he wanted to do right then was put his head in his hands and scream. He had visions of standing up, beating his chest like some miniature King Kong, and smashing up the whole department. He looked longingly at his steaming coffee before closing his eyes, searching for that elusive zen people on the TV were always talking about.

Dean pulled his head out of his monitors and grinned. It was the smile of a bastard revelling in someone else's misery. 'You best hurry,' he said, the smile on his face making his eyebrows raise. Carl wanted nothing more than to rip them off and make him eat them. 'He was in here at half-eight looking for you.'

I would fucking kill you with your own pen, he thought as his colleague turned back to his screens. *If I thought I could get away with it...*

'Today, Riggs,' Rod shouted through the open office door.

Carl gripped his cup and took a deep swig, not banking on the liquid still being not far off boiling point. As he scalded his mouth, he spat it all out, back into his cup.

Brilliant, he thought. *A burnt tongue and another coffee I can't drink. Today is the day that just keeps on giving.*

2.

'CARL, I KNOW you've only just got in, but I need a huge favour.' Big Rod looked lost sitting behind the desk in his office. He was the IT manager and—as he liked to tell as many people as he could, as often as he could— he was the person where the IT buck stopped. Although, in reality, that was nothing but a pipedream, as he was really nothing more than a sycophant to the upper echelons of higher management. He thought the departmental mission statement, under Rod's leadership, should read: We Jump, You Tell Us How High.

The poor man knew everyone in the department called him Big Rod, but he wouldn't do anything about it—or more likely couldn't, as he didn't have the backbone, or the balls, required for the confrontation.

He also stood at five foot five in his Cuban heels.

Not that this was a bad thing; he wasn't a bad person, and he was a decent boss, at least until one of the other managers in the business asked him to do something for them, something outside the remit of the department, or if there was something wrong and one of them complained, then he would jump exactly how high and in what direction that particular manager wanted him to. Plus, he was very good at making departmental shit roll downhill.

Carl huffed. 'Rod, don't make me do anything I don't want to do, not today,' he moaned as he sat in the chair on the opposite side of the too big desk. 'I've got a shit load on already. I've got to get that blade server upgraded in Server Room One. That *has* to be my priority today.'

Rod looked at him. He was grinning, but it wasn't from humour; it was more like embarrassment. Carl knew the look. He knew he was about to be shit on, and from a great height. 'What is it?' he asked, his chin hitting his chest as his head fell.

'Gerard has been in this morning.'

Carl slumped even further. He put his head in his hands and emitted a low growl. He knew what was coming.

'He was talking about his laptop. There seems to be some ...' The small man fidgeted as his eyes darted towards the window.

Remind me to invite you to our next poker night, Carl thought with an inward groan.

'... issues with it,' he continued, ignoring Carl's body language.

'And it has to be me? Today?'

Rod nodded. 'He's asked for you directly.'

'He always does.'

'That's because you're the only one who he can talk to. You should be glad; you're the only one he trusts.' He shifted his head, indicating the rest of the team. 'The others are ... well, you know.'

Carl knew what he meant. The others were all socially awkward.

The truth of the matter was they weren't, but they put up a good pantomime that they were. Carl was a people person, no matter what way he looked at it. He could talk to, and get along with, anyone from any walk of life. The others just hid it better than he could.

He pushed both his fists into his eyes and grimaced. 'Is it the same laptop?' he asked, already knowing the answer. He looked up, glaring, challenging Rod to tell him the truth.

Rod nodded, refusing to make eye contact with him.

Carl took in a deep breath through his nose, filling his chest and making quite a loud noise doing it. 'Seriously?'

'Yeah. He asked me as a special favour—'

'Christ, Rod, how many *special favours* are you going to do for this man? Has he come up with the excuse that it was his son again?'

Rod shuffled in his seat. 'He's the managing director, Carl. The CEO. He's a VIP. If we keep on his good side, then our budget—'

Carl stood. 'His good side? The guy hasn't got a good side. He should be in fucking prison, Rod, and well you know it. You didn't get to see the'—he paused, remembering some of the images he found on Gerard's laptop the last time this happened— 'things I saw last time. The only VIP he is, is a Very Insistent Pervert.'

'I know, I know. I'll sort out some'—he leaned in over his desk and whispered— 'some extra time off for you if you do this one thing for me, this one time.'

This piqued Carl's attention. Time off sounded good. The less time spent in the office, the happier his life was. His shoulders slackened and he sighed. 'All right, I'll do it. But I want at least a week off, in October,' he demanded.

Rod's face beamed at the news, then it fell again. 'There's one small complication, though,' he continued reluctantly.

'There always is.'

'There's quite a bit of, erm …' Rod bit his lower lip as his eyes went distant, trying to think of a word. '… data he needs getting off the machine. Apparently it's all rather sensitive. So, make sure you back everything up before wiping it.'

'What kind of sensitive data?'

Rod shrugged. 'I don't know. Financial stuff, I think, also some personal stuff. So don't upload anything to the network; work from removable media if you can.'

Carl could sense he had just been dismissed, and to be honest, he wanted out of this office as soon as he could; it had gotten far too uncomfortable for his liking.

~~~~

Gerard Medley was the CEO. He was as corrupt a man as Carl had ever met. He also had a penchant for the more illegal side of pornography. This would be the third time Carl had saved this laptop, the company network, and the CEO's professional (not to mention public and personal) life by running a deep wipe on the machine. The software he used was on the illegal side too. It was an old Ministry of Defence program that overwrote the digital media in the machine, four hundred times, with zeros, completely erasing any access to data—or, in Gerard's case, filth— from anyone who might have an appetite to retrieve it.

Each time, the excuse he made was that his son had returned from university and gotten onto his laptop. This just didn't cut it. It never cut it back in the day when his son was sixteen (and therefore not at university), and it didn't cut it now when his son was mid-twenties, married to a man, and living in Canada with an adopted child.

Carl was feeling more than reticent as he trudged down the corridor towards Medley's office. The large, intimidating door had a sign on it reading Gerard Medley – CEO. Please knock before entering.

Probably because he doesn't want people catching him wanking, he thought.

He knocked on the door and waited.

There was no answer.

In his mind's eye, he saw him, a man in his late fifties, a completely bald head, and a stern ruddy face, sitting in front of his laptop, his trousers by his ankles, with a sock over his erection, enjoying himself a little too much to CCTV footage of the women's toilets. He shook his head, trying desperately to clear that image away, but he knew there was no deep wipe software he could use on his brain, and the image would be back to haunt him, probably tonight while he was trying to get some sleep.

'Coming,' came a voice from the other side.

This made him chuckle.

As the door opened, Carl had his fist bunched in his mouth, attempting to stem his laughter.

A thirtysomething-year-old woman opened the door. Carl noticed she was looking a little flushed, as if she'd just been doing something strenuous. *I wonder what that might have been,* he thought, trying his best not to laugh.

'Oh, Carl,' Leanne Riley smiled. 'Are you here for the laptop?'

Carl smiled and rocked on his heels. 'I am.'

'Come in, boy,' a deep, Queen's English, public school accent shouted from inside. 'I just had Leanne here under the desk, yanking on my wire,' the voice continued.

Carl grinned as he passed Leanne. She was a pretty woman, but she had a real downtrodden look to her, as if she'd been coerced into doing a lot more than normal PA duties. She fixed a lock of hair behind her ear as she actively avoided his glance, staring at the floor, stepping back to allow him access to the office. The air inside felt heavier than it did in the corridor, like there was a moist misty cloud hanging in the ether, making everything feel damp, foul, and murky.

'I just couldn't get the little bugger up,' Gerard continued, getting up from the desk that was too large for the small room.

'I've heard that's a real problem these days,' Carl answered, trying to stifle a giggle. 'It's a good job Leanne was about, to give you a hand. You know, to help you get it up. Us mere mortals usually rely on little blue tablets.'

The joke was lost on the older man.

19

'Well, here you are, boy. I'll tell you, that lad of mine is a real tinker. Every time he gets his grubby mitts on technology, it's all bums and boobs. You know how boys are, eh?'

It's not the bums and boobs I'm worried about, boy, Carl thought as Medley passed the laptop over to him. *It's the other stuff.* 'I'll have it back to you in no time.' He smiled, taking receipt of the machine. Even the touch of it made him feel grubby. He wasn't one for becoming attached to machines, he knew they were only there to serve a purpose, but he couldn't help feeling sorry for this one when he thought of everything it had been forced to witness.

In his mind he thought he could feel the thing pulse. It reminded him of that odd film from the seventies, *or was it the eighties?*

Long live the new flesh, he thought with a grin.

'Good lad,' Gerard said in a condescending tone, snapping him out of his reverie. 'Make sure I have it back by tomorrow afternoon. I have a business trip to Bangkok in a few days, and I'll need to prep for it.'

'I bet you do …' Carl said as he turned to leave the office.

'What was that, boy?' Gerard asked, his voice inflecting on the last word.

Carl turned back, realising he'd just spoken aloud what he thought he was thinking. 'I said I'll see what I can do. I might just get you a new machine, as Rod was saying there is a lot of… erm, data, on this that you don't want to lose.'

Gerard looked at him, squinting. 'Well, OK then, see that you do that. And, as I said, I have to have a machine back by tomorrow. Do you hear me, boy? No later.'

'Loud and clear, sir. Tomorrow,' Carl said, turning and hurrying towards the door.

Leanne followed. There was a pleading expression on her face, it made her look like she needed help getting out of there, out of the office, the building, maybe even the country, and never, ever coming back. All Carl could do was smile and nod.

Once he was in the corridor and the office door closed, trapping Leanne inside, he leaned against the wall and breathed deep. The air tasted sweeter somehow; there was no oppressive, underlying stink.

He held the laptop as if it was something diseased, something filthy in his grip. It was no longer throbbing, which he thought was always a good thing, laptops were not supposed to throb. The machine had a feel to it as if it were something best used flushing down a toilet. He already had an idea of the things he'd likely see when he opened the Pandora's Box of this hard drive. Things that were going to make him want to shower for at least an extra ten minutes longer than normal, and possibly in bleach.

~~~~

'Carl, the network is slower than ever.' The annoying voice of Alan Bryce was behind him, he was following him.

Carl began to walk faster.

'Hey, Carl, your team didn't do too good last …' Eddie, the football bore, called out to him; he ignored him, almost bursting into a run to get away from these men.

'Hi, Carl,' the new girl in Engineering—he couldn't remember her name—called. He stopped and smiled at her. 'Are you OK, chicken?'

'Yeah. All good. I was just saying hello,' she replied, smiling, looking back at her monitor. He noted she was looking at a page selling bikinis.

'Well, all right then,' he said, prising his eyes away from the pictures of hot young women in flimsy outfits, wondering what she would look like in one of them. 'If, erm, if you need anything, and I mean anything, you know where my desk is, don't you?' he said with a smile. As he fumbled his words he looked back the way he had just come. Alan and Eddie were glaring at him.

Carl shrugged and pointed at the girl. 'Look at her and then look at the kip of you two,' he said. 'Who would you speak to?'

With that, he turned and walked back towards the IT department, stopping only twice—to eat cakes that had been left on the side for people's birthdays, whose names he couldn't remember.

Such was life working for the IT department.

3.

AS CARL GOT back to his desk, his phone was ringing. He heard it even before he stepped into the room. He looked around at the others, his supposed colleagues, who were all busying themselves doing other things, anything other than answer his phone. He shook his head and sat down, placing Medley's laptop next to his monitor. He picked up the phone. 'Morning, IT,' he stated. *A little piece of my soul dies every single time I say that,* he thought.

'Good morning, IT,' the chirpy voice answered. 'Who am I speaking to?'

'Carl.'

'Steve…' Carl's eyes rolled again. He knew it wouldn't be the last time today. '…my computer's not working,' the voice continued.

Carl sat back in his chair. 'Yeah, my name's Carl, and I kind of guessed that would be the case, as people don't tend to ring to tell us everything's working correctly,' he answered.

The person on the other end of the line didn't catch his sarcasm.

As he listened, he absentmindedly powered up Medley's laptop.

'Yeah, well … I'm going to ask you the most obvious question now. You're going to laugh, and then make the same joke everyone else does when they ring IT. When it works, you're going to ask me why you didn't think to do it in the first instance. Are you ready? OK. Here goes. Please turn the machine off and then turn it on again. Yes, I'll hold while you do it.'

He covered the phone mouthpiece and spoke into the air. 'For fuck's sake. These people,' he hissed.

In the time it took for the person on the other end to reboot their machine, he'd logged on to the laptop with the administrator's account. The moment it booted into the operating system, Carl was confronted with a screen filled with pop-up windows, a sure-fire indicator that whoever had been using this machine had been frequenting unsavoury, and often malicious websites.

'For fuck's sake,' he sighed.

A furious retort from the other end of the phone blasted his ear.

'No, no … I wasn't talking to you,' he backpaddled. 'I'm working on another laptop while sorting you out. Oh, that worked. What a surprise. I did tell you it would.'

As he was furiously battling with the pop-ups and trying to placate the user on the other end of the phone, one of them caught his eye. It was a type he'd seen any number of times before. It was designed to look like an important DOS Prompt Screen, as if it was an official, and integral part of the computer's operating system. The designers had gone to great pains to make it look as genuine as they could, scaring the unwitting users into clicking on it, thus allowing the virus it carried to infect the whole system, and beyond.

But it was the syntax that caught his eye.

Normally, this type of pop-up would say something about a system wide infection and click here to prevent operating system shutdown, blah, blah, blah. But this one was different.

Error: The function LIFE is not responding
Terminating function
Press any key to reboot system …

It wasn't the normal reference he would have expected on a blatant scam. He looked at it a little closer and hovered the mouse over it. A small red X appeared that he had to chase with his cursor to kill. It was replaced with an advert for a woman selling any, and all, of her orifices to the highest bidder.

Forgetting about the odd pop-up, Carl looked at this new advertisement. *I bet Medley's put in a few speculative bids for that, the filthy fucker.* He chuffed.

'Right, so it's working, yeah? Excellent … Well, maybe next time you could do that *before* you call us? Yeah, you have a good day too … You bellend.' The last part was added after the handset was back in its cradle. Carl stood up, stretched, and regarded the rest of the team. There were six of them in total, including him.

'So, no one fancied answering the phone just then?' he asked aloud.

Tasha hid behind her monitor. The only acknowledgement Dean offered was a middle finger salute behind his head.

Bryan sat in the corner with his headphones on, ignoring everyone and everything, including the phones. He was an odd one. He never spoke to anyone if he could help it but was always the first there at a department night out or the Christmas do, where he drank far too much and did a whole year's worth of talking in one night.

Charles sat next to Bryan. He had never really liked Carl, or so Carl thought, anyway. He always seemed to be jealous that he pretty much got away with murder with the users and he would complain and bitch about him when he thought he wasn't listening. Carl knew all this, and in truth, he didn't really like him back.

He hadn't expected an answer from Charles.

Jodi was the token in the department.

He knew how that sounded, but it was true. She was the only bit of glamour that was sorely needed in the drab surroundings of a mostly male, and mostly nerd-infested department. Dean had made the mistake, a long time ago, when Rod was recruiting, of mentioning that they should get a girl in the department. He'd actually said *a bit of skirt.* When Tasha had squeaked that she was a woman, Dean had said the, now immortal, words that has since gone down in office lore: 'No, I meant a real woman.'

It hadn't gone down well. If Tasha had balls, she would have taken this up with Rod, maybe even HR and gotten rid of Dean, but she didn't, so she hadn't.

Jodi steadfastly refused to answer any phone other than her own, as she loudly told anyone who would listen. 'I never spent four years in university to become someone's PA.'

Carl's retort was usually something about the course she did being a two-year BTEC in domestic sciences, making scones and sponge cakes. He would then ask how it took four years to complete.

It was fair to say there was a reasonable amount of animosity and ill-feeling within the group. But they worked well together when they needed to, and there were very few complaints about them.

'You got Meddling Medley's laptop again?' Dean asked without even turning around.

'Yeah. He's fucked it up again with dodgy porn and general nastiness.'

'He's a filthy bastard. He puts me to shame. You know we should probably report it.'

'Who to?' Carl asked. 'He's the head honcho.'

'I mean to the authorities. The police. There's got to be illegal stuff on there.'

Carl watched as the computer turned itself off. He shook his head as it bounced right back on again. 'Apparently, he needs *stuff* off it for a trip to Bangkok, so I can't just wipe it. I've got to go through it, I'm probably going to image it and give him a new machine.'

Dean turned away from his monitors, allowing Carl to see his permanently squinted face for the first time that day. *I'm glad he spends all day looking into that monitor, the ugly bastard,* he thought with a smile.

'You'll get the photos of Leanne,' Dean replied—the naughty spark in his eyes made him look like what Carl thought the troll, the one that lived under the bridge, must have looked like to the Billy Goat Gruff family. What he said piqued the interest of Charles, opposite him.

'I'll do it for you,' Charles said, standing up in a snap.

'Sit down, you perv,' Carl replied a little too loud.

Charles's face flushed but he did what he was instructed.

'Mate, you need to get yourself on some of the websites Meddling gets himself onto. Maybe they'll take your mind off that weird obsession you've got going on. If you want mucky photos of her, just ask.' Carl laughed. 'They'll all be on my external drive.'

Dean was giggling as he buried his head back into his monitors. Carl watched Charles's eyes flick over to the small red box he was pointing to.

Jodi was stifling her laugh too.

'You're wrong in the head, you,' Charles said before tearing his eyes from the external hard drive. 'One of these days, you're going to go too far … and I'll be there, watching and laughing.'

'I hope you are, mate,' Carl replied. 'I really hope you are.'

The laptop on his desk was not fully rebooted, but all the pop-ups were back advertising their filthy and depraved wares. Carl was impressed with some of them. 'I never thought that dirty-old-man would have it in him to access this many sites,' he laughed. He noticed that the same pop-up he'd seen before was back. It was languishing behind a page offering *chicks with dicks* and *angry skinheads, waiting for you.*

As he looked at it, he exhaled through his nose with his mouth closed tight. It was odd that the same pop-up had come back; they were usually randomised. For some reason, it stood out from the others, even though it was just a simple screen, a black square with stark, white writing made to look like a command prompt. It offered the exact same message as before, only this time, there was more text at the end of it.

Error: The function LIFE is not responding
Terminating function
Press any key to reboot system ...

This was followed by another message:

Turn them off, then turn them on again ...

He was certain the end bit hadn't been there earlier. For some reason, one he couldn't fathom, the message irked him. Pop-up messages in general were garbage, and everyone—*or almost everyone*, he thought—knew that clicking on them caused nothing but trouble, but there was something different about this one, something that was making him want to click it. It was like it was calling to him.

He didn't *want* to click it; he felt like he *needed* to click it.

The cursor hovered over the black box in the centre of the screen. Perspiration was seeping from the pores in the palm of his hand as his finger caressed the mousepad. Everything in his being, everything in his twenty years of working in an IT environment, was shouting at him *not* to click it. He knew if he did, he was validating his network connection to a group of cyber-terrorists somewhere, but there was a compulsion, something was willing him to do it.

Suddenly he was in the middle of a strange out of body experience. He felt as if someone else, someone outside his own consciousness was attempting to coerce him into clicking on the icon. He couldn't stop himself. In his head, he was rationalising this compulsion. *It's not connected to the network,* he thought. *Or the internet ... What's the worst that can happen?*

He didn't want to do it, but a crazy voice in his head—or was it coming from somewhere else? —was telling him to, commanding him, instructing him.

Now, he *wanted* to click it.

He was *going* to click it.

There was nothing anyone in this office—or maybe even in this building—could do to stop him from clicking it. Nothing except the mantra of *do not click on pop-ups* being drummed into his head ever since university, all those years ago.

He looked around the room.

No one was taking any notice of him. Dean was in his own little world of monitoring software. Tasha was on the phone. Jodi was scrolling through fashion websites, Charles was ignoring him, and Bryan had his headphones on, doing whatever Bryan did every day.

His finger continued to hover.

His hand was shaking, and he could feel a drip of perspiration trickling down his cheek.

His phone rang.

The shrill sound cutting through his odd trance. It made him jump.

As he did … he clicked on the pop-up.

A panic rose within him. His heart began to pound, and more sweat began to bead on his brow. His vision tunnelled, and his focus was on the screen, his eyes were wide.

Nothing happened.

Nothing, except the fact that the small black box was gone.

A shiver ran through him as he stared at the screen. It was still filled with adverts for every sexual perversion known to man, a lot of them new to him. *Angry skinheads?* he questioned.

'Are you going to answer that phone?' Dean asked without turning around.

'Uh?' he replied, looking at his desk as if it was the first time he'd ever seen it.

'The phone,' Dean growled. 'Answer it. It's doing my head in.'

'Oh, yeah,' Carl muttered, picking up the receiver, not taking his eyes from the laptop screen. 'Good morning, IT,' he said automatically. A voice spoke to him from the other end. He never listened to what it was saying. 'Have you tried turning it off and turning it on again?' He swapped the receiver over to his other hand, and the other ear, while his gaze remained transfixed on the screen. 'Did that work?' he asked. 'Good, thanks for calling,' he continued without listening to what the person said. Without waiting, he slammed the phone back down onto its cradle.

He hadn't noticed that at some point, he'd stood up. He looked around him, before sitting back in his chair, returning his stare to the small screen.

The room had taken on an odd feel. All the noises—the normal everyday noises of computers, telephones, muted conversations—were muffled. It sounded as if they were being conducted underwater. The overhead lights had dimmed, but the screens of the computers around him were glowing brighter than usual. They reminded him of streetlamps on a dark, rainy night. The normal sounds he'd heard, only moments ago, were replaced. The muffled conversations were now whispered conspiracies. The whirring and hums from computers were now muted clangs, like old machinery kicking into life, rubbing against each other. The eerie sounds hung in the air, interspersed with muffled screams, and sickening wet tears.

'*Carl* …'

His name was whispered within the conspiracies. He turned to see who was calling him, or talking about him, and was surprised to find himself alone. Where there had been people only moments before, there were now only glowing visages, silhouettes, shimmering ghosts.

'*Carl* …' the voice whispered again.

He spun, hoping to catch who was calling him. There were cracks in the monitor screens that Dean always had so much interest in. The plastic covers were splitting. A viscus red liquid was seeping between the cracks.

Blood, Carl thought.

At that moment, this was his only rational thought.

Then he saw something else. There was something behind the screens. He couldn't see it directly. It was blurred by the glowing and the blood, but it was there. It was long, thin, and … otherworldly.

A part of him knew it was something hideous, something evil … and very old.

~~~~~

Rod pushed the screen down on the laptop that Carl was looking at, snapping him out of the horrible daydream he had found himself lost in.

'Is this Gerard's?' the small man asked.

Carl jumped from his seat. As he stood, he gripped the sides of the desk for some much needed support. He looked at Rod, before casting his glance further afield, around the IT room. His eyes were wide, and wild.

Everything was as it should be. It was completely normal. Everyone was there, was doing what they had been doing before he clicked on the pop-up box. Dean's screens weren't cracked, there was no blood seeping from them, and the ghosts he'd seen at the desks were gone, replaced by normal, everyday people. People he recognised and knew.

Pushing past Rod, he went to Dean's desk and, shoving his disgruntled colleague to one side, he touched the screens.

'What the fuck are you doing?' Dean spat. 'You'll get greasy prints all over my monitors.'

Carl slid his fingers up and down the screens, looking to see if he could feel any cracks and if there was anything nasty lurking behind them. Something hideous like he'd seen moments ago.

There was nothing.

'Are you quite finished being a knobhead?' Dean asked, opening a drawer, and removing a spray and a cloth.

Carl snapped his head around to look at him. 'Eh?' he asked as if he had only just noticed he was there.

'I asked what the fuck you're doing, Carl.'

All he could do was look at Dean, aware that Rod was behind him with his arms folded, watching these events with interest.

'Carl, are you OK?'

Carl's eyes were squinting as they crawled around the room. He was shaking his head as if he had a particularly nasty spider in his hair. 'Did anyone see anything funny just then?' he asked, stepping back towards his own desk.

'Only you being a tosser,' Dean replied, spraying one of his screens before wiping it with the cloth. 'You've got some greasy hands there, mate. I don't want to know what you've been doing?'

'Are you sure you're OK, Carl?' Rod asked again.

Carl fell onto his seat, making it hiss in protest at the unexpected weight on it. He was grinning like a villain in an old black and white movie, blinking and laughing. 'Yeah, I'm good. I think I might have just had an acid flashback to when I was in 'Nam.'

Tasha poked her head up over her monitors and looked at him. 'You've been to 'Nam?' she asked. There was more than a little awe on her face.

'Yeah,' Carl replied. 'Birming'nam! Fucking awful place.'

Tasha tutted before hiding back behind her screens.

'I'm all right,' he said, looking up at his boss. 'I think I just need some decent coffee, without fucking sugar in it.' He mentioned the sugar part louder than the rest of the sentence, making sure Tasha heard him. 'I'll get onto Gerard's computer now. He can have a new one this evening.' He was shaking his head as his attention returned to the laptop before him. 'He's one dirty bastard.'

Rod glared at him while looking towards his office. 'You can't say that,' he snapped. 'He's the boss, remember.'

Carl shook his head and chuffed. 'Everyone knows it, and well, he can't fire me, can he? I've got more dirt on him than the FBI had on Nixon.'

'One day, you're going to get yourself in a whole load of trouble; you know that, don't you?' Rod warned, leaving the room.

'Yeah, but not today, eh?' he shouted in response.

Rod's only reply was to offer him a middle finger.

'Very professional,' Carl shouted, grinning as he logged on to his own computer. He looked at the time in the corner of his screen and went to roll his eyes but stopped himself just in time. He didn't want that to become a habit. 'In what parallel universe is it not even half ten yet?' he mumbled, opening his emails.

4.

At one o'clock, Carl had lunch. He was back at two, even though he should have been back fifteen minutes earlier. By three o'clock, he'd finished backing up Gerard's computer onto removable media, so as not to corrupt the network, restored the image onto a brand-new machine— one he knew he'd be seeing again, and again, and again—and dropped the new model off at his office, where an overworked, and harassed looking Leanne gratefully and enthusiastically accepted it. He then stored the old machine in the build room to work on later.

By five o'clock, the day was winding down. He'd been involved with several idiotic calls from another office. He'd been invited to three pre-meeting-meetings and declined them all. *I hate meetings at the best of times,* he thought. *I'm not going to sit in a pre-meeting where all they talk about is what they're going to talk about in the actual meeting. What a colossal waste of time.*

He was now the only one left in the office. He enjoyed the six o'clock shift, as it pretty much gave him the last hour of the day to do what he wanted.

That usually meant his hobby.

Writing graphic novels.

Normally, he wrote horror, but he was currently in the process of writing a funny story about a naughty, rude reindeer who was one of Santa's best. When people asked him what he was writing and he told them, they would usually look at him as if he had two heads and one of them had just said he'd killed their mother. His answer to that look was, 'You just write what comes into your head.' He never forced his muse. He had never claimed to be an exclusive horror writer.

So, with the phone quiet and the department empty, he settled in to write some panels.

He had been lucky enough never to suffer from writer's block; his ideas flowed rather freely. However, today he just couldn't get into the swing of it. The day had been such a drag that it had sapped almost all of the creative juices he needed out of him. Wearily, he got up from his desk and walked the short distance to the toilets. After he had done his business, he made a point of washing his hands. He always did. There were so many others he worked with who he'd personally witnessed just waltzing out of the toilets after shaking, or even wiping, without a cursory rinse of their hands. He was always wary of going anywhere near *their* computers.

As he washed, he looked into the mirror above the sink. What he saw there made him step back a little. He was not looking good, kind of rough around the edges.

That's what working in the fucking IT department does for you.

This morning, after he'd been in the shower, he'd dressed in the clothes he'd pressed the night before, and fixed his hair as he did every morning. Only now, he looked like he'd been dragged around a forest by his ankles. His hair was sticking up at almost every angle possible, and his t-shirt was close to resembling an elephant's foreskin. His face was sallow, and he was sure he could see the beginnings of dark rings forming underneath his eyes. 'Jesus, Carl, you need to get yourself a bit of sun,' he mumbled, as he dried his hands. Releasing a deep sigh, he wrapped his hand in his t-shirt, gripped the bathroom doorhandle and exited the bathrooms.

He bumped straight into Gerard Medley.

'Ah, Carl, isn't it?' the older man asked with a smile that the Cheshire Cat in that cartoon—the one that had freaked him out as a child—would have been proud of.

'Erm, well, yes. I haven't changed it since you saw me this morning, so I guess it still is.'

The sarcasm went over the CEO's head. 'I say, boy, when you were clearing that laptop, you didn't find a little folder thingy hiding in there did you? It would have been called WORK.'

Carl shrugged. 'I don't know, probably. I transferred everything to my external hard drive. You won't have lost anything.'

'Ah, good. There's a few, you know, personal files in there,' he said with a wink.

Carl was suddenly sure this man had been a lizard in a past life. He repressed a shudder as he smiled.

'I'm sure I can rely on your … digestion in these matters, can't I?' He sleazed, tipping him another wink, and tapping the side of his nose, like the worst Santa Claus he'd ever seen in his life.

Carl nodded. *It's discretion, you fucking moron,* he thought, smiling. 'Of course. Yeah, I understand completely. You can rely on me, sir,'

Gerard beamed. 'Good man, good man. Keep it up then, sir. I'm off to play with a few holes. I'll speak to you in the morning then.'

Carl looked at him, his brows knitting in close to each other.

'Golf, my boy,' the older man laughed—there was a silkiness to that laugh that gave Carl goosebumps. With that, he pushed past him, making his way towards the exit.

He has to know that the first thing I'm going to do is look at that file, Carl thought, making his way back to the IT department.

He looked at his watch. It was five fifteen. He smiled and sat back at his desk. He interlaced his fingers and stretched them, cracking a few to release his tension. It was time to get some writing done. As he unlocked his computer and fired up his file, he did a double take.

Before he went to the bathroom, he was roughly on thirty-seven thousand words. He knew this, as he was a stickler for word counts—he took note of it at every given opportunity, usually every five minutes or so.

The word count was standing at forty thousand words.

I never wrote three thousand words before going to the toilet, he thought. With a ruffled brow, he clicked on the file and scrolled upwards and began to read.

The naughty reindeer had just gotten into trouble with Santa for knocking a lever in the toy factory, and all the Action-Man toys were now being produced wearing pretty bridesmaid's dresses.

Santa was scolding the reindeer.

All of this he remembered writing.

But that was where it changed.

The naughty reindeer produces a small knife from out of nowhere. He leaps on the big, jolly man, grabbing him in a headlock. Santa struggles to free himself from the beast's grip, but the reindeer is too powerful. 'I need to do this for The Master,' the mischievous young reindeer says, his eyes milking over with a thin white film. 'He needs the sacrifice of the innocents to enable his rebirth into this realm.'

Carl sat back. His jaw was hanging open as he read the text before him. *That would make a fucking brilliant story,* he thought, *if I was writing a horror. But this is a kid's story.*

He highlighted the text and was ready to delete it but stopped himself, deciding instead to cut and paste it into another file. A thought occurred then, causing another shiver to run the length of his spine and goosebumps to raise all over his exposed flesh.

It was a feeling he was now getting rather used to.

'Who the fuck wrote this?' he asked aloud, turning to look at the empty desks around him. He'd only been in the toilet five minutes, tops, and the conversation with Gerard couldn't have been any more than two. There was absolutely not enough time to write a descriptive murder scene of just a little less than three thousand words.

Something in the text caught his eye as he pasted it into a new document. Something he *knew* he hadn't written.

Just as the naughty reindeer ripped Santa's second eyeball from its socket, the red of his blood poured out. It was stark against the white of the snow beneath them. It made the giant man's suit appear as if it was melting.

This is fucking good stuff, he thought again.

The impish reindeer turned his bloody muzzle to look into shot, breaking the fourth wall. With a wolfish grin, filled with the misery of every child's greatest hero, he spoke to Carl.

No, not to me, Carl thought—or hoped. *To the reader.*

'The Master needs you to turn them off, then turn them on again.' The reindeer giggled, dropping Santa's lifeless body into the melting red snow. He then turned his attentions to the cute little house with the smoke pluming from the chimney. His sights were set on Mrs Claus and those fucking annoying elves.

'Turn them off, then turn them on again,' Carl mused. 'What the fuck does that mean?'

He continued to read.

You know what it means, Carl. You tell everyone every day to do it,

34

The passage was answering him.

Carl pushed himself away from his desk, leaping out of his chair for the second time that day. As he did, he inadvertently pressed the DELETE button on his keyboard. It removed all the text that was still highlighted.

His whole body was shaking as he leaned into his desk. He looked closely at the blank document. Breathing deep, shaky breaths, he grasped his mouse and minimised the document. He wanted to look at the original file below it. The text had been cut from this one too. He clicked the UNDO icon, but all it did was change something he'd typed earlier.

He stared at his screens. His tongue was touring his teeth as he pondered what he'd just seen and read. His eyes flicked to the word count at the bottom of the document. It was back to thirty-seven thousand.

'Am I going mad?' he asked, spooking himself with the sound of his own voice.

He looked at the clock again. It was almost half past five—there were still another thirty minutes before he could leave. Suddenly, he had no appetite for writing about naughty reindeer. *It turns out the little bastard was naughtier than I thought.* He decided he wasn't going to spend the next half hour in this little room on his own, so he forwarded the desk phone to his mobile and took a stroll around the office.

The main office was four long corridors making up a huge square. One full revolution of it had been measured as a quarter of a mile. He usually made at least eight revolutions a day, keeping his steps up and getting him out of the department, and therefore work.

He knew there would be precious few people around at this hour, but there were always some, and after the strangeness of the day, he wanted, or he needed, the company of others. Usually, these were people with no personal interests other than work, or the ones who were visiting from other offices for meetings and the like. As he made his way around, he tutted at all the machines that had been left powered on at the desks. They had recently been on an environmental drive, wanting to save the planet. They, as the IT department, had been tasked with reminding people to shut their machines down of an evening. It had been embraced by most of the staff, but there was still a few who were missing the point.

He counted four heads still working in the otherwise deserted space, but there were three machines in the first bay of the open plan office that had been left on.

He made his way over, intending to shut them down and therefore save the planet. As he wiggled the mouse on the first, he received the familiar company logo and the message to press CTRL + ALT & DELETE. He did as commanded, awaiting the log-in screen that would allow him to power the machine down safely.

However, another command box appeared, one he'd not seen before.

He looked at it, cocking his head. He wasn't used to boxes popping up *before* he logged on. *There must be something wrong with the network,* was his first thought, looking up to see if the few heads he'd seen earlier were working. These were the kind of users he thought of as frequent flyers and would have run squealing to the IT department at the slightest hint of network issues.

As they were all working, doing whatever these engineers did, and not moaning or whining about the systems, he knew everything must have been running fine.

He read the white text inside the little black box.

Error: The function LIFE is not responding
Terminating function
Press any key to reboot system ...

He heard the throb in his head before he felt the thud of his heart pounding in his chest.

Turn them off, then turn them on again ...

'What the fuck?' he whispered.

It was, word for word, the same message he'd read in the pop-up box on Gerard's laptop.

That's not possible, he thought. *That was just a stupid advert; phishing, that's all. This machine must have caught a virus.*

He went to click on the box, but it disappeared as soon as the mouse moved across the screen.

He sat down and entered his administrator credentials.

The palms of his hands were wet as he waited for his profile to load. When it did, he ran a quick diagnostic on the machine.

It took a small while, but eventually, it reported there was nothing infecting it. No viruses, no trojan horses, no malware… nothing.

He then ran a deep scan; this one would take about ten minutes, so he decided to try to close down the other machines in the bay.

Each one popped up with the same box.

Error: The function LIFE is not responding
Terminating function
Press any key to reboot system ...

Turn them off, then turn them on again ...

He bit his bottom lip as he looked at the other two screens. *What the fuck does that mean?*

Going back to the first computer, he looked at the report the scan had generated. The anti-virus check was almost sixty percent complete and, up to now, it hadn't caught anything.

He pondered the other machines in the office and wondered if he should check them all.

'I can't be arsed with that,' he said as the run completed. 'No viruses, everything's tickedy-boo! Fuck this, I'm going home.'

He closed the three machines down by the power buttons and made his way back to the IT department. He saved his reindeer document and closed his machine down too. Removing the phone forwarding from his mobile, he grabbed his bag, and his coat, and made for the exit.

As he walked out the phone on his desk began to ring. He thought about answering it. He looked at his watch; it was five minutes to six. *That's a nope,* he thought and left the building.

5.

'ARE YOU SURE there's nothing wrong? You're awfully quiet.' Amy was looking at him from the other end of the couch. The kids were in bed, and they were enjoying a glass of red wine. It was a Tuesday night ritual, just the one glass on a Tuesday night as a reward for making it through the two hardest days of the week.

'I'm good. It was just a mad day at the office today; you know what it's like,' he replied, taking a sip of his rioja.

'It's Tuesday night, Carl. We're not supposed to bring work home with us on a Tuesday,' she warned him.

'I know. And I really don't want to. I think I'm just knackered. I'm sure I fell asleep at my desk or something before … I had the weirdest daydream. It was like a—'

'Do you want to write, Carl? Is that what it is? If you'd rather spend time with your little reindeer than your wife, that's cool with me. I'll watch that programme about the maternity hospital you hate.'

Carl shook his head. 'No, writing that comic is the last thing I want to do tonight.'

'Then what's up with you? You're a right miserable bastard tonight.' She gave his leg a playful slap as she got up and walked past him on the couch. 'Do you want to break our routine and have second glass? There's at least another one each in that bottle.'

Carl swigged the little bit of liquid that was still in the bottom of his glass and smiled as he lifted it towards her. 'You're a lifesaver.'

She snatched the glass and made her way into the kitchen. He got up and followed her. He leaned into the counter and sighed.

'You are doing my head in,' she said, unscrewing the lid of the bottle.

'I didn't get a chance to do that server upgrade today,' he said in a moody way.

'Is that what's pissing you off? You need to get yourself a life, love,' she laughed, handing the half-full glass back to him. She leaned into the counter, sidling up next to him, and chinged his glass.

He loved the sound of half-full wine glasses changing. It made him smile, but there was very little humour in it.

'No, it's not that. I had to wipe the managing director's laptop again.'

'Was it filled with filth again?' she asked.

He widened his eyes. 'Yeah, it was.'

'The same kind of stuff?'

He chuffed a laugh, but it wasn't accompanied with a smile. 'Maybe worse. I swear that man is as big a deviant if ever I saw one. I think he makes that Vinny Savelle fella look like the Pope.'

Amy was looking at him, her eyes expectant and longing to hear more.

'No, it's not that. I just had a bit of a moment in work, that's all.'

She sipped her glass and looked at him. 'A moment?'

He nodded. 'I'm not sure if I fell asleep or not, but it all went a little weird in the office. Everyone disappeared, and there was blood coming out of Dean's screens.'

'Dean, who never takes his head out of his monitors? I'm not surprised there was blood coming from them.'

He smiled. 'No, it wasn't like that. There was a voice, and there was something … odd, it was kind of hiding behind the screens.'

'Something odd? Was it one of the others messing about? You know what they're like.'

Carl shook his head. 'No, it couldn't have been any of them. This thing was inside the screen, like it was in a film, trying to get out.'

Amy leaned over and put her hand on his forehead. 'You need your bumps feeling, you do. You're working too hard; that's all that's happening.'

He ducked away from her touch. He shook his head and put his wine down on the counter. 'There was something else too. This is going to sound mad.'

'Crazier than something trying to get out of one of your mate's screens to eat you? Try me.'

'Well, I clicked on a pop-up box on Gerard's machine. It was an accident, but it was right before the crazy stuff happened.'

'Oh,' Amy laughed. 'You accidently clicked on one of that weirdo's sex adverts?' She made air quotes over the word accidently.

'No, this isn't a joke. It *was* an accident, and it wasn't a sex advert.'

'So?' she asked, sipping her drink.

'So, it was a stupid message on the pop-up. Like one of those that try to scare people into doing stuff on their machine. A load of rubbish, really. But then I saw the exact same message on three of the machines on the network just before I came home.'

Amy pouted and shrugged her shoulders. 'Is it a virus or something?'

Carl shook his head and picked up his drink. 'Listen, it's nothing. Just me going mad, that's all. Maybe I am working too hard.'

Amy smiled. 'Maybe you're spending too much time in the North fucking Pole with that stupid reindeer,' she said, returning to the lounge.

Carl sighed and drained his glass. 'I'm not up for watching any telly tonight. I'm going to get a shower and an early night.'

Without taking her eyes from the TV screen, Amy shouted back into the kitchen. 'I'm not having sex tonight.'

'What?' he asked.

She turned to him with a smile. 'The only time you have a shower before bed is when you're expecting sex. I can't be arsed with any of that tonight.'

Carl laughed. 'I'll be well away before you get up there anyway. So, you can hold on to your virtue for another night, young lady. And just for the record, this is *me* knocking *you* back.'

He was still smiling as he made it up the stairs.

~~~~

He stripped off and walked along the landing.

'Don't leave your dirty undies in the bedroom,' the shout from downstairs filtered up.

He turned back, picked up his dirty underwear off the floor, and dropped them in the washing basket in the corner of the bathroom. He turned the shower on, put his towel on the rail next to the cubicle, and tested the water. It was just right. Hot and steaming. *Just how I need it,* he thought stepping into the hot flow.

As he began to lather his tired body, right after he submerged his head under the spray to wash his hair, a noise disturbed him.

Normally, noises in this house didn't worry him; it was usually one of the kids going to the toilet, or sometimes Amy cleaning up after him, or something else mundane.

Only this noise was different.

It was a wet *shlopping* sound.

Shlopp? he thought as he massaged shampoo into his hair. *What the fuck sort of word is that?*

Then he heard it again.

Shlopp!

It sounded like something wet slapping against the tiles of the bathroom floor.

He opened his eyes to look out of the steamed glass wall of the shower cubicle, instantly regretting it. The sting of the shampoo running into his eyes was terrible.

'Oh, you dickhead,' he cursed as he rubbed them. In his hurry to rid himself of the insufferable pain in his eyes, he forgot about the shampoo he still had on his hands. All he managed to do was rub more into them, and the sting became unbearable. He lifted his head towards the stream of water.

He opened his sore eyes.

He jumped out of the spray.

'What the fuck?' he shouted.

The water was still warm and steaming, but it had turned into a thick, flow of something that looked like…

Blood!

'Jesus Christ,' he cursed, trying to get out of the way of the vile downpour.

'Carl …'

He blinked the gore out of his eyes and opened them again.

The water was just water again.

'Carl …' The voice that was calling to him was nothing more than a whisper.

Then the odd noise happened again. It was another wet *shlopp*. The bathroom filled with a strong whiff. It was in the steam, it was coming from the shower head, it was coming from his wet, naked body.

It was the worst stink of fish he'd ever smelt.

Carl gagged. He hated the smell of fish, but this was on a different level. It was like fish that had been cooked days ago, weeks maybe. *Hell,*

41

years! There was even an underlying stench, one he couldn't identify, but he thought it might be decay, like rotten bodies in a mass grave. He remembered going fishing once with his dad. When they had gotten to the lake, his father had opened his tackle bag, only to find a fish he'd caught last time had been left inside for the whole of the winter.

That day he had thrown up.

He'd hated fish ever since.

This stink was exactly the same.

With his hand over his mouth, trying to stifle a gag, his eyes scanned the misty room, searching for the source of the stench. His gaze fell on the washing basket; He wasn't sure, but he thought it might be twitching.

Another slapping noise echoed through the fog, and there was another whisper.

'Carl ...'

'Hello?' he whispered back, feeling more than a little bit foolish, and more than a little bit vulnerable, as he was naked and covered in suds. 'Who's there?' he asked through clenched teeth. He didn't really want to open his mouth in case he swallowed some of the vileness in the room.

'Tommy? Is that you?' he asked, hoping that it was just his youngest son doing one of his infrequent sleepwalking stints.

There was no answer.

He wouldn't call me Carl, he reasoned. His eyes were drawn back to the washing basket as it twitched again.

'Carl ... You know what you need to do.'

He didn't know if he'd heard what he thought he'd heard. He wondered, hoped, that it was his ears playing tricks with him. He'd read somewhere about people associating voices with white noise, like static or *running water*. He tried to convince himself that's what it had been.

He turned the shower off. As he turned, reaching for the towel on the rail next to the shower, he caught another whiff of the cloying stink now filling the bathroom. A build-up of saliva filled his mouth. *I'm going to hurl,* he told himself.

The washing basket twitched again.

Only this time it moved.

My dirty undies can't do that, he thought, trying to rationalise what he could see. *And they don't stink like that either.* The last bit he thought might be a stretch. After the day he'd had, he thought stinking underwear could be a distinct possibility.

'Carl … you need to turn them off and then turn them on again!'

Slowly, he moved his hand away from the towel. *What if whatever is in the washing basket is under the towel too.* This thought wasn't what he wanted bouncing around his head. Leaning back into the cubicle, he lifted his leg and kicked the towel.

It moved.

He was convinced that his heart skipped a beat as his skin tightened into goose bumps.

Then he realised it was just his foot kicking it making it move. With a dart, he reached and grabbed it. Quickly giving his face and hair a wipe, he wrapped the towel around his waist, being careful not to take in too deep a breath. He didn't think he could handle the taste of the decaying fish in his mouth.

The washing basket moved again; it was accompanied by the now familiar *shlopping* sound. Even though the room was wet with the steam from the shower, he felt a prickle in his skin, one that he associated with breaking out in a sweat.

'What the fuck?' he whispered. 'What's going on here?'

The basket twitched again.

His eyes were bugging from holding his breath far too long as he looked around the small room for a weapon, anything he could use against the fishy abomination living alongside his dirty underwear.

He grabbed the toilet brush. He had to shake some beige water from it, and some drying bits of toilet roll, before he could wield it like the weapon he intended, or wanted, it to be.

Feeling less brave, or confident, than he'd felt in his entire life, he reached the brush towards the twitching basket.

With his other hand, he took the towel hanging around his waist and lifted it to his face. He took a deep, relieved breath into the fabric, hoping it would filter out most, if not all, of the fishy stink.

It didn't.

It hardly even scratched its surface.

'Carl … turn them off, then turn them on again.'

He poked the rapidly twitching basket, and it fell onto its side.

Dirty washing spilled onto the tiles of the bathroom floor. The exodus charge was led by his recently added underpants, as the floor filled with underwear, t-shirts, and socks.

There was nothing else.

Nothing!

He removed the towel from his face and took a tentative breath. The smell along with the fishy tang were gone.

'Turn them off … Then turn them on.'

The whisper lingered for a few moments before it too disappeared into the retreating fog from his hot shower.

Carl was left standing in the bathroom with shampoo still in his hair, a towel around his waist, holding the toilet brush over his head, ready to strike at anything that might crawl out of his undies, or Amy's panties.

He'd never felt so stupid in his entire life.

~~~~

'Are you awake?'

Carl stirred in his light sleep. He opened his eyes. In his twilight dreaming he saw a hulking shadow leaning over him, its head was too big for its body, and instead of arms it had wildly flailing tentacles.

He was just about to scream, remembering his fear in the bathroom, when the shadow suddenly became Amy shaped.

'Are you asleep?' she whispered again.

'Not now,' he growled, his mouth sticky with sleep. 'But I was,' he mumbled, wiping the drool he could feel from the side of his mouth.

'Sorry, I thought you'd be watching the telly,' she said slipping into the bed next to him. She was cold, and she insisted on cuddling right into him. His warm body responded to her chill by breaking out in goose bumps, accompanying his sharp intake of breath. 'Fuck's sake, Amy!' he snapped.

'I was only joking about before,' she purred. 'You know, about not having sex.'

Even through his fuzzy brain, his body responded to the word *sex* in the only way it knew how.

'Oh, well I can see you're up for it too,' she giggled as she brushed a hand along his obvious erection.

He could smell the wine on her breath, but that didn't bother him. He could still taste the wine on his breath, mixing with the mint toothpaste he'd used. *Maybe this is what I need to get my brain away from all the shit that's going through it.*

The pep-talk he was giving himself became moot when she started kissing his neck. He was past the moment of no return. When she was in a mood like this, he knew he was powerless to do anything about it.

As she kissed him, he felt her fingers slide underneath his pyjama bottoms and wrap themselves around the shaft of his rock-hard penis. As she squeezed, his stomach muscles cramped along with it, sending beautiful tingles through his body, distributing their warmth all around. It culminated in a small 'aah!'

'You still like that after all these years?' she whispered in between bites to his neck.

'You know I do,' he whispered.

'What about if I do this?' she said, moving down his body, caressing his skin with her lips. As she bit down on his nipples, the 'aah!' made a comeback, and she giggled as her head moved further down his body. He knew where she was going, and his feet began to twitch in anticipation.

Her lips continued their tour as her hand slipped from the bottom of his erection to cup his balls. The twitch in his feet had spread; now his legs were at it too. He loved this feeling.

A shiver ripped through him as he felt her tongue brush around his tip, and he closed his eyes and lay back into the bed.

'You can come in my mouth if you want,' she whispered right before he felt a wet warmth engulf him.

In her mouth? he thought excitedly. That was normally a treat reserved for birthdays, anniversaries, Christmas, and, occasionally, Father's Day. As long as he'd remembered Mother's Day and gotten her something nice from the kids. *I must have been good in a past life,* he thought as he relaxed, allowing her to do what she did best.

Suddenly, the urge to enter her, to thrust himself inside her, was overpowering. He eased her head from his crotch, kissed her, just to let her know that he was man enough to do it after she'd had his cock in her mouth.

She responded with her tongue.

Apart from a rogue pubic hair in his mouth, and him having to fish it out, he was having the time of his life.

She flipped over onto her back and, with a mischievous grin, pushed him down between her legs. He went willingly, kissing her stomach, her bellybutton, and nibbling at the insides of her thighs.

Then he got to where he wanted to be.

The stink was awful. It smelt like salt, and dead, rotting fish in filthy, shitty seawater …

His stomach flipped as she grabbed the back of his head and pushed his face closer to the source of the reek.

He resisted.

Fuck me, he thought. *It's the same smell as in the bathroom.*

He had never known her to have so much strength in her hands. It was too much for him, and try as he might, he couldn't wriggle free. He was glad it was dark because if the stink was anything to go by, he didn't even want to think what he was being forced into eating.

His erection wilted. His whole body was repulsed, and for the second time that night, he could feel a build-up of thick saliva in his mouth.

He could feel his breath bouncing off her cold, wet flesh and he was struggling—in vain—to get away from the all-encompassing tang, but it was no use.

Then he saw a light.

It was coming from right in front of him.

He opened his eyes, attempting to push back against her, but she was just too strong. The strange light illuminated her. Between her legs, where he would expect to see the delicious lips of her labia, something he loved to gaze at, there was an impossibly huge opening … It was so big; he questioned his sanity.

Maw ... that was the only word he could conjure to describe it.

It was a gash with thick, dirty water spewing from it in rhythmical pumps, or waves. The odd light emitting from deep inside her was bringing something forth. Inside Amy, his wife, the woman he loved was something that glowed in the darkness, something luminous that gave off a sickly green light as if it were submerged in filthy seawater.

It was something hideous.

He wanted to scream, but to do that, he would have to open his mouth, and he had no intentions of letting whatever that … *thing* might be get anywhere near him.

The light was all wrong. First it was green, then it was blue, before finally turning purple.

Then he saw it.

It was the product of a bad dream. It looked like something out of a programme he had watched years ago. It was a natural wildlife show called *Terrors of the Deep*!

It was a thick, undulating tentacle.

It looked like a tongue as it flexed and squirmed its way out of the tunnel that used to be Amy's vagina. There was an intelligence to it, like it had a purpose.

A thought occurred to him, one that had no place in his terrified brain.

'Turn them off, Carl. Then turn them on again ...'

It wasn't his voice he could hear. It wasn't like any voice he'd ever heard before in his life. It was the sound of a million voices, a hundred million maybe, all of them telling him the same thing, all at the same time.

'Turn them off, then turn them on again.'

With one final push, his wife's incredibly strong hands pushed his head into her wet, fleshy cave with the putrefying water and the cloying stink. As his face touched the pink horror, he succumbed, he had little choice. Then he screamed.

The moment his mouth opened; the tentacle slithered inside.

He could feel it wriggling in his throat.

As he tried to scream, his mouth filled with Amy's dark, vile liquid.

~~~~

He woke.

It was light outside.

He looked at his clock; it read five forty-seven.

Amy was next to him; her mouth was open, and her throaty snore was emanating from it.

He had a massive erection.

In a panic, he felt underneath the covers. They were dry, and there was no stink.

A dream, he thought with relief. *A fucking dream.*

He got out of the bed and crossed the room towards the bathroom. He knew there was no way he was going to be able to relieve his screaming bladder while his dick was still so hard, but nothing he could do would get rid of the damned thing.

He kicked the bathroom door closed and took himself in hand. He closed his eyes and tried to think of something rude that Amy had done in the past, but all he could see each time he closed his eyes was a large pink cave with stinking, filthy water gushing from it.

That did it for him, and the erection began to fade away to nothing.

Relieved, he emptied his bladder.
It turned out to be a most fitting start to the strangest day of his life!

6.

CARL DROVE TO WORK

CARL DIDN'T THINK he was in any fit state to drive to work today. He was tired, exhausted, and his brain space felt like it belonged to someone else. He'd drifted his way through breakfast, ignoring the demands of the two children who were present—he could honestly say that if someone had told him they were not his own children, he wouldn't have been able to argue the point. But mostly, he'd been avoiding the glaring looks from Amy.

If the truth had been known, he wasn't ignoring her, he just couldn't bring himself to look her in the eye. Each time he did, he was reminded of the huge gaping maw, the tentacle, and the filthy, stinking water spewing from her vag. The feel of it in his mouth might have ruined sex for him for the rest of his life.

It wasn't a joke; he was seriously worried about whether he would ever be able to make love to that beautiful woman ever again after that dream.

I just need some rest, he thought as he sat in traffic on the motorway. He'd been running too late to get the train today. He'd stopped being angry about the frequent traffic snarl-ups en-route, as he'd been doing this commute for over ten years now and it had never been any different. All he could do was silently shake his head at whatever idiot thought that four lanes moving into two at a major junction was a good idea.

A shiver ran through him again as another flashback to his dream hit him. *Was it even a dream?* This question burned him. *I'll book some holidays as soon as I get in. I'm overworked and overtired. Maybe I should let up on this reindeer story too.*

The truth—he knew it was the truth but really didn't want to admit it—was that after yesterday's escapade with the phantom writing, he didn't know if he wanted to continue the story at all.

I'll book a few of days and take Amy and the kids somewhere nice.

He smiled at that idea. It had been a while since they'd been on a family vacation. Some well-earned R and R was overdue.

He flicked the radio on and selected his favourite music station, setting the volume up loud he opened the window. The heat of the morning was becoming a little stifling.

It got worse as the heavy air from the stationary cars around him almost suffocated him. He was just about to wind the window up again when he heard it.

'Turn them on, turn them off again ...' the radio sang to him.

Instantly, his pulse was pounding in his head and sweat lined his palms. He looked at the digital readout on his radio.

'Turn them off, then turn them on again ...' it read.

He was glad he wasn't moving, as he might have swerved all over the road and caused a bad accident.

He blinked his eyes, not surprised to feel the sting of sweat caressing his balls. When he looked back at the readout, it was back to normal. The screen informed him that the song playing was Genesis, and they were singing 'Turn *IT* on,' not turn *THEM* on. He laughed aloud when he realised his mistake, then went to wind the window back up as he realised how shrill and crazy the laugh had made him sound.

The driver in the next car glared hard at him. She was smoking a cigarette out of the window while holding a coffee cup in her other hand. *And she's looking at me as if I'm the menace,* he thought with a smile.

Turning the radio off, he gripped the steering wheel and took a deep breath. The traffic was moving again, slowly, but at least he was getting away from the woman driver who was still looking at him, while talking on her phone.

He kept his eyes ahead as she glared at him as he passed.

He shifted his car into second gear as the flow began to edge a little faster. He looked at the clock on the dash; it was still only a quarter-to-nine. He had plenty of time to get into the office and start work on the server upgrade he had planned for yesterday. *Thank you Rod, and Gerard.*

The traffic slowed again, and as he reduced his speed pulled the gear down from the fourth he had only just slipped into, back down to second.

He looked up at the sky. The morning was warm, but the sky was moody. A heavy cloud cover, a mixture of light and dark greys, lay thick in the sky, promising, or maybe just threatening a coming storm. There wasn't even a hint of blue up there.

A digital road sign loomed overhead. Huge orange letters told him what he already knew: ACCIDENT AHEAD. There was always an accident at this junction. He pondered why they even bothered with the expense of the massive signs when all they did was tell everyone what they already knew. His eyes idly flicked back towards the sign. The letters were dancing about up there, making him squint. He blinked, thinking his eyes were going funny, or he had more sweat in them.

Then his heart was no longer in his chest where it belonged. It was now deep in his stomach, making him feel like he needed the toilet. It was a similar feeling to being on a ride in a theme park. The letters were all blinking off and on. Each time they reappeared they were jumbled. He could tell it wasn't a glitch, it was much more than that. He knew exactly what they were going to read when he looked back up.

He wanted to keep his gaze away from it. He looked everywhere else other than up. He turned to his right and caught the eyes of the same woman who had glared at him earlier. She was still looking at him as she ate a sandwich, another cigarette in her other hand, as she shook her head.

He thought about flipping her a one-fingered salute but then thought better of it. *You're better than that,* he thought, wanting to laugh, but couldn't knowing the sign was still above him. She saw him laugh and offered him a grimace as if he were filth on the bottom of her shoe.

This made him laugh more.

Then, without thinking, he looked up.

He wasn't the least bit surprised to see what the sign read.

TURN THEM OFF, THEN TURN THEM ON AGAIN!

He blinked and gripped the steering wheel tighter. He was suddenly cold, shivery as if a summer flu had hit him, hard. He was shaking his head, sweat flinging off him with each movement. He looked back up. He had high hopes that it was going to read simply, ACCIDENT AHEAD.

He was bitterly disappointed.

CARL... TURN THEM OFF, THEN TURN THEM ON AGAIN!

He looked around again. The woman in the car was back on her phone, a little bit of lettuce was stuck to her lip as she was talking. By the way she was side eyeing him, he was obviously the topic of the conversation.

51

He looked behind him. The man in the car behind was idly picking his nose, as if being in the car hid him from everyone else and no one could see his disgusting little habit. Even in his burgeoning panic, he knew he was just as guilty as the man for picking his nose and flicking the booger out of the window. A man and a woman with two kids were in the car behind the nosey woman; they were all singing a song they obviously enjoyed.

No one was looking at the sign.

He gripped the steering wheel again. The car felt oppressively hot now. He looked at the temperature gauge; it read seventeen degrees. That wasn't too warm, even though the morning had been warm. Sweat was dripping from his brow and his armpits. *Am I having a stroke?* he asked himself. He opened the window again. As he did, the woman in the car next to him flinched, as if he might jump out of his seat, into her car and attack her.

He had no intentions of attacking anyone, but he did want to jump out of the car. He could feel it closing in on him. The steering wheel felt closer; the peddles beneath his feet felt as if they were getting nearer—he could no longer stretch his leg out fully. The back seats were encroaching, invading his personal space.

He covered his nose, anticipating a thick fishy stink.

His head began to spin, and he felt like he might vomit.

The same noise he'd heard in the bathroom echoed through his head. *Shlopp!*

He didn't want to look as he knew he was going to see something wet, something horrible, something that had spewed from Amy's vagina would be slapping the glass of the windows.

He spun, not wanting to, but needing to see where it was coming from.

The cars that had been all around him, hemming him in, were gone. They had been replaced with water, dirty, green water. His car was totally submerged. He could see rock formations, old wrecks of ancient ships, all with green plankton gripping them, waving like victorious flags in the wicked current he could feel buoying his vehicle.

He wasn't alone.

Something was hiding, lurking in the murk all around him. It was big, it was powerful...

It was old.

He removed his hand from his nose. The anticipated stink was indeed there, thick, and wet, *like going down on Amy,* he thought.

His stomach churned. He felt it flip, roll over. This time, there was no saliva buildup in his mouth before he vomited. Thick, foul, and bitter water streamed from his mouth, and his nose. The stench of fish doubled, trebled, quadrupled, as thick, green tinted water flowed.

Through tear-streamed eyes, he looked up towards where the sign should have been, but it had been replaced. It was now nothing but a dark, shadow shifting in the filth.

Something was lurking. Something was seeing him.

A beep from somewhere made him jump.

He opened his eyes. There was no vomit down the front of his shirt, there was no water around him, the sign above him read ACCIDENT AHEAD, and the cars that were back around him were now moving.

There was a large space before him where the traffic had begun to flow.

He looked in the rearview mirror and saw the angry face of the man who had been picking his nose.

He offered him a wave as an apology, put the car in gear, and began moving off.

He spared one more look up to the sign above him.

It hadn't changed!

7.

'CARL, HAVE YOU seen this error message before?' Cheryl on reception asked him as he walked through the main doors. 'Jesus,' she continued as he looked at her. 'Are you OK? You look awful.'

'Yeah, well, thanks for that. I was feeling great until about five seconds ago.' He offered her a smile that wasn't convincing anyone, least of all, himself. He ran his fingers through his hair, not entirely surprised that it came away wet from the sweat caused by the heat of the morning, and the strange occurrence in his car. 'I'm just feeling a little bit'—he paused for a moment before continuing— 'out of it!'

He made his way behind the reception desk and leaned into the screen Cheryl was pointing at. 'Margaret had it this morning too. I've never seen it before.'

Normally he would have made a dirty joke about Margaret *having it* this morning, but the chill that tore through his body as he looked at the black box on the screen, ripped the joke from his breath. It was the same message he'd seen yesterday on the machines that had been left on.

Error: The function LIFE is not responding
Terminating function
Press any key to reboot system ...

Turn them off, then turn them on again ...

He swallowed hard as he looked at the white words on the black background. He turned to Margaret. 'You got the same message?'

The younger girl's eyebrows raised as she nodded.

'Did you ring IT?'

'No,' Cheryl replied. 'It's only just happened on mine. Just as you walked in.'

He looked at Margaret's console. The same message was on her screen. It felt like an accusation, like it was pulsing at him, eating into his brain.

'Did it just flash up? I don't know what's going on, but I'm seeing this message everywhere,' he said, looking at the younger girl. 'Did you do anything different this morning when you logged on?'

Margaret shook her head.

'Me neither,' Cheryl interrupted. 'All I wanted to do was print this document. It said, print spooler service not active. What's a print spooler? She's getting the same thing.'

Carl looked at her as if he'd never seen her before in his life. 'What?' he asked, shaking his head. 'What are you talking about? Print spooler?'

'That message there,' she said, pointing to her screen.

The black message was gone.

It was replaced with a small grey box that read: PRINTER ERROR: PRINT SPOOLER SERVICE IS NOT ACTIVE!

Carl's brow ruffled as he looked at the screen. He then looked back at Margaret's screen. The black box had gone from there too, replaced by the same grey one as Cheryl's.

'Are you sure you're OK?' Margaret asked, looking up at him from her chair. 'You're pale.' She put her hand over her face and moved her chair away from him. 'You're not coming down with something, are you? I'm away next week. I don't want your germs all over me.'

Carl looked at her, then back at the screens, and then at Cheryl. Both women were backing away from him.

'I'll … I'll, erm, I'll have a word and see if the printer service is running on the server. I've got to do an upgrade today anyway.'

As he walked away from the reception, both women watched him stagger off down the corridor, both of them were shaking their heads.

'Carl, this is getting stupid now!'

Oh, fuck off, Bryce; I don't need your mithering today, he thought as he was accosted by the same man as he was every day.

'The network speed. It's atrocious. I can't get anything done today. Everyone's complaining. All the printers are down too. What are you guys doing about it?'

'Alan, I haven't even got to my *fucking* desk yet,' Carl spat. His voice louder than he thought it had been, and a number of users looked up from their machines, excited at the drama unfolding before them.

Bryce looked like he had been slapped, hard.

Carl took a deep breath. 'Look, Al. I'm sorry for shouting. I'll have a look at the server when I get to my desk. I think I just need a strong coffee.'

'Well, while you get your coffee, we could be losing a tender worth millions here,' Alan snapped back.

Carl knew there was going to be a complaint going in about him. Right then, he didn't care. He turned away from the angry man and stormed off towards his department.

He ignored a few other calls of his name, even the female ones. All he wanted to do was get to his desk and try to sort out what the fuck was happening in his life. Something strange—not to mention scary—was occurring, and he had absolutely no idea what it could be.

~~~~

'Medley called for you,' Charles said with a smirk the moment Carl stepped into the office.

'Can I even sit down before you start giving me the shit?' Carl snapped. There was time to see Charles laugh before he disappeared back behind his computer screen.

'What did he want?'

'Something about files on a data drive. He said he was talking to you about it last night, said you'll know what it's about,' Charles continued from behind his screens.

Carl leaned back in his chair and put his hands over his face.

'Are you OK?' Tasha asked, popping her head over her monitor to look at him.

Carl dropped his hands and looked at her. He liked Tasha, but sometimes she just annoyed him for no reason whatsoever. 'No, Tasha, I'm not,' he replied.

'Do you want a cup of coffee?' she asked. 'You look a bit ...'

Carl waited to find out what he looked like, but when it didn't come and her voice petered out, he decided to ask her. 'A little what, Tasha?' he snapped, instantly regretting it. Shouting at Tasha was the equivalent of kicking a puppy when you were angry.

'Erm …' she mumbled.

Carl closed his eyes and raised a hand. 'I'm sorry, Tasha. You're right; I am feeling a bit off. I've just had a mad couple of days. It's nothing. But, in answer to your question, no, thank you. I don't want a cup of coffee.'

Tasha smiled—it looked a little nervous—and hid herself back behind her monitors.

'I'm never going to get that server upgrade done, am I?' It was a rhetorical question, and everyone in the office knew it.

He unlocked his drawer and removed the hard drive he had used to back up Gerard's laptop. He was just about to plug it into his work computer but stopped himself at the last moment. Whatever filth had been on that hard drive, he didn't want it to infect the network.

He got out of his seat and made his way over to the storeroom to pull out a spare machine. He dug an operating system drive from his drawer and began building it as Gerard's new laptop as a stand-alone machine. He then took another older, spare machine and dumped the corrupted files onto this one, leaving it off the network.

'Is there anything wrong with the print servers?' he asked the room as the laptop began to build.

'There's something wrong with everything, mate,' Dean said without turning around. 'Print server, proxy server, data servers, backup servers, the whole network is going tits.'

'Alan Bryce just collared me on the way in, like he does every day,' Carl continued.

'That guy needs a life,' Dean laughed. 'Tell him there's more in Heaven and Hell than can be found in his work computers.'

That's rich coming from you! Carl thought with an internal smile before turning back to his own machine.

As he waggled his mouse, his monitor came to life.

There, in the centre of the screen, just over the instructions to press CTRL+ALT+DELETE, was the dreaded black box. It was displaying the exact same message as it had on the other machines.

Error: The function LIFE is not responding
Terminating function
Press any key to reboot system …

Turn them off, then turn them on again …

Carl spun on his chair and addressed the room. 'Have any one of you ever seen this message before?'

Everyone ignored him.

Everyone except Jodi, the one he expected the least out of. 'What message?' she asked, standing up to look at where he was pointing.

'This one.' He pointed to his screen but wasn't the least bit surprised to see the box was gone.

'Fuck, it's gone!' he sighed as he looked back.

Jodi shook her head and sat back down. 'I can't help you if there's nothing to help with,' she mumbled.

Carl glared at her as he logged on. He opened up his Internet search page, on his own machine, and entered the message. The function LIFE is not responding.

There were several hits. The first ones were all sponsored links wanting to take him to online shops to buy exotic perfumes called LIFE and FUNCTION and so forth. Others were about films, books, and albums that featured either the word LIFE or FUNCTION.

There was nothing about a computer error.

He clicked his tongue and typed again. Command prompt. The function LIFE is not responding …

Again, there was nothing.

He sat back and stared at his screen. He couldn't believe he didn't get at least one hit.

His phone rang. Acting on autopilot, he picked it up. 'Good morning, IT,' he offered chirpily—a lot chirpier than he felt.

The sound on the other end sounded like a mobile phone that had been dropped into a swirling river.

His first instinct was to drop the receiver.

Which he acted on.

This alerted everyone in the room, and they all stopped what they were doing to see what was happening. He felt the glare of everyone's eyes on him. Slowly, he picked up the receiver and put it tentatively to his ear. The same bubbling, gurgling noise emitted from it.

This time, he put the receiver back in its cradle slowly. As soon as it was down, it rang again.

He was still the centre of attention, and it seemed that him answering the phone might be the best entertainment on offer today.

He stared at the device for a few moments.

'Are you not going to get that?' Charles asked, pointing at the phone.

Carl looked at him as if he had snuck up on him while in the shower, doing something he shouldn't be doing. 'What?' he asked, his voice dry and wavering.

'The phone, numbnuts. Are you going to answer it, or what?'

'Oh, yeah. Of course I am.'

'Well, hurry up then. The noise is doing my head in.'

'Good morning, IT,' Carl said, notably less chirpy than before. He was expecting the underwater sounds.

'Carl,' the male voice on the other end of the line shouted. 'Sorry, mate, I just tried to call but my signal's crap. It's Billy from on-site.'

He felt the unease and tenseness loosen in his stomach; it was like a huge weight had been lifted from him when he realised the last call hadn't been anything to do with what was going on around him. 'Billy, how are you, mate?'

The conversation went on, and Carl fixed the problem he had. When he finished, he logged the call on his system and turned his attention back to the stand-alone laptop next to him.

It was pretty much done.

He inserted the drive from Gerard's laptop and browsed the file structure. Ignoring all the system folders he headed for the one he was looking for. It was on the root of the drive and as Gerard had said, it was called WORK.

With the oppression of some existential dread building in his stomach, he double clicked the yellow folder.

As he did, the lights in the office dimmed.

He spun around in his chair again as the stink from his bathroom and the place he didn't want to think about—between his wife's legs—was back.

He was also alone in the office.

'TURN THEM OFF, THEN TURN THEM ON AGAIN!'

This time, the voice was not a whisper; it was a shout, one that boomed from everywhere, all at once. He put his hands over his ears, hoping to drown out the horrific disembodied voice, but it was to no avail.

'CARL ...' There sounded like a bubbling effect to the voice now, as if the person speaking was doing so from the depths of some long dead ocean.

'YOU CAN'T IGNORE ME, CARL. I AM THE MASTER, AND I WILL BE OBEYED!'

The stink was as strong as it had been in the car. He looked out of the window, and instead of seeing the windows of the other wing of the building, there was nothing but water. Dirty, filth-strewn water.

'DO YOU SEE ME NOW?' the voice asked or demanded. 'TURN THEM OFF, THEN TURN THEM ON AGAIN, CARL. THE FUNCTION LIFE IS NOT RESPONDING!'

There was a shifting outside. Something huge and shapeless lurked in the murky shadows. *Is it the same something that was outside the car?* he thought. Then another thought occurred to him. *The function LIFE? Did the voice just say that?*

Something hit the window, hard.

Carl screamed, and looked around him, trying to see who might have heard his indiscretion. There was no one there, just the same vague ghosts he'd seen before. Once he controlled himself, he looked out the window, trying to see what it might have been that hit the glass.

Then he saw it.

Or part of it at least.

It was long and muscular, and emitting a slight glow that cut through the darkness. The sickly green and yellow luminescence was familiar. He didn't want to think about where he'd seen it come out of before, but the same salty tang of blood and seawater filled his mouth.

'Get the fuck away from me!' he whispered, scraping his fingernails down his tongue in an attempt to remove the vile taste.

'What the fuck are you doing?'

Carl stopped backing away from the window at the side of his desk and turned towards the new voice.

It was Dean's.

He was stood next to his PC; Charles was behind him, as was Jodi. Tasha was looking at him from her desk, twitching, playing with her hair as if not knowing what to do with herself.

Carl spun on his heels. Outside the window was the familiar view of the offices opposite them. There was no water, no glowing muscular tentacle, and no shapeless mass lurking in the near distance.

'Are you OK, mate?' Dean asked in a conspiratorial whisper.

'What's going on in here?' Big Rod asked as he entered the office to see a stunned looking Carl, looking pale and more than a little frightened.

'Carl just jumped up and told us to get the fuck away from him,' Tasha said from behind her screen.

Rod looked at him; Carl returned the stare.

The smaller man indicated towards his office. 'Can I have a word with you, Carl? In my office!'

As he walked out, Carl looked at the faces of his colleagues. They all looked concerned except for Charles, who was smirking, and Bryan, who still had his headphones on.

~~~~

'I'm just going to ask, Carl. Have you been drinking?'

Carl sat down without being invited, which prompted Rod to find his own chair around the other side of the table.

All Carl could do was sigh.

'I've just had a phone call from HR. Apparently, you told Alan Bryce to fuck off this morning.'

Carl leaned forward in the chair and put his head in his hands. 'Rod, I think I'm going mad, mate. I keep seeing this message come up on the computer screens. I've searched for it and can't find anything related to it. But it's—'

'I'm sorry, Carl,' Rod interrupted, looking at his watch. 'I've got a meeting I need to go to with the head of finance. Can we do this another time?'

'What? You just asked me to come in here,' Carl said, his voice at least an octave higher than it normally was.

'I know, I know. I just need to get this out of the way. We'll chat a bit later, OK?'

Carl got up and walked out of the office. As he got back to his desk, he looked at the folder on the laptop screen, the one he'd opened before he'd had another … *another what?* he asked himself. The only word he could think of was *episode*.

'Carrie rang for you,' Tasha said over her monitor. 'She wants to know if you can go around and sort her out.'

For the first time that day, a smile broke on Carl's face. 'Oh, I think I can manage that. Did she say what it was about?'

'Nope, just something popping up on her screen. She only wanted to talk to you.'

He made an exaggerated pained face as he locked his computer and left the department.

~~~~

Carrie Carson worked in the marketing department, which was on the opposite side of the square from where the IT department was located.

As Carl took off to look at whatever problem Carrie had, he would have to pass through the open plan offices of the rest of the floor. Normally, he didn't mind the excursion, but today, with everything that was happening to him and all the moaning about the slow network, he was dreading it. *I'll start that server upgrade I've been threatening while I'm around there,* he thought. This made sense, as Server Room One was located close to the marketing department, next to the men's toilets.

He mentally prepared himself as he walked through the corridors.

'Carl …'

He ignored the first shout.

'Carl …'

And the second one—he could tell by the voice it was *that dickhead* Bryce.

He continued walking and heard his name being called at least five times. Once he reached the end of the first corner, he was in the executive suite, and it was unlikely he would be accosted in this part.

He was wrong about that.

'Oh, Carl?' the female voice called from one of the doors. He recognised Leanne, Gerard's assistant's, timid voice.

He turned and offered her a false smile. 'Hey, Leanne. Did you want me? Well, I know you probably do, what with you being female and all …'

The joke was lost on her.

'Not me, as such. Gerard was just asking me about the files from his machine. Do you have them?'

'I do, but I've had to build another laptop to retrieve them. Whatever virus was on that hard drive would have knocked out the entire network if I'd have plugged it in. So, I'll have them probably in an hour or so. I'm just off to the marketing department to do a call. I'll give him a shout when I'm finished there.'

'OK then. You won't forget, will you?'

'Turn her off, Carl!'

He was stunned into silence.

Had that voice come from inside his head? He looked up at the ceiling to see if there was anything there, but all he could see was a wireless router flashing away. *Could it be coming from that?* he thought.

He cleared his head and swallowed before looking back at her. 'Right, I'll ring you in a bit. I have to go …' He almost ran from the CEO's door, leaving a lost-looking Leanne watching him go.

He walked quickly towards the other corner and beyond it into the marketing department.

'Riggs,' Richard—the youngest and cockiest member of the marketing department—shouted out to him as he opened the door and let himself in. 'You come to make our computers work better?' he asked sarcastically over the office.

'The computers only work as well as the idiots using them, Dick,' Carl replied without even thinking.

Richard's face flushed red, and he put his head back down towards the document he was reading.

'Carrie, what seems to be the problem, chicken? Or did you just get me around here for nefarious purposes?' he asked as he approached the desk of the most desirable lady in his life—*apart from the wife,* he reminded himself.

This made him think of last night, and a cold sweat covered his body.

Carrie spun in her chair and beamed at him.

I swear that she's as into me as I am to her.

'It's my computer,' she said with a giggle.

'Do you know what? I must be psychic. I knew that was what the problem was going to be, what with the call into the IT department and all. People just don't ring us to say, *Carl, my computer is working perfectly; do you want to come round and see for yourself?* Maybe afterwards we can go for a drink and then run off together into the sunset, never to be seen again.'

Carrie was laughing.

'Well, there is Ray in engineering. He rings us all the time, but he's not really my type; if you know what I mean?'

Carrie reached out her hand and playfully slapped him. The contact of her skin on his caused a tingle to surge through him.

She is into me!

'This pop-up box keeps coming up,' she said, her face becoming businesslike as she looked at her screen. 'It says something about rebooting my system.'

Carl went cold. 'It says what?' he asked, leaning in to look at her screen. The alluring smell of whatever fantastic, and sexy perfume she was wearing was lost on him now.

Is she seeing the message too?

'I've got it up for you.'

Normally he would have retorted with something along the lines of, *Well I've had it up for you for years now,* but this didn't feel like the time for jokes. If she was seeing the message, then maybe, just maybe, he wasn't going mad.

When the sexual innuendo retort never happened, she clicked a few pages, minimising them, and a small black command prompt box was underneath.

He looked at the text, his heart pounding in his ears.

AUTOUPDATE FAILED ...
TYPE OK TO REBOOT MACHINE >

It wasn't the same pop-up.

He felt all the breath in his lungs dispell. He couldn't breathe. He wanted to cough, to choke, but all he could feel was his face turning red, and then blue. His vision began to swim, and he could feel his legs wobbling beneath him.

'So, should I just type OK, then?'

'What?'

'Should I type OK?'

'Oh, erm, yeah. Make sure you save everything you have op—' He stopped talking as he looked at the screen again. It was flashing. White then black, the text the opposite of the colour of the screen.

TURN HER OFF ...

THEN TURN HER ON AGAIN>

TURN HER OFF ...

THEN TURN HER ON AGAIN>

Over and over again it flashed.

'Are you sure you're OK?'

He was getting a little pissed off with people asking him if he was OK. He snapped his head around to look at her. 'Can you see that? On your screen?'

She looked where he was pointing and shrugged. 'The pop-up box I was telling you about? Should I type OK?'

Carl stood. The screen was still flashing.

TURN HER OFF ...

THEN TURN HER ON AGAIN>

TURN HER OFF ...

THEN TURN HER ON AGAIN>

It's only me who can see it! This thought unnerved him more than he could possibly imagine. 'Hm?' he asked when he heard her voice.

'Are you paying attention? Should I type OK or not?'

'Fucking type it if you want to. I'm not here to tell you what to do,' he snapped and walked off towards the door. As he did, he looked back once to see Carrie, Richard, and the other four members of the marketing department all looking at him. That wasn't what was bothering him, though; it was the flashing on all the screens he could see.

Every screen was flashing just like Carrie's.

TURN THEM OFF ...

THEN TURN THEM ON AGAIN>

TURN THEM OFF ...

THEN TURN THEM ON AGAIN>

He pulled the door open too fast and narrowly avoided hitting himself in the face with it, then left the room at full speed.

When he was in the corridor, his breath lost him again. He could feel his throat tighten, constricting his air. He was hot, too hot. He pulled at the polo-shirt he was wearing, and the two buttons that were closed popped off. He heard them bounce on the floor as the walls of the corridor began to change colour. They went from the dull cameo beige that followed you around the whole square, to a dark, dirty, mouldy green. It looked like seaweed was growing from the floor to the ceiling. Filthy, decaying rot, like something that had been wet for hundreds, maybe even thousands of years.

The stench was back too.

No matter how many times he smelt it, it turned his stomach. It was the stink of decaying clam chowder that had been mixed with shit.

'TURN THEM OFF, THEN TURN THEM ON AGAIN!'

The voice disappeared, as did his panic attack, the green on the walls, and the smell.

He bent over, his hands on his hips, and breathed deep.

'Are you—'

'Don't you fucking dare ask me if I'm OK,' he snapped at whoever it was asking him.

It was the football bore—at that moment, Carl couldn't even remember his name. He stepped back and held his hands in the air in surrender. 'Whoa, don't shoot the messenger,' he laughed. 'You look how Crystal Palace looked when Everton turned them over last week.'

'Well, I'm glad you can find a funny side to this,' Carl growled.

The football bore put his hands down. 'Do you want me to get a first aider?' he asked, seeing that Carl wasn't joking.

He took in a couple of deep breaths, and held them for a few moments, before releasing them through pierced lips. He shook his head. 'No, I'll be fine. It's just fatigue. I haven't been sleeping lately. Listen, I'm sorry for snapping just then; I'm just overly tired.'

'I hear that,' he replied, slapped Carl on the shoulder and walked off, back down the corridor. 'If you're sure you don't need a first aider?'

'No, thanks. I'm fine, honest, fella.' Carl felt a little embarrassed that he couldn't remember his name, but there were too many people for him to remember in the office.

He picked his buttons from the floor and looked at them. *It looks like I'm sewing tonight, then,* he thought, putting them in his pocket.

He staggered along the corridor, past the reception.

'Carl, are you—'

He held up his hand to stop the question and continued walking.

He ignored the shouts and jibes coming his way about the speed of the network and the general performance of the computers. He needed space, a little bit of quiet, somewhere he could catch his breath.

He got to his desk, and Jodi looked over at him. 'Rod—'

'Will just have to wait,' he interrupted, grabbing the laptop off his desk and marching off in the direction of the IT meeting room. He walked, slamming the door behind him.

Once inside, he leaned against the door and banged the back of his head on it. He sat at the table and rested his head, relishing the cold wood against his hot brow.

He didn't hear the door open, so when Rod spoke, he jumped.

'Carl,' his boss whispered.

Carl winced, as he almost expected him to say, 'Turn them off, then turn them on again!'

He was relieved when he didn't.

'Carl, I'm sending you home, mate. You look like shit, and you're snapping at people left and right. That's not like you. So, before you get yourself into trouble, go home.'

Carl looked at his boss and smiled. He nodded as he walked out, taking Medley's files with him.

8.

THE DRIVE HOME was uneventful. He kept his windows tightly closed, telling himself it was because the air-conditioning in the car worked best with them closed and it was a hot day; but in reality, he didn't want to slip into another daydream and allow the water to stream into the car and drown him. Nor did he fancy the idea of a long, luminous, muscular tentacle wrapping itself around his neck and killing him while he drove.

When he got home, he was surprised to see Amy's car still on the path. He squinted at it through tired eyes, just to make sure it was really her car.

It was.

Why is she home?

He had to concentrate to remember what day of the week it was.

Is it Tuesday? Or Wednesday? Either way, she should be in work!

He parked the car on the path and got out, bringing the laptop with him.

He spared a glance up towards the bedroom window and was sure he saw a flick of the curtains. He dismissed it and dug in deep for his keys.

As he entered the house, he heard a lot of panicked thumping around upstairs. At first, he thought it might have been burglars, but then he remembered Amy's car.

'Honey, they sent me home from work. I don't know if I'm sick or not, but I've been having these weird daydreams. Sickly fish smell everywhere. Amy, are you up there?'

'Yeah, Carl. I'm coming down now,' her voice filtered down. She sounded out of breath.

'How come you're home?' he asked as he went into the kitchen to put the kettle on. He put the laptop on the counter and filled the kettle with water. 'Do you want a cup of tea?'

'Erm … no,' she replied.

He then heard her coming downstairs. It sounded like there was more than just her up there.

He grabbed the laptop and walked out of the kitchen.

Amy's hair was a mess, looking like it had been hurriedly brushed, and her face was red, flushed.

Her clothes had been put on in a hurry.

A man walked down behind her.

Carl didn't recognise him, but his face was flushed too, and he looked worried.

'Who's this?' he asked.

'Erm … remember you said the internet was slow; well, Mark here, well he …'

The house went dark as if the sun had passed behind a thick cloud and had decided to give up on trying to brighten the day. The stench from between her legs was back, only this time, there was another stink behind it, nearly as thick and as bad as the smell of fish.

But somehow worse.

He'd smelt this before, only the once, but he remembered it to this very day. When he was a younger lad, he had gone to Amsterdam with his mates. They'd all wanted to smoke weed and go to the strip joints. One of his mates found a peep show where you paid a euro to enter a booth. In there you could watch some old, and bored looking prostitute getting it given to her by a younger man, degrading herself for the humour of the paying patrons.

Well, that was the stink he could smell now.

It was the thick, physical stonk of the peep-show booths.

It was the reek of dirty, sordid sex.

'TURN THEM OFF, CARL, THEN TURN THEM ON AGAIN!'

It wasn't his own voice whispering to him, it was too loud for that.

The vile, wet slap—*shlopp*—of something hitting glass or another hard surface came again.

SLAP!

He could see patterns on the walls, as outside the window, the greeny-brown of the dirty water was back. He could see the mammoth black shadow skulking somewhere in the murky depths.

SHLOPP!

The wet sound came again.

~~~~

He woke up in bed. It was getting dark outside, and panic blossomed through him. *The kids,* he thought as he looked at the clock.

It was seven minutes past eight.

'Shit,' he mumbled sitting up and grabbing his mobile phone. He looked at the last dialled number; it was his mother's.

He didn't remember ringing her.

He looked at his text messages.

There was one from his mother. It read, 'I've got them. They're OK to stay tonight. We'll get them to school in the morning. Ring when Amy gets home from her meeting.'

Meeting?

He then looked at the next message; it was from Josh, his son.

'Dad, I asked nan to lend me a tenner to go to the football tomorrow with school, is that OK?'

He'd replied to this one.

'Yeah, that's cool.'

He scratched his head and looked at the phone before putting it back on the side table. He looked for Amy.

She wasn't next to him.

He remembered being sent home from work but nothing about getting home or going to bed. 'I'm getting worse!' he mumbled as he got up out of the bed. 'Amy,' he shouted out of the room.

There was no reply.

'Amy, are you in?'

He looked out the window and saw her car was not there. She must have gone to her mother's. *Or is at that meeting,* he thought. *The one my mum was talking about.*

He wrapped a housecoat around himself and made his way down the dark stairs. Something about the house troubled him. It was too quiet and far too dark. He thought about the whispered voices he'd been hearing and the daydreams he'd been having. Everything in his instincts screamed at him, telling him he didn't *want* to go downstairs, but he knew he had to.

Without turning a light on—he wanted the dark right now—he made his way into the dining room. He could see in the gloom, the laptop he'd brought home from work.

It was on the table.

He sat down and pulled it closer to him.

There was a crack on the lid he was sure hadn't been there earlier. He traced his fingers along it.

It felt wet.

I hope it's not broken, he thought.

He flipped it open and pressed the power button. To his relief, the laptop powered up and the screen hadn't been damaged.

He entered his credentials, and the operating system opened up on the folder he had copied over yesterday before the world had gone mad.

Something occurred to him then, causing him to break a small smile. He hadn't seen the message that had been plaguing him. He nodded, acknowledging this fact, and proceeded to open the folder.

Inside were a number of text documents, each one named MASTER #1, MASTER #2, MASTER #3, and so on, up to MASTER #7.

They weren't large files.

The way Gerard had insinuated the importance of these files, Carl had expected photographs or videos of some depraved shit, something involving animals or, God forbid, children.

But it was just text files.

He double clicked on the first file. MASTER #1.

The application associated with the file opened, and he saw that it was indeed just text.

He started to read.

DAY #1

I don't know what happened!

I believe I'll need to keep a journal of what has been happening to me over the last week, even if it is just for my own sanity, or even amusement. I've seen things that might make a lesser man's hair turn snowy white. Wonderous things, and terrible at the same time. I believe I might have stumbled on something I cannot understand, or even comprehend.

It started a few nights ago. Brenda had gone to bed early with one of her heads, but I had some work I needed to finish for the upcoming Bangkok trip.

I know some people are laughing that I'm going to Bangkok, and to be fair, I will be having my share of fun while I'm over there, and why shouldn't I? But it will be a business trip first and foremost.

I started working but soon got bored, and my wandering fingers found their way towards that damned internet icon in the corner of my screen.

The naked form has always been a weakness of mine, and tonight, with Brenda drugged up to her eyeballs, I fancied a small dalliance!

'I knew he was a dirty old bastard,' Carl laughed as he made his way into the kitchen. He opened the fridge door, the light illuminating him and the dark room behind him. He removed a can of beer and pulled the ring-pull. He took a long swig of the cold, fizzy liquid. He belched loudly before putting the can to his head. It was still warm in the house despite the lateness of the evening.

He got back to the table and pulled the laptop closer to him, ready for some insight into the perverted mind of their managing director.

Despite what people think, I do know a little about computers, and I was able to disable the proxy settings that are enforced on the work's laptops. That is why I insisted I was made an administrator on my own machine.

I then connected to my own little VPN, the one that scatters any trace routes to my IP address. I grinned as I gained access to the more delicate, and delicious areas of the Dark Web. My own little delights.

Carl pouted as he read this little titbit of information. 'The old bastard has been faking his uselessness for years,' he laughed before continuing.

I was hungry for filth, and there is nowhere better on the planet. Anything I want, any dark requests and fantasies are catered for, right there at my fingertips!

I entered my information, including the company credit card details, into a certain site where my dark odyssey usually begins. Who doesn't like a little torture porn at the end of a hard day in the office?

Oh, the images it showed me. How they tickled and aroused me. There was one woman who looked just like poor old Leanne. It was fun to imagine it was her tied up in that chair.

I bet she would enjoy it!

Watching as the poor girl was beaten and cut with a rusty knife was stimulating, but that kind of thing can only get you so far along. I wanted something juicy ... I wanted to push myself, to view something even I would think was wrong!

'What the fuck?' Carl whispered in the dark. He toyed with the idea of closing the lid on this laptop and calling the police.

He drummed his fingers just below the keyboard as he thought about his next move. He took another swig of beer and screwed his mouth into a tight hole. *I've come this far; I might as well finish the first entry, at least.*

He took another swig of his drink and continued.

I did a quick search, and the usual stuff popped up. Normally I would have been titillated by the wonders on offer, but tonight ... tonight was different. I hungered for something on a different level.

A file offered itself to me.

It was from a location I'd never seen before, from a user I was not familiar with. His handle was simply HP.

HP? Carl thought. *HP?* It sounded familiar. *Where have I seen HP before?* He looked at the laptop he was on. The logo emblazoned across the top of the lid answered his question. 'Fucking weirdo's flights of fancy,' he mused. 'Would the guy's name have been Dell if he was using a different computer?' He laughed, amusing himself with his rubbish joke.

He continued to read the shocking, yet compulsive text.

I entered the forum and was happy to find I was the only one in the chatroom, other than HP himself. I introduced myself, giving whoever it was the usual passwords and codes that were used across the Dark Web to let them know I was not an agent of the authorities attempting to subdue people's fun.

He asked me if I believed in cosmic horror!

It sounded like something I wanted to see, so I told him yes, cosmic horror was probably something I could handle.

He sent me a file.

As it arrived in my download folder, I won't lie, my heart raced. I could hardly control the shaking of my fingers as I clicked on it.

A whole new world opened up to me.

I saw filth!

It was real filth. Not the watered down rubbish I was offered elsewhere. This was everything to me.

I witnessed the most basic of depravity. There were videos, pictures, there were interactive demonstrations of masked people (their genders were deliciously indecipherable).

I immersed myself completely, and I must say, I had the most wonderous of nights.

HP invited me back. He told me someone called The Master would like to meet me, as he thought I had what they needed to usher forth the new order.

This all sounded so wondrously naughty to me, so obviously, I accepted the kind offer.

As I closed my laptop and wiped myself, I was refreshed, revigorated. I felt like a new, different man. Making my way up to bed, I thought of introducing

Brenda to my new paradigm. I knew she would be illuminated by it.

Carl was surprised that he'd finished his beer. He crushed the can and got himself another. He sat back down at the table and looked at the file structure before him.

He hovered his cursor over the file called MASTER #2 and debated if he even wanted to read what this file had to offer. The first one had been such an insight into that dirty old bastard's dark mind.

He decided he did.

DAY #2

Oh, God. Please forgive me.

The things I did to Brenda last night.

Heaven knows, she's a good woman and did not deserve the defilement I inflicted upon her. The poor woman was already asleep when I got to the bedroom. But after the delights HP had awakened in me, I knew I had to wake her to them too. She simply *had* to experience the disgusting pleasures shown to me in the videos.

How could she not have enjoyed them?

Even the strong drugs she'd taken could not prevent her from waking during my depraved acts.

When I had finished, when I had had my fill, I forced more of the sleeping drugs upon her.

As she dozed, crying, I cleaned her up and went to sleep in the spare bedroom. I didn't want to sleep on the wet, slippery bedsheets. She wouldn't mind; she was out of this world anyway!

Hah ha! Talk about cosmic horror!

Carl's eyes had widened as he read the passage. He picked up his latest beer and was again surprised to find it was over halfway empty.

How the Hell could this sick fuck laugh about raping his own wife?
He wanted nothing more than to close the laptop and go to bed. Tomorrow,

when he got into work, he'd take the files to Rod. Surely, he'd know what to do with them. If he was too chicken shit to do something with them, he'd take them to HR.

HR sounded too close to HP, for his liking.

'But …' he whispered in the dark after a beery belch. His eyes shifted from side to side, as if he was looking to see if anyone was witnessing his enjoyment, *is that what it is,* of these horrific texts.

The house was quiet.

He knew he shouldn't continue; but he did!

> I worked from home today. There was just no way I could drag myself away from my new obsession.
>
> As I got out of bed, I was aching delightfully from head to toe. It was my muscles remembering my physical exertions. I could only imagine how poor Brenda was feeling today. In her drugged state, I fed her even more pills. I didn't want the good lady to suffer any more than she needed to. Also, with her asleep all day, it would give me leave to do anything that I wanted to do.
>
> I poured myself into my online activities. Delicious, sickly pleasure after pleasure assaulted my eyes. I am pleased to report that I am almost raw down below from incessant rubbing, but it's nothing a little petroleum jelly cannot sort.

Carl thought he would never get that vision out of his head. He retrieved himself another beer before continuing to read.

> Eventually, HP introduced me to this MASTER character. I am not too proud to admit that I was a little nervous at first. HP had informed me of his role in this whole Dark Web adventure I was undertaking.
>
> Apparently, he is something of a God character, so far as I can ascertain. He was cast away with the four winds over a millennia ago, and his endgame is to get back into prominence as soon as he can.

Reboot: A Cosmic Horror

I do enjoy a little role-play.

He is a stickler for what he called 'the old ways.' It all sounded rather pagan to me, definitely pre-Christian anyway. Ritual sacrifice, the eating of cleansed flesh, fornication that pleases the Gods, that kind of thing.

Anyway, HP and The Master informed me of a way that he could return. It's more than a little eccentric, but it sounds like good fun.

He told me that in this modern age, not many people knew about the 'old ways', and these practices would probably be abhorrent to them anyway. That is why he resides in the Dark Web, waiting for someone to awaken him, to guide his hand back into the prominence he truly deserves.

I must say it all sounds like a lot of fun.

He promised he would send me instructions that would facilitate his rise, or, as he called it, his return.

I am awaiting his communication.

In the meantime, I am just off to have some fun with poor old Brenda.

He wanted to delete the files he'd read. He wanted to delete the whole folder, to smash the laptop against the wall until it was in pieces on his floor, never to be used ever again, and then burn the house down where he had read them.

But he knew he wouldn't.

There was something in the ramblings of the obviously deranged, not to mention perverted, old man that was mesmerising. He felt he needed to read more.

Carl wondered if he was supposed to find these scribblings, if this dark knowledge was supposed to be imparted upon him. It was a horrible idea, but he couldn't deny the semi-erection in his trousers any more than he could deny his longing for just one more beer.

He looked at the clock. It was nearly ten o'clock, but maybe due to the sleep he'd awoken from earlier, or even the beer—he didn't want to acknowledge that it could be the scripts opening up before him—he wasn't in the least bit tired.

He also didn't want to acknowledge the fact that he wanted more. He wanted to know more about the debauchery Gerard Medley was revelling in. He grabbed another beer from the fridge, noting there were only another three of them left, and returned to the table, to the laptop, and to the titillating files on the screen.

He clicked on the third file.

Day #3

What a glorious day.

I don't think I'll be getting any disturbance from Brenda today. I think I may have enjoyed myself a little too much last night after my dalliance with HP and The Master.

There was a moment where I think she may have stopped breathing altogether, but it passed, and she is once again sleeping off my extravagances.

She's a game old bird, but then, she doesn't really have much choice in the matter ... he he!

I have awoken today to a message from The Master; he has sent me the file he promised.

I have opened it and read it, but alas, it makes little sense to me. I feel I am only getting snippets of the details he is demanding.

There is a manual included in the message. I have opened it up and will attempt to start the proceedings this very evening.

I am going back online in a moment or two, once I have finished this journal entry, but I need to go into the office today, I have an idea of how to decipher the messages The Master is sending me.

I will finish this off later tonight.

Day #3 - addendum

Reboot: A Cosmic Horror

I spent a couple of glorious hours on the Dark Web with my two new friends. I have to say that HP and The Master do know how to revel. They put me to shame with the videos they have sent me.

Just to my taste too.

I do enjoy the defilement of young boys!

I spent a fruitless few of hours in the presence of Leanne. I'm still convinced I'll be able to persuade her to join me in my revels. She is a quiet girl, yet I have heard say that empty vessels make the most noise.

Hah ha!

Brenda will not be joining me tonight. I have had to keep her in an enforced comatose state. I do believe it will take more than a few days for her wounds to heal before she could be seen again in public.

But now that I have the manual, I feel like I might perform a little test run at completing the steps.

There may well be another addendum to this journal tonight.

Day #3 Addendum #2

Brenda is incapacitated.

I tried to follow the steps in the manual, but it was to no avail. I'm thinking I may need assistance in my dark little adventure.

I turned her off, but the old dear would not turn on again, no matter how I tried.

I must go and clean up my mess now.

I'm wondering what I shall tell the children about their mother. Hopefully, I won't have to worry too much about it once The Master returns.

They will understand then.

They will ALL understand.

Carl had read enough.

Had Gerard killed his wife under the instruction of this *Master* person?

Was he reading fact or fiction?

If it was fact, Carl told himself that he would ring the police first thing in the morning, ask them to go to Gerard's house and ascertain the whereabouts of his wife, Brenda.

If it was fiction, then he thought it was brilliant writing. He never would have thought the old man would have enough imagination to conjure up such flights of fancy.

As an IT professional, he'd heard tales of the Dark Web, but he had never, not even once, thought of accessing it.

I've got my kinks, but I'm not that …

He stopped thinking for a moment.

He stopped moving.

He was frozen to the spot.

When it passed, he opened the laptop again. It opened on the MASTER #3 file. There had been something in there that had caught his mind's eye. Something he'd overlooked.

He rescanned the text, hoping *not* to find what he was looking for.

But it was there. In black text on the off-white screen.

I turned her off, but the old dear would not turn on again, no matter how I tried.

He turned her off, he thought. *But couldn't turn her on again!*

Carl sat back in his chair. He couldn't do anything other than stare at the screen. He shivered as cold air enveloped him, bringing the inevitable goosebumps.

He read the words again.

'TURN THEM OFF, THEN TURN THEM ON AGAIN!'

The voice haunted him.

For the first time in a good few hours, he realised he was alone in the house. Amy hadn't come home.

Or has she?

He closed the lid of the computer. As he did, he noticed something thick and slimy lining the crack of the casing. The dark gooey substance was over his hands now too.

The lack of light from the laptop screen hampered him identifying what the substance was. However, there was a strange, but somehow familiar, smell to it. His pulse was throbbing in his temples as he rubbed his fingers together. The substance was thick, it was sticky but not quite liquid.

He stood and looked at the empty beer cans next to the computer. They had the same darkness covering them.

He looked over to the fridge.

The darkness was all over the handle, and over the floor where he'd paced back and forth.

He looked down at his feet.

It was all over them too.

Oh fuck, no, he thought, trying force himself to breathe.

Oh fuck, no! Oh, fuck no! Oh, fuck no!

He looked at the light switch on the wall. In the darkness, he could tell there wasn't any of the dark substance on it.

You know what it is, Carl. Just admit it. You know what it is.

He swallowed.

He looked back at the laptop; he could just about make out the crack along the top of it. The crack he knew hadn't been there when he left work.

He closed his eyes and flicked on the light switch.

The brightness from the ceiling lights illuminated the back of his eyelids for a few moments before he dared himself to open them.

When he did, he wished he'd kept them closed.

Permanently!

The room was awash with dark brownish-crimson.

It was unmistakably—

Blood, he told himself. *You knew it was all along.*

What he didn't know was where it had come from. There seemed to be an awful lot of it.

He remembered he hadn't been home alone. When he got back, Amy had been there with someone called … Mike? Mark? He couldn't remember.

He did remember falling into some sort of horrible daydream, hearing the voice whispering to him and the sounds of the tentacle slapping against the floor.

A movement from outside the kitchen caught his attention. He whipped his head around so fast that he thought he would be feeling it in the morning. 'Amy?' he shouted, leaning back, and gripping the door. 'Amy, is that you?'

There was no reply.

He left the lighted kitchen and walked into the darkness of the hallway. He fumbled for the light switch, found it, and flicked it on.

He realised what the movement had been the moment the room was lit.

The body of Amy's *friend* had fallen, sliding down the wall to finally rest with his head in Amy's lap.

Both of them had deep, dark, dripping holes where their eyes should have been.

There was a scream within him. He could feel it. It was just that he couldn't give birth to it, no matter how much he wanted to. There was no breath left in his body, and he felt like he might choke, or even suffocate. He grabbed at his throat, attempting to release whatever, or whoever, had a grip on his neck stopping his airflow, but there was nothing there.

I don't do panic attacks, he thought.

Well, you do now, he retorted in his own voice.

~~~~

He woke at the kitchen table. He didn't understand how he had gotten there from being in the hallway, but at least he was breathing again. His hands were filthy, as was the table and the cans before him.

The laptop's lid was up, and the screen, smeared in blood, was displaying another one of Gerard's text files.

Even though his eyes were stinging, and his head was swimming, he was compelled to read.

Day #4

Who would have known it was so bloody messy to get rid of a dead body? I know Brenda had a penchant for boxes of chocolates, but bloody-hell, woman, would it have hurt you to do a little exercise now and then?

I have been on to HP and The Master. They were asking how I was getting on with my manual. I had to tell them that it wasn't at all how I had expected it to be.

The manual said that I needed to 'turn them off'. This part could be done in any way I wanted. There was also a small note to tell me that I should have any amount of fun with them before, and after.

I'll tell you now ... I did!

Hah ha!

So much fun.

So, as per instruction, I retrieved a screwdriver from my toolbox and took it to my dear lady wife's eye.

Carl thought about Amy's eyes, and her friend's too. Another shudder ripped through him.

It took some gouging, I'll tell you that, but when the eyeball itself popped, it did so with such a satisfying release. Having watched this kind of thing multiple times on videos on the Dark Web, doing it myself brought on a burst of breathlessness and, dare I say it, an arousal, the likes I have never experienced before.

Once it popped (and I very nearly did too, hah ha!), then I went to work on the other one. It was a good job Brenda was already dead, as I couldn't imagine trying to access the eye socket while the vessel was still thrashing and the like.

Vessel? Carl thought, as yet another shudder crawled through him.

As the second eye popped, the instructions advised me to take a long metal skewer, or use a longer screwdriver, and insert it into the brain via the left eye socket. Once that was completed, I was to do the same with the right. This would create an input and an output.

That took some work, I can tell you. There is quite a bit of cartilage and bone to work through, only using a hand-held tool. I toyed with the idea of using one of my power-tools but thought better of it. I wouldn't want Brenda's brains splattering all over the wall.

Imagine trying to clean all of that up.

After a little while, I managed to get the sockets to the required length, but this is where it all fell apart, I'm afraid. The Master had instructed me to insert a five-meter ethernet cable into the left eye, connected to the broadband router I use in my home. He then wanted me to do the same with another five-meter ethernet cable but this one into the telephone line-in.

I'm buggered if I know what an ethernet cable was, and even if I did, I'm sure I'd not have one.

It looks like my plans are scuppered for tonight ... Maybe if I ask around in work.

Day #4 addendum

No good asking around in work. The Master and HP have just informed me that the vessels need to be turned on within an hour of their turning off.

Ah well, at least I can have a little fun with the body, when I get home. Just a little bit for old time's sake before I dispose of her. HP has requested I video myself engaging with Brenda. He thinks I might want to use it for nostalgia purposes (I just think that he wants to watch, the dirty old bird!).

Carl walked over to the bodies of Amy and her friend. *What was his name?* he thought, shaking his head. That was when he noticed the four ethernet cables lying next to the bodies. The ends of each of them were gored and dripping with the thick drying blood of each victim. He traced the cables and saw they were going into his wireless router.

There was another wire, one he'd missed a moment ago. The reason he missed it was because the plastic sheathing of the cat 6 cable was red and had been camouflaged by the blood. This cable ran from Amy's eye into Marcus's—*or Mike's, or whoever's, I don't* really *care anymore.*

He braved a closer look.

There, on the floor next to Amy's body, was a screwdriver. It, too, was covered in gore. Some of it he could identify as blood, the rest of it was … well, he couldn't really tell what the rest of it was.

'YOU TURNED THEM OFF, CARL. BUT YOU DIDN'T TURN THEM ON AGAIN!'

'Master?' he whispered, looking up towards the ceiling.

'YOU HAVE A NEW MESSAGE!'

Carl heard a familiar noise coming from the laptop in the kitchen. It was the *DONG* that signified the arrival of an email. It was a normal, familiar sound, one he'd heard a million times before, when life had been so… *so what, Carl?*

So normal, he answered himself.

He looked at the machine and cocked his head. It wasn't connected to his home network, not via a cable, wireless, 5G, or anything. It was impossible for the machine to retrieve an email.

With his head throbbing and his body feeling as if it had aged fifty years overnight, he made his way back to the kitchen. He lifted the lid on the bloody laptop and looked in the corner. There was a small yellow envelope.

He did indeed have mail.

He opened it.

It was from an account called MASTER@OLDEGODS.NET

He'd never heard of this account before. Every instinct in his body told him not to open it. The good voices in his head told him to go and clean himself up, have something to eat, then call the police and hand himself in as a double murderer.

He opted for the opening the message option.

Apparently, he'd been chosen to be the conduit of the Gods. His was the honour of opening the gates to allow the 'Old Ones' back.

All he had to do was to follow the instructions (attached)—

He looked; there was indeed a text attachment.

—and his job would be complete.

~~~~

The smell was back. It was thicker and closer than ever. He could feel it, like a slow-moving liquid dribbling through a tube in his nose. He could taste it on the back of his throat.

It was vile.

But it seemed he was getting used to it. It no longer made him want to retch.

His body was surrounded by dirty green water, with a brownish tint to it, yet he could still breathe. Every time he opened his mouth, the bilious liquid rushed in, complete with the lumps and the gristle of whatever was discolouring it, filling him up—*with the filth of untold millennia,* he thought.

This surprised him, and he wanted to keep hold of it, maybe for his next book, the one where the Olde Gods come back from an alternative realm to sacrifice Father Christmas and his naughty reindeer.

He was cold, yet comfortably so, as he floated in the grime. He was aware of movement around him. He couldn't see who—or what—it was, but he could tell they were there. Huge, monstrous, lumbering beasts, unhindered, as he was, by the dirty water and the thick stench.

The rhythm of the ebb carried him away, and his worries floated with him, on the flow.

9.

LIGHT WAS STREAMING in from the window. The curtains hadn't been closed, and it was hitting him right in the eye.

Carl scratched his head and sat up. Amy's side of the bed was empty. He pouted a little at this, as he was always up before her, and she was always there.

He listened for any sign of life from the house.

There was none.

That can't be, he thought as he eased himself out of the bed, scratching somewhere else, somewhere men from the dawn of time have scratched first thing in the morning. 'If Amy's up, then the kids should be up too,' he reasoned. Then he remembered that the kids were staying over in his mother's; he'd sorted that out last night when he'd ...

Killed Amy!

The realisation of what was waiting for him downstairs hit him like an eighteen wheeler truck, with a full trailer.

He'd bashed her over the head with the laptop he'd brought home from work. *Her boyfriend too,* he thought bitterly. He stopped at the door to the bedroom, his hand gripped the handle as everything came flooding back. The blood, the files, the gouging of Amy's eyes, and her boyfriend's—*who the hell was he, and what was his name?*

He didn't remember going to bed, but that was the least of his worries.

He crept down the stairs, as if not wanting to wake anyone up. His eyes were half closed, not entirely knowing what he was about to find.

He was hoping that the murder fairies had been in the night and cleaned the whole mess up, and he could just get ready and go to work as if nothing had happened.

When he peered around the door to the living room, he had to double take.

The room was clean. In fact, it was spotless.

I didn't clean that up, he thought, suddenly thinking that maybe he should believe in murder fairies.

He looked into the kitchen. The cracked laptop was sitting on the table. The lid was up, but the screen was off.

The beer cans he knew were next to the computer were gone.

He turned, casting his eyes into the hallway, realising that he'd walked past where her and her gentleman friend's bodies had been placed, *and worked on,* he thought.

There were no bodies, and no gore to go with them.

He knew there'd been gore, blood, and other jelly-like substances dripping from their eyes, and the wounds on their heads where he'd bashed them in with the laptop. He distinctly remembered forcing ethernet cables into those empty sockets.

Did that happen?

He hoped beyond all hope it had all been a dream, a bad dream, a fucking awful dream. One that was along the lines of the horrible fishy dreams that he had been having in work lately. Relief flowed over him as he stepped into the living room, ready to flop onto one of the chairs and ring in work, sick.

It was then he realised it hadn't been a dream.

The two chairs in the corner of the room had been pushed together. The bodies of Amy, and her anonymous boyfriend, had been placed on them. An ethernet cable was running from his wireless router into the guy's left eye, then from his right eye into Amy's left eye, then from her left eye into the wall socket where his internet connection came into the house.

He felt the gorge of vomit, hot and thick, in his throat. But he swallowed it, stopping it from springing forth and ruining the carpets.

His eyes flicked past the hideous scene and settled on the router sitting on the sideboard beneath the window. The little green light that indicated the speed of the network was flashing rapidly.

Data was being passed across the network.

From where? he thought, looking out of the living room towards the laptop on the kitchen table.

Tentatively, he made his way towards it and rubbed his finger on the trackpad, bringing the computer to life. A familiar command prompt box was on the screen.

>The function LIFE is performing within expected tolerances
>The function MASTER V2.1 is downloading

Progress 2%..........

'What the fuck?' he asked the empty room.

He looked at the network connection icon; it was reading that it was currently connected to a network called AmyMarkOne.

'AmyMark? What the fuck is AmyMark?'

As he stared at the screen, the realisation dawned on him what AmyMark was. 'Holy shit. That's his name; Mark,' he whispered.

The *dong* that would forever be associated with receiving email, chimed from the speakers of the machine. It was too loud in the silence of the house.

YOU HAVE A NEW MESSAGE … flashed up on the screen.

It took him a little while to control the cursor enough to be able to click on it. When he did, the email programme opened up, displaying two messages.

The new message was from the same address as the first message. MASTER@OLDEGODS.NET

He double clicked it, his breathing was fractured as he waited, what felt like an eternity, for it to load onto the screen.

> Hi Carl.
>
> Thanks for agreeing to the terms and conditions for downloading MASTER V 2.1
> We hope you enjoy your new overlord.
> If you have any queries relating to your new ruler, please do not hesitate to contact us on the link below.
>
> Yours
>
> HP

He looked at the link in the message and saw it had already been activated.

He looked at the command prompt. The ellipses were moving along the small box, indicating that whatever was downloading was still in progress, but the indicator was still showing two percent.

In the background, he noticed Gerard's file MASTER #4 was still open.

He took a deep breath before opening the file MASTER #5

Day #5

I spent the rest of the night enjoying the delights my deceased wife had to offer. I always thought that when a corpse entered a rigor mortis state, they stayed stiff until they began to decay. How happy I was to find that this was not the case.

We danced and played into the small hours. I did things to her that she would never have allowed in life, well, at least until I forced her to (hah ha!).

I had more conversations with HP and The Master. They really are a mine of information.

They informed me I needed to download and install a file called MASTER V 2.1. They sent me an email with the necessary files attached.

I did try to connect, but alas, I was informed that my failure to turn Brenda on again in time would hinder the connection required to download the application.

Maybe I'll go and hunt for another plaything.

Day #5 addendum

I contacted Leanne. I told her I needed her to meet me at my home with some files or other from my office. I told her it was rather urgent.

The daydream of having her as my new plaything sent a delicious shiver down below. I do love the corruption of an innocent.

However, my daydream was cut short; as it was Friday, and she had already left the office and turned off her mobile phone. I'll be having words with her on Monday morning, mark my words.

Now, this left me at a bit of a loss.

I'm eager for what The Master has in store for me but frustrated with my lack of ability to perform the functions.

I'll go out tonight. There's a place I've frequented before. It's a place of ill-repute where I'm known (that is a good joke), and I'm certain I will be able to coerce someone back here with me.

I've been studying the manual, and I'm confident of being able to turn them off and then turn them on again.

I'll see how I do tonight and report back in the morning. Hopefully, I'll have enough power to download The Master's files.

Carl was horrified.

Not only had this maniac killed his wife, he was now actively on the hunt for someone else to kill. He felt useless. He was reading the ramblings of an obviously deranged individual, and there was nothing he could do about it.

Obviously deranged? he questioned himself. *Here I am sitting on a computer that's being powered by the dead bodies of my own wife and her lover. And I'm judging him!*

The irony of the situation was not lost on him.

He wanted something to drink. Something hard, stiff, and strong, but he had an idea he'd need to go into the office today after all, and the last thing he needed as a newly ordained multiple murderer was to be pulled over for drunk driving.

He opened a plastic bottle of water and took a long swig, finishing off well over three-quarters of the liquid before coming up for breath. He looked at the bottle, shook it, then finished the rest. He closed his eyes and allowed the cold water to run through all his tubes.

The little black box on the screen was still reading two percent, but the progress dots were still working. Data was being sent, something was downloading, only it didn't seem to be downloading fast enough.

He sat back down at the table and opened one of the other files within the folder.

MASTER #6

Day #6

Rubbish.

I'm just not cut out for this network stuff.

I thought I was good at computers; well, getting onto the Dark Web does take a bit of guile, but apparently I have the knack for turning the people off, just not turning them on again.

I purchased some ethernet cables from the local computer shop, as I wanted to be ready for when the time came. I really didn't want The Master to be disappointed in me. I was surprised to find that ethernet cables are the same computer cables we use in work. If I'd have known that I could have arranged for Leanne to bring some around from work yesterday. Maybe I would have had some fun with her too.

Ah well. We live and learn.

I went to the club and bumped into an old friend. I have known her for a few years now; she enjoys the same ... interests as I do.

We got talking, and I asked her if she had ever heard of The Master. She told me that she loved being a submissive and she was up for playing some of the games I wanted to. We agreed on a safe word (the word was COSMIC, ha ha, it was a good joke) and agreed to meet back at my house after I told her my wife would be a willing partner too (after all, she was in no state to refuse, was she?).

Reboot: A Cosmic Horror

Once we got back to my house, she complained about a strange smell. Realising it must have been Brenda rotting away in the living room, I quickly informed her that Brenda and I had been experimenting with a little sacrifice play and had bought some recently slaughtered meat.

That seemed to strike a chord with her, and she took my word for it. (Note to self: I need to explore this sacrifice thing a little more. It was a total fluke as an excuse, but it seems I might have hit on a thing.)

Once she was relaxed and I'd brought her a drink, we got to chatting about the life of a deviant and the things she'd been asked, and willing to do.

They opened even my eyes.

Apparently, necrophilia, which I'd had a dalliance with over the last few nights, was more popular than I would have believed.

Anyway, I told her about The Master's programme on the Internet, and it piqued her interest, so I invited her into the living room to help me set it up.

I must admit that the stench from in there was stronger than I thought it would be, but for some reason, this only excited this strange young lady.

I opened the door to reveal Brenda. Her eyes were gored out, turning them into deep, black pits. She was lying on the couch, naked and already turning quite Purple. I realised, with some chagrin, that I hadn't cleaned her up from this morning's activities and was more than a little embarrassed to see my seed dried upon her bluish-purple face.

The lady then panicked.

It was obvious this might have been a tad too much for her, as she began to push back, away from the door and the abhorrence inside.

I had no choice but to push her back in.

I gave her an almighty shove, and she fell, stumbling into the room, falling onto poor Brenda.

The scream was hideous.

This got me thinking that she might have been lying to me and really hadn't done half the things she'd admitted to. Ah, well. It was too late for her now. She had suddenly found herself right in the thick of it.

I must say, it's a good thing my job affords me a nice house in its own grounds because the screaming and squealing from this feisty one could have woken the dead.

I realised my pun; I must keep that one for The Master and HP to read. I believe they might get a real kick from it.

I slit the screaming girl's throat with a knife I had already hidden in the room. I always keep a little something handy because you never know when you'll need it.

With the woman now silent and bleeding out on my floor, I retrieved the manual sent by The Master and the ethernet cables I'd purchased.

I really hadn't thought about defiling the woman as she lay dying, the thought of being inside her as the light in her eyes flickered and dimmed was a sweet elixir, but I couldn't bring myself to do it. I mean, there was Brenda, in the same room, staring at me with her empty eyeholes. Something about her unnerved me. I did think about removing her before taking the bleeding woman, but I didn't. I wanted Brenda to be a part of everything that was happening.

I owed her that much.

The woman was making some of the most absurd gurgling noises as the life ebbed from her body. I wanted to get to my job at hand as soon as I could, but I was transfixed watching the stranger die. I had the urge to masturbate, and I was feeling the familiar twinge in my trousers, when I received another message from The Master *on my computer. He wanted me to video what was occurring and upload it for him and HP to observe.*

I did.

To my disappointment, neither one of them were happy with what I was doing.

Apparently, the blood is the vessel that allows the network to flow.

Once again, I had fallen short. My victim was no good for what I needed to do.

I've decided to move Brenda out of the living room. She doesn't need to witness what I intend to do.

'It's the blood that keeps the network flowing?'

The sound of his own voice surprised him in the silent house. He looked at the black box on the screen and was not surprised to see the progress hadn't changed from two percent.

'It needs more power,' he mused. 'How do I get more power to it?' He sat back on the kitchen chair and rubbed his hand over his chin. He got up and made himself a bowl of cereal. On his return, he regarded the wired corpses of his wife and her lover.

'It's the blood that allows the network to flow,' he mused again as he spooned a heap of cereal into his mouth.

'Where do I get myself more blood?'

He opened the last file in Gerard's folder. MASTER #7. He noted this was only a short entry.

Day #7

I don't think I have it in me to do this on my own.

After defiling the woman, I realised how tired I was and forced myself to retire.

I was plagued with persistent dreams.

Awful ones.

The Master and HP came to visit me in my sleep. Hideously deformed monstrosities they were, but I recognised them as kindred spirits. They informed me that now I had started down this path, there was no other way for me to go. I had to complete the mission that had been given to me. They showed me some of the wicked and delicious delights that would be mine if I was to be able to download the Master V2.1 application.

I truly do want, and I believe deserve, what they have shown me.

It should be mine, all of it.

However, I have come to the conclusion, after moving the body of the woman and remounting the body of my beloved Brenda back into the lounge, that I need help.

I toyed with the idea of inviting the rather splendid form of Leanne to this little party, after all, she will do pretty much anything I ask of her, the timid little mouse. But I think it needs to be someone strong of character and with a knowledge of networking.

I have an idea of who would be perfect to partner with, in the conclusion of this mission.

I will request him when I get back into the office tomorrow. In the meantime, I'll fill my laptop with filth to disguise the hidden Dark Web application.

It will be so good to have a compadré to share this mission.

Oh, the fun we will have!

'That dirty old bastard,' Carl spat as he read the last paragraph. 'It was his intention to bring me in on this all along.'

He looked back into the living room as he thought about what the old man had said. *He wants me in on this.*

He shrugged. There had already been at least four murders associated with this application.

'I wonder …' he pondered as he swallowed another spoonful of breakfast.

10.

CARL SHOWERED AND got himself ready for work. Before he left, he thought about bringing the cracked laptop with him, but then thought if he did, it might break the connection to his new *network* and the Master download would be disrupted. He needed to know what would happen when it was fully installed on the laptop.

He locked the house up tight. He didn't want anyone having any suspicions of wrongdoing happening in there and letting themselves in. He knew his mother had a spare key.

'Hey, son, how are you doing?' he said into the hands-free audio system in the car.

'Dad, what's happening? How come I'm staying at Nan's all of a sudden?' the teenage boy on the other end of the phone asked.

'It's just for a few days, kiddo. Your mum had to go away on a project in work, and my hours this week are going to be mad. We just thought best that you stayed there. You'll be home in a few days, and everything will be different.'

Yeah, really different, he thought, but he didn't entirely know what he meant by that.

'I've tried ringing her, but her mobile is off.'

Turn it on again ... he thought with a smile. 'She had to go to Scotland; you know what the signal's like up there. She can never get a connection. I'm sure she'll ring when she gets a moment. Listen, Josh, I've got to go; I'm just getting into the server room, and I'll lose my own signal. You going to be OK to look out for Tommy?'

'Yeah. If I have to,' he replied sullenly. 'But you might have to reimburse me for some expenses.'

Carl laughed. To his ears, it sounded so fake, but he hoped it would convince his son. 'Well, we'll talk about that when I see you in a couple of days. OK?'

'OK. I'll speak to you later.'

'You will, son.'

He sincerely hoped that last bit was true. He loved his kids; whether or not they would still love him when they found out what had really happened to their mother, he'd have to wait and find out, but for now, he was content. *Everything will be different when The Master comes anyway,* he convinced himself.

~~~~

'Did you speak to Gerard yesterday, before you went home?' Rod asked as he walked into the office.

'Jesus, Rod. *How are you, Carl? You feeling any better, Carl?*' He snapped.

'Yeah, yeah. Time for the niceties when I stop getting my dick chewed off by the big boss.'

'Well, maybe you want to start taking your dick out of his arse more often, eh?' Carl replied, sitting at his desk, and logging on to his computer. He watched as Tasha, who had been watching this exchange with some interest, dropped her head and laughed.

'What did you say?' Rod asked.

Carl knew there was no real malice in his question; he thought the man genuinely hadn't heard him.

'I said, I'll go and see him right after I've logged into my computer. By the way, I *have* to do that server upgrade today. It needs to be done by the weekend, and I'm fucked if I'm coming in on Saturday to do work I could have done through the week.'

Rod looked at him. His eyes were narrow, as if he *did* know what he'd said to him but didn't want the confrontation. 'OK, get on that, but after you've spoken to Gerard. He's anxious as hell about these files. You do still have them, don't you?'

'Yeah, I've got them,' Carl answered, wiggling the external drive in the air towards his boss.

'Well, all right then. Get them to him, and I'll take you off the telephones. Just get that server upgrade done.'

'All over it, boss man,' Carl replied, not looking up from his screen.

He could feel Tasha still looking at him, laughing. 'Tash,' he whispered. 'Can you come and have a look at this for me?'

She got up from her desk and walked around. 'What is it?'

'What do you see there?' he asked, pointing at his screen.

She shrugged and pouted. 'Your log in script running and your email opening. What am I looking for, Carl?'

Carl shook his head. 'Nothing. I think I might be going a little mad.'

He looked back at his screen where the black box was sitting in the centre. White letters were flashing, they read:

TURN THEM OFF, THEN TURN THEM ON AGAIN!

Today, he thought it might have been good advice.

'OK, I'm going to see Medley, then I'm going to be in Server Room One all day. If anyone needs me, that's where I'll be. OK?' He was speaking to the whole department.

Only Jodi and Tasha even reacted. Jodi nodded her head as if she didn't care, *which she doesn't,* he thought. And Tasha looked up at him as if she wanted him to take her with him, her eyes pleading with him to free her from the monotony of the office.

He smiled and walked out of the department.

~~~~

'Is he expecting you?' Leanne asked timidly from behind her desk. She always had the look of someone who had been pushed to her limits, or at least very close. Carl had always associated it with the look of PAs to managing directors of large companies worldwide, but today, there was something different about her. She had a little-girl-lost look in her eyes, as if something, *or someone,* had pushed her that much closer to that edge.

'Yeah, he is. I've got some files from his old computer. He needs them for his trip to Bangkok, apparently.'

She blinked a few times, rather rapidly, as she consulted her computer. Carl breathed deeply as he regarded at the young girl. She was pretty; she could be very pretty if she put her mind to it. She looked like the kind of girl everyone would be amazed at when they saw her on a night out. Plain Jane in work, wild disco diva on a Saturday night.

You don't understand how close you came on Friday night, do you? he thought, remembering the Master files he'd read. *It could have been you lying on the carpet of his house with your throat slashed, your eyes gouged out, and that dirty old bastard doing things to you that no man should ever do to another human being, alive or dead!*

'Yeah, he'll see you now.'

'Uh?' Carl asked, looking at the girl as he snapped back into reality.

'Mr Medley. He'll see you now. You can go in,' she said, indicating towards the office door.

'Oh, right!' he laughed. 'That *is* what I'm here for, after all.'

His heart went out to her as she laughed before putting her browbeaten head down, as he knocked on Gerard Medley's door.

'Come in,' the old man shouted from the other side. With one more look back towards Leanne, he opened the door and entered the office.

The room was dark and musty. It wasn't at all like it had been the last time he'd been here. Then, it had been bright and airy. *Something has happened to this guy since I was last in here,* he thought with a knowing smile.

'Carl, thanks for coming. Please sit down. Do you want anything? I can get the lovely Leanne to make us some coffee.'

'No, I'm OK. Really.'

As the door closed behind him and he took his seat, Gerard got right down to business. His face changed, his smile faded into a grin, and his eyes regarded Carl from hooded lids. He reminded him of Jack Nicholson in that film about the haunted hotel. 'Did you bring the files?' he asked. It was almost a whisper but not quite.

Carl nodded as he put the external drive on the desk and pushed it towards him. Both men looked at it.

There was an accusation hanging in the room, one neither man wanted to address but both knew they had to.

Carl folded his arms and looked into Gerard's eyes. He said nothing.

Gerard fidgeted with the knickknacks on his desk.

Carl watched as his eyes flickered from the drive to him and then to the door. The old man licked his lips and then bit his top lip with his bottom teeth.

'How's the wife?' Carl asked. 'Brenda, is it?'

The old man's eyes brightened then, and his grin widened. 'I take it you read them then?'

Carl nodded, his eyes never leaving the older man's. He watched as they continued flicking around the room.

'And?' Gerard asked eventually.

'And, I think you are a sick old fuck. I also think this world would be a better place without perverted pieces of shit like you in it.'

Gerard's face twitched with the insults. 'Yet here you are. No HR department, no police, just you and the files. Did you make copies?'

Carl nodded.

Gerard lifted his head, breathing in at the same time. 'And what have you done with them?'

'They are on a laptop in my house.'

'What laptop?'

'The same one that is currently attempting to download Master V2.1.'

The old man's eyes widened, and his jaw fell slack. 'What?'

Carl's expression didn't change. 'You heard me.'

Gerard nodded. 'I did. I'm just a little … shocked, that's all.'

'Why are you shocked? You wrote in the journal that you were going to get me to help you, for me to become your little accomplice. You set it all up so I would click on that file, didn't you? You knew, somehow, that clicking it would set me off on a journey. The visions I've been having, the stink I've been smelling. It's all because of you, isn't it?'

Gerard looked down at the table. 'You've known me for years now, Carl. You've been fixing my'—he paused as if thinking how to phrase what he was about to say—'computer troubles for years. You know I have needs, impulses, urges, yet you still cover up for me.' The old man shrugged. 'You were the obvious choice.'

'How did you do it?'

'I knew you'd read the journal if I put it in your mind that I really needed those files. Your complicity allowed me to introduce you to HP and The Master. I never wrote in there about my meetings regarding using you. You would have been repulsed. But, as we put the seed into your brain, you became a willing accomplice.'

'How do you know I'm an accomplice?' Carl asked.

Gerard put his head down and closed his eyes. He looked like he was ready to light up a cigarette. 'How's Amy?' he asked eventually.

'What?' Carl asked. He felt like this meeting had taken a different direction, one he wasn't quite ready for.

'I asked, how is Amy?'

The moist feelings underneath his arms began to spread, and he could feel perspiration dripping down the side of his body.

'I … erm!'

'Don't stutter, Carl. You told me your *other* laptop was currently downloading Master V2.1. You wouldn't have been able to connect to their network without the flow of blood. So, it's my guess that in your house, the amiable Mrs Riggs is sitting there with holes where her eyes used to be, and an ethernet cable running through her. Am I right?'

Carl didn't answer. In fact, he couldn't answer. Right then, he couldn't even breathe.

Gerard was grinning. Carl knew then that the power had shifted; the old man now had the upper hand. He reached out to grab the drive that was on the desk and wasn't at all surprised to see his palms were soaking wet.

'I …'

'I'd leave that there if I were you,' Gerard said, reminding Carl of the old man who owns the nuclear company on that cartoon that's never off the television.

Carl complied. He had to; this old man was scaring him now.

'So,' Gerard continued. 'It's my guess that you're here because you are only hitting around one percent of the download.'

'Two, actually,' he whispered, pulling at the collar of his shirt.

The old man sat back in his chair, raising his eyebrows. 'Two?' He nodded.

'Yeah, but it seems stuck on that. It's been on two since yesterday.'

'So, tell me, Carl, who is the other victim? I really hope it wasn't one of your children.'

The grin on Gerard's face was knocking him sick. The old man was reading him like a book.

'It's, I was, erm …'

'Come on, boy, spit it out. You can tell me. I've shown you mine,' he hissed as he leaned forwards on the desk. 'Now it's time for you to show me yours.'

Carl paused before continuing.

'It's my wife's bit on the side. The bitch was having an affair. But I didn't do it. It was an accident. It was in a dream, or something.'

Gerard leaned over his desk even closer and grabbed Carl's hand. Carl tried to pull it away, but despite it being slick with sweat, the old man had a pretty decent grip on it.

'Don't you worry, my boy.'

This disgusting old man calling him *my boy* turned his stomach.

'You're safe here with me. Your secret is safe. We have the knowledge and the understanding of HP and The Master behind us. He's told me what we need to do, and I know they've been sending you messages too.'

'Messages?' Carl asked, knowing exactly what the old man was talking about.

'Yes, Carl. Messages. You've seen them. I know you have. They told me. You need to turn them off and turn them on again, Carl. The Master needs more power than he currently has. I failed to connect to my network. You didn't. You know exactly how to work it. We just need more … juice.'

The way he had said the word *juice* turned Carl's stomach again. This man really was a lecherous old bastard. The trouble was, he knew exactly what he was referring to. But he was having trouble with just how cold he was about it all.

Gerard pushed a button on his desk, and the cowed voice of Leanne filtered through the speaker. 'Yes, Mr Medley?'

'Leanne, could you bring us in two coffees and a plate of biscuits? Make them the nice chocolate ones. Mr Riggs and I are going to be in here a while. We have quite a bit of business to attend to.'

There goes my server upgrade, Carl thought as Leanne agreed to make the coffee.

11.

IT WAS OVER an hour and a half later that Carl staggered out of the office of the managing director. His face was pale but either angry or determined; Tasha couldn't tell which.

She wanted to catch up to him to see what was wrong with him. But by the way he was striding down the corridor, he didn't look like he wanted, or needed, company.

Tasha, with a laptop tucked under her arm, that she was dropping off for Carrie in the marketing department, looked from the managing director's door back to Carl before walking off in the other direction.

She did note that Carl was heading in the direction of Server Room One. *He must be going to do that upgrade he's been going on about,* she thought.

12.

'CAN YOU SEND out an outage to the business for me?' Carl asked over the phone.

Jodi looked at the receiver as if it had just asked her to send nudes. 'What? Me?'

'Yes, Jodi. You. I'm going to be taking one of the servers down for a short while. There'll be intermittent access to certain data files for the rest of the day. I'll flip it over to the backup server and sync them tonight. You got that?'

Jodi nodded at the phone.

'You got it, Jodi?'

'For fuck's sake, Carl! Yes, I got it,' she shouted and slammed the phone down.

'Dick,' she mumbled.

Rod was in the office as she slammed the phone back into its cradle. He looked up from his conversation with Charles. 'What's the matter, Jodi?' He knew exactly what the matter was with her; she was rubbish at her job and she didn't want to be there, but they were stuck with her for the time being, until he could find another department that would take her and manage her out of his. 'I'll tell you what, why don't you see this as a learning opportunity?'

Jodi looked at him with the nudes expression back on her face.

Rod stood up to his full height, which wasn't very high, but it was evident he was not going to step down on this. 'A learning opportunity. If you're going to stay in this department, and I truly want you to…' he lied. '…then you're going to need to understand the workings of everything. This is a chance to learn from Carl. He's been here the longest and knows everything that's worth knowing. So, why not go and watch him and learn something?'

Jodi just stared at him.

Rod nodded. 'I'm serious. Go and watch him upgrade the server.'

Jodi's eyes flicked around the room. There was no one else taking any interest in what was happening, therefore no one to plead her case to. She huffed as she locked her computer. She stood, grabbed her bag and jacket from the back of the chair, causing it to spin, then glared at Rod as she stormed out of the office, almost banging into Tasha as she walked in.

'What's the matter with her?' Tasha asked after the Jodi had left.

'I've just asked her to work with Carl on the server upgrade.'

'Well, that'll be a frosty server room to work in,' she commented as she sat down.

'What do you mean?' Rod asked.

'I just saw Carl storming out of Gerard's office, heading to Server Room One. He didn't look in a good mood at all.'

'Fuck,' Rod snapped, as he headed back into his office.

'Hey, Leanne, is Gerard in?' Rod asked, gripping the telephone handset in his white-knuckled hands.

'No, he's just left. He has a meeting with the senior heads of engineering in ten minutes. He wanted to grab a bite to eat beforehand. Is there anything I can do for you?'

'Has Carl Riggs just been in the office?'

'Carl? Yeah, he left just before Gerard. Why?'

'How did they both look as they left?'

There was silence over the line for a little while. 'They both seemed fine. They were in there for about an hour. I took them coffee and biscuits.'

'Biscuits?'

'Yeah, chocolate ones.'

Rod exhaled as he released his extra-tight grip on the handset and sat down, relieved Carl hadn't had one of his moments and upset Medley.

Charles looked at him from the other side of the desk. 'Is this meeting over?' he asked.

Rod had forgotten he was even there.

13.

JODI WAS FUMING. She'd planned her day out to the smallest detail before coming into work. First, it was coffee and a little flirt with the young apprentice electrician. Then she'd walk around the building fluttering her eyelashes at the other men. She knew a lot of them were too old for her, but she wouldn't mind a sugar daddy—as she had access to the HR records as part of her IT administration privileges, she knew how much money a lot of these older men were on.

Next, she would return to her desk. She had some serious shopping to do online. She'd booked a holiday for the week after next, and needed some serious bikini action if she was going to bag herself a man who would look after her and keep her from doing this—or any other—job.

Then it was lunch. In the pub.

The engineers usually bought her a couple of drinks if she was nice to them, which she always was.

After that it would be a lazy afternoon ignoring the phones and emails.

It was all going so well, she thought as she stormed down the corridors heading towards Server Room One.

~~~~

Carl was pacing around the small, cold server room. It was freezing due to the three air-conditioning units blasting out their frigid air, keeping the servers, switches, and other infrastructure from overheating. There were four huge cages in the room. Three of them were empty, ready for when the new kit arrived, earmarked for making the next floor live, in a couple of weeks. The new kit would allow this server room to become the primary data centre for all the remote offices around the UK, and even some other parts of Europe.

Before that could happen, the old servers needed to be upgraded to the latest operating systems. It was a job Carl had done on numerous occasions in the ten years he'd worked here.

He was an old pro.

He'd been looking forward to it. It meant a full two days away from his desk and the needy users around the office while he managed all the individual processes involved in bringing everything up to date.

But now, his mind was not on the job at all.

The moment he walked into the room, all the screens, of which there were twelve in total, began to flicker.

TURN THEM OFF, THEN TURN THEM ON AGAIN!

The words flashed in between the blinking command box telling him that the function LIFE was not responding. There wasn't even a function he knew of called LIFE.

How can HP or The Master be getting to me here? he questioned as the screens continued to flash at him.

The pulsing was hypnotic. He could feel his brain swimming behind his eyes. Each time he turned his head, he could feel it following behind a few moments later. This effect was making him sick; it felt like the worst hangover ever.

'Carl …'

The voice was thin and whispery. The only thing he could liken it to was grease-proof paper being crumpled. The smell was back too. The thick, dirty fish stink. In other circumstances, in his dizzy state, the stench would have tipped him over the edge, he would be hurling into a bucket or a toilet bowl, but he must have built a tolerance to it now because it was doing the opposite. It was stopping his head from spinning and was actually settling the churning in his stomach.

The room was dark from the mirrored windows, but it had taken on a darker, other-worldly feel. Strange shadows were dancing on the walls, green silhouettes that made it look, and feel, like he was underwater. There were other things in the reflections too. Old things, things that had been banished from this realm for hundreds of thousands of years, maybe even millions of years.

And for good reason.

He had an inkling The Master was near.

He looked at the hardware stacked in the only cage that was full. The initials HP emblazoned all over them were glowing on each one. He was sure they used to be silver, but now they were a filthy, sickly green.

'Carl ... you know what you have to do.'

He sat down on the tall stool that was used for working on the servers. It bounced a little under his weight; the buoyancy did nothing for his already dizzying head and sensitive stomach.

'You know what to do to serve The Master, Carl. Reboot them. Turn them off, then turn them on again in His name.'

Carl bowed his head. The flickering of the screens and the dancing shadows on the walls had put him into a strange dream-like state. He felt susceptible to suggestion, vulnerable.

He must obey The Master.

'Yes, Master,' he whispered, a thick drool of saliva dripped from his lower lip before landing, with a splat- *or was it a shlopp*- on the raised metal floor.

'You know what to do,' the voice came again. 'You have done it before. You must do it again.'

Carl nodded.

He knew exactly what to do.

It made the bowl of cereal he'd eaten for breakfast spin in his stomach; it made his brain bang against his skull; it made his skin crawl with the cold itch of sweat, even in the freezing room.

Yet he knew what he had to do.

'Will you do it, Carl?' the voice continued. It was thin and tinny; it sounded far away, but not too far away to not be menacing. 'Will you? Can you turn them off and turn them on again? Are you willing to serve your Master?'

'I am,' he whispered.

'I need you to convince me, Carl,' the voice continued.

'I am,' he said louder.

'Convince me, Carl,' the voice demanded.

He stood from the stool and raised his hands in the air. 'I WILL ... I WILL. I'll TURN THEM OFF AND THEN TURN THEM ON AGAIN,' he shouted.

The laughter ringing in his head came from everywhere, all at once.

~~~~

Jodi gave a coy smile to the man in his forties who was stood at the printer. She dropped her head and darted her eyes away at just the right moment; she really was a master in the art of seduction. She knew she would be getting her drinks paid for her come the Christmas do in a few months' time.

She turned down the next corridor, the one that housed the executive suite. This one always gave her the creeps. She'd made a mental note when she started in this job that if she was ever stuck on the late shift and was leaving the office on her own, she would take the other way to the reception. She never, ever wanted to be caught, on her own, with Gerard Medley. She didn't think there was anyone who gave her the creeps more in the whole world, than he did.

That's one sugar daddy I can live without, she thought as she hurried past the door to his office.

As she turned the corner to the corridor where Server Room One was located, next to the gent's toilets, she saw her current favourite walk out, wiping his hands on the back of his trousers.

She grinned as he saw her.

'Hello, beautiful.' He beamed as he his eyes eventually made it to hers, after roaming all over her body first.

'Well, hello yourself,' she replied. This was the one she'd had her heart set on flirting with this morning. *Funny the way fate twists itself,* she thought, feeling somewhat proud of her deep philosophy.

'I was going to come and see you,' she said, batting her lashes.

'I was hoping you would. I was trying to think of some way for you to come and sort out my *hard drive.*' The words hard and drive were spoken as if to emphasise his erection rather than the storage facility on his desktop computer.

Jodi knew it, and she loved it.

'Well, good things *come* to those who wait,' she replied. The emphasis on the word come was also meant to mean something else.

Chris got the message and grinned like a cat who had gotten to the milk first and had stolen all the cream at the top.

They stopped for a few moments, just talking silly things. She giggled and pawed at him shamelessly, before eventually they walked away from each other. Chris was fixing the front of his trousers as he went.

This made her smile. *Definitely one for the future,* she grinned, continuing on to her destination.

Server Room One was the fourth door along on the left. She closed her eyes and tried her best to control her anger and frustration at the thought of spending the rest of the day in a cold server room with that boring old fart, Carl. Odds on he would be singing stupid songs all day, songs she knew would stick in her head for days, and he would tell his ridiculous stories about the children's books he wrote ... *or draws, or colours in ... who the fuck knows, or cares?*

A shout from the other side of the door snapped her from her little day-nightmare. It sounded like Carl was talking to someone in there. *But why would he be shouting like that?* she thought. Her heart was beginning to pound, and she considered going back to find Chris, or anyone, to find out what was happening.

She looked over her shoulder, but the corridor was empty.

Blowing her cheeks up, she keyed in the security number and turned the little knob.

It didn't open.

Closing her eyes, she cancelled the last entry and did it again, envisioning the number in her head.

It still didn't open.

'Fuck,' she cursed as she dug into her handbag for her mobile phone. Flicking it on, she opened her notes. She knew she wasn't supposed to write the codes for the doors into the app, *but fuck them,* she thought. *How am I supposed to remember all those numbers?*

She found the number for Server Room One.

She cursed; she'd been one number out.

Tutting, she inputted the correct number and turned the knob.

She felt the door unlock, so she pushed it open.

~~~~

Carl heard the lock being activated. He stopped raving to the voice in his head and turned towards it. Whoever was trying to get in had gotten the code wrong.

The smell in the room disappeared instantly.

He heard whoever it was give it another go. Again, they got it wrong.

The green shadows, with their hidden mysteries and monsters, disappeared, presumably to the same place the stink went.

A few moments passed. Carl held his breath, hoping whoever it was had gone. He looked at the computer screens around the room. They were still blinking the same message.

TURN THEM OFF, THEN TURN THEM ON AGAIN!

He closed his eyes and clenched his fists. He mentally willed the person, whoever it was, to just go away, mind their own business, and leave him be to complete his server upgrade.

The lock activated again. This time, they'd gotten the number correct.

The knob turned, and the heavy wooden door began to open.

14.

'YES, WELL, WE'LL see about all of that when I get back from Bangkok. I believe the Asian market will see things a little differently in a couple of days' time,' Gerard said as the meeting concluded. He was followed out of the room by three other people, two women and one man, all of them wearing the expensive clothing of executives of the company.

'Why's that, Gerard?' one of the women asked with a wan smile on her face. 'Do you know something that we don't?'

'I might,' he replied without turning back to look at her. 'I think we'll be seeing a lot of change happening in the markets in the next few days.'

The male executive was shaking his head and grinning. 'Come on, Gerard, you old bastard, tell us what you're thinking,' he laughed.

'That will be for me to know and you lot to find out,' he grinned.

A strange noise distracted the executives. All three of them turned towards the sound. It was a thud, followed by a short-lived muffled scream.

'What was that?' the other woman asked. 'It sounded like a—'

'Maintenance,' Gerard interrupted. 'They're doing work in the server room. Something about upgrading the network. It sounds like one of those IT monkeys has just caught his finger on something.'

The three executives laughed. 'Cretins,' the man replied. 'If they used one fifth of their intellect, they'd be climbing that ladder instead of sitting around wanking to Wonder Woman and *Star Wars*!'

All four of them laughed.

Good boy, Carl, Gerard thought as he reached his office door. *Turn them off and then turn them on again ... just what The Master ordered.*

'Leanne,' he snapped. 'I need to see you in my office in ten minutes. Bring tea and biscuits. I'll be needing you to take some things down.'

'Erm, yes, sir. I'll get the tea on the go now.'

'Good girl,' he said with a leer as he closed his office door behind him.

15.

THE FIRE EXTINGUISHER came from out of nowhere.

It smashed Jodi square in the face, knocking her back, out of the server room and into the corridor. She just had time to make a small squeal, possibly of shock and/or pain before Carl's arm reached out, grabbed her, and pulled her back inside.

The rounded bottom of the red metal tube had caught her on the bridge of her nose, shattering it.

He muffled her yelp with his hand, hopefully before anyone else in the office could have heard it. If anyone asked, he'd say he'd stubbed his toe on the corner of the server cabinet. 'Yes, I'm aware I yelped like a little girl,' he'd say. 'But fuck, it hurt.'

Jodi's eyes were already swelling as they spun wildly in their sockets. He didn't know if she could see him, but he didn't care. His heart was racing in his chest, and it seemed, everywhere else in his body.

He looked up from the twitching woman in his grasp to the computer screen beside him. It was flashing faster than ever, in perfect rhythm with the pounding of his heart.

TURN HER OFF … it flashed.

THEN TURN HER ON AGAIN … it continued.

The room was intermittently darkening and lightening. The smell of the sea and the thick decaying fish stink was back, then it was gone, then it was back again. His head spun as blood gurgled out of Jodi's twitching mouth, and broken nose.

The fire extinguisher had made short work of her features, smashing them, pulverising would be a better word to describe it. He didn't understand how he knew this, but he was informed that small, sharp splinters of bone had broken off with the force of the hit. These had pierced her brain. She wasn't dead physically, but she was—as he could tell from the uncontrollable rolling of her eyes—brain dead.

Dark pink froth continued to bubble from her mouth as her blood mixed with thick saliva.

TURN HER ON AGAIN! TURN HER ON AGAIN! TURN HER ON AGAIN!

The screen was flashing so fast that the words were almost permanent.

'Do it, Carl,' the voice ordered him, the voice he'd come to think of as The Master's voice. 'Do it. Turn her on again. You know how to do it. DO IT NOW, before it's too late.'

Carl nodded. He was burning up despite the cold air blowing from the three air-conditioning units. 'Yes, Master ...' he muttered. 'Yes ... right away!'

Unceremoniously, he dropped the twitching body of Jodi onto the metal floor and winced as her head hit the tiles with a resounding THUNK. *She won't care,* he thought. *She wouldn't have felt it anyway.* He reached over towards the bench next to the empty server cabinets and opened the toolbox residing there.

His hands were shaking as he fiddled with the plastic snap that kept the lid closed; his slick fingers kept flying off it. He paused for a moment, took in a shaky breath, calmed his thrashing heart, and tried the snap again.

This time, it opened.

Inside, he saw what he was looking for.

Sitting prominent, on top of all the other tools, was a long-handled screwdriver. The yellow and black grip housed a lengthy shaft that tapered to a flat edge at the top.

It was a perfect tool for what he needed.

He grasped it, wrapping his fingers around the handle, getting used to the ridged feel of it in the sweat-lined grip of his palm.

He held it up to look at.

Once again, the room turned dark. The green reflections of underwater were dancing on the walls again. He could feel the presence of something hiding in the depths, creating the shadows he was seeing. Again, he had the feeling that this was something powerful, something commanding.

Something *old.*

'You know what to do, Carl,' the voice whispered. 'There's no going back now. She's already been turned off. All you need to do is reboot her. Turn her on again. You've done it before.'

116

He could feel the sting of tears in his eyes. He wanted to talk, to reply to the voice, but the sob trapped in his chest was stopping words from escaping him.

'I ...' was all he managed.

'Don't think about it, Carl. You did it last time. You can do it again. The Master commands it.'

'I don't remember doing it,' he whispered. His words were shaky, barely legible, but the voice, the whisper, understood him.

'You blocked it from your memory, but believe me, you did it. You took the screwdriver and plunged it into the eyes of your wife. You did the same to her lover.'

'I didn't ... I loved Amy.'

'That doesn't matter anymore. She didn't love you. Do you think she was thinking about you when she had Mark's cock in her mouth? When he pulled her hair back so he could watch as his dick exploded in her face, in her mouth, the same mouth you kissed when you got home. The same mouth she kissed your children with. Do you think she was thinking about how lovely your wedding day was when she allowed Mark to do the things she would never let you do, Carl?'

His eyes were fixated on the long shaft of the tool in his hands. As his breathing grew shallow, and fast, he altered his grip on it.

'Take it, Carl. Reboot her ... Plug her in. Turn her on again. You know you can do it.'

He looked at the body of Jodi lying on the floor. Her nose was swollen and dark, as were her eyes and lips. Her face was a total mess. *Did I do that?*

'Yes, Carl, you did, and glorious work it is too. Now, take the tool and finish it. Plug her in. Allow her life blood to power the network. Bring The Master home, Carl. Bring him home.'

Breathing so fast that the room itself was spinning around him, as if he were the only constant in the whole world, he fell onto his knees and cradled Jodi's head in his arms. She was warm, and he could feel her fluttering pulse in her neck. He looked into her eyes, but knew they were not seeing him. They were long gone, seeing somewhere else. They were glazed and vacant. She had the blank stare of a fish lying on the ice in a supermarket refrigerated counter.

The briny smell of the same counter emanated from her.

Her eyes were filling up with water, like on the cartoon about the cat and mouse who hated each other, when the cat had drunk too much water. He could see deep depths within them. A trickle of dirty liquid began to pour from her nose. Then her mouth fell open, and out of it came a wave of filthy, scummy brown water.

He was about to drop her head when he blinked and the water disappeared, but the stink remained.

He held the screwdriver to her eye. It was difficult to grip the shaft, as his hands were shaking so badly. He overcompensated, and the flat blade of the driver ripped into the skin of her forehead.

Jodi didn't even flinch.

'She's already as good as dead, Carl.' The voice filled his head again. 'You need to make sockets so you can network her. Plug her in to the network, Carl. Let the blood do its thing. Download the Master V2.1 file. It makes sense, Carl. It's going to happen anyway; it might as well be you who sees The Master's favour.'

Carl's hands knew what was going to happen even before his head did. The voice, coupled with the strobing effect of the screens flashing their message at him, was too powerful to resist.

This time his aim was true.

He didn't strike her face; the blunt blade of the screwdriver entered into her right eye.

As the metal shaft pierced her eye with a satisfying pop, she bucked. It was only a feeble subconscious attempt to escape what was happening to her, but it was still a fight for whatever life she had left.

He suddenly felt the urge to cry.

He wanted to cry for this poor girl who hadn't asked for this to happen to her today. He wanted to shed tears for his work colleague, who had come in filled with dreams, both long and short-term. She was probably looking forward to the coming weekend, the plans she had with her friends and family. She might have arranged to meet a nice man or woman. They might have hit it off, they could have settled down, bought a house, raised a family. He'd taken all of that away from her. Her life was snatched out of her hands with a fire extinguisher and a screwdriver in a cold server room by a raving lunatic who was hearing voices.

The tears came.

They weren't for Jodi; they were for him.

It felt like only yesterday that he'd been a loving husband, a great father, and a funny work colleague.

What am I now?

'You're a hero,' the voice in his head said. 'You're the brave one. The one ushering in the new regime. You're a pioneer, Carl, and you'll be long remembered and *rewarded* when The Master comes.'

He looked up at the screens. They were still flashing in perfect sync; but the message had changed.

PLUG HER IN … NETWORK HER!

He cursed Gerard Medley for getting him into all of this, but the curse was in the back of his mind. All that mattered now was forcing this screwdriver into the back of Jodi's brain and feeding an ethernet cable into her head.

He pushed the shaft deeper into her eye, her shifting beneath him slowed, before stopping altogether.

Jodi was dead.

She wasn't the first person he'd killed in service to The Master, but it was the first one he remembered.

Spurred on by the flashing and the voices, he forced the screwdriver even deeper into head. Once he'd forced his way into the cartilage, it was easy going to get the rigid shaft into the softer tissue of the brain.

He was careful of its passage; he didn't want to go too deep and end up with the screwdriver coming out of the back of her head and stabbing his thigh beneath it.

Juice, blood, and other thick, sticky substances trickled out of her, as well as the dark, fresh blood from her nose. He didn't want to get any on him, as sooner or later he was going to have to go back to his desk. It would be difficult to explain how he became covered in blood and gore while upgrading the operating system on a data server.

Once the handle of the screwdriver was banging against the skin of her eye socket, he knew he'd gone far enough.

Gently, he lay Jodi down to rest on the metal floor and went to search for what he needed.

A console cable.

This would form a direct connection from what he was now thinking of as her eye-port, straight into the back of the main switch, and then into the network.

The long blue cable was in the top drawer, where he knew it would be. He slipped around the back of the cabinet and unlocked it. He located the primary switch and plugged the bloody cable into the console port. He then threaded the cable around towards the first of the empty server cabinets. He opened the door and looked inside.

He nodded. It was perfect.

There was plenty of room in there to hang her body.

He dragged his former colleague around to the open cabinet. He needed to lift her up and hang her from the small rail that ran the length of the cabinet, the one normally used for cable management. It looked sturdy enough to hold a few bodies.

A few? he thought.

There was box of moist paper wipes—used to clean the screens—on the top of the cabinet. He reached up, retrieved a handful, and proceeded to wipe the gore from Jodi's face.

Once she was clean, he hoisted her up and, tying a spare network cable around her neck, hung her in the cabinet.

He then took the other end of the console cable and forced it into the empty eye socket.

The sound as it entered tickled him. It reminded him of jelly being spooned into his bowl for dessert, by his mum.

It made him smile.

Shlopp ...

Where've I heard that noise before, recently? he thought absently as he forced the cable far enough in to hear the satisfying click of the small plastic lever locking it in place.

He stepped back to admire his handiwork.

Perfect, he thought.

A change in the message on the screens caught his attention.

TURN HER ON AGAIN ...

He pondered on this for a moment before an idea came to him.

He went back around to the cabinet and rebooted the switch that the console cable was connected to.

He didn't care about the detrimental effect this would have on the network, or that the people out there would lose unsaved data, and emails wouldn't send. There would be a few minutes of outage. They had been warned, he was upgrading the network after all.

As the switch came back online, so did Jodi.

Carl watched with a mixture of fascination and more than a little horror as her body began to spasm as the switch drew power from her.

He logged on to the main server to check the network speed.

It was faster than it had ever been.

Alan Bryce might be fucking happy for once, he thought with a wry grin.

Then the telephone rang.

He looked at it as if it was something foreign that had just appeared from out of nowhere rather than a device that had been in the room all this time. He wiped his hands on the back of his jeans and picked it up.

'Hello!' he greeted whoever it was.

16.

THERE WAS A knock on his door. It was only a feeble one, and he smiled to himself. 'Come on in, Leanne. You know you don't need to knock.' Gerard closed the drawer he'd been looking in as the door opened and the delicious, timid, innocent figure of his secretary, and PA, entered carrying a tray. On the tray were two steaming cups and a small plate of biscuits.

He was pleased to note they were coconut rings. He wasn't a cheapskate by any stretch of the imagination, in fact he was rather extravagant with his money, but he liked what he liked. The coconut rings on the plate were of the variety that came in a long pack, usually found in the supermarkets, retailing for less than one pound. But they were the most delicious things when dunked in a hot cup of tea. He enjoyed the game of dunking and eating them as fast as he could, before they broke off, falling back into the hot cup and ruining the drink.

He loved to live life on the edge.

'Come in, come in, and sit yourself down,' he greeted her. He would have stood, but his erection was stronger than it had been for years, and it might have given the game away too soon.

He noted there was a pad and pen on the tray. *You're not going to need them,* he thought with an inward smirk. *That was not what I meant when I said you would be taking things down!*

'You wanted to see me, Mr Medley?'

'Yes, Leanne. Please sit.' He indicated the seat opposite him.

She smiled and looked away as she sat.

She put his cup of tea on his side of the desk and hers next to her, then put the biscuits on the desk and the tray on the floor.

Gerard took a biscuit and ate it. 'Hmm, I do love coconut rings,' he commented, spitting a few crumbs as he spoke.

Leanne smiled and took a sip of her tea.

'Leanne, I'm just going to get to the point here. I'm not one to beat around the bush.'

She picked up her pad and pen and looked at him. He could see the fear in her eyes, and it excited him.

'I'm going to have to let you go.'

Her eyes widened and her mouth dropped. 'What?' she whispered.

'I'm letting you go. To be honest, you're a fucking terrible PA; I only hired you because you have nice tits.'

The poor girl blinked rapidly, and her head jerked in irregular spasms.

That was when he stood up.

His erection was more than evident.

He clucked his mouth. 'So, you see, we have a bit of a situation here. I really need a PA, someone who is more than willing go that extra mile. And, well, I just don't see you as that person.' He put his hands on his hips and pushed his crotch forward.

'Mr Medley, I …' she gasped.

'Now do you see my problem, Leanne? Do you see it?'

She shook her head, her shoulder length hair swayed with the movement. He could see her anxiety beaming from her eyes and knew he had her exactly where he wanted her.

She was a single mother with a five-year-old child and a deadbeat ex-husband. This job was her only source of income, and the business creche took care of her child when she wasn't in school.

Leanne was completely at the mercy of this company, and therefore, him.

'The problem I see here is that anyone else, and I mean anyone'— he unzipped the fly to his trousers— 'would take the opportunity presented before them. They would grasp it with both hands, throw themselves at it, so to speak.'

He reached into his fly and removed his fully erect penis.

Leanne's eyes were wide. He rather enjoyed the tears that were filling up within them. It turned him on even more.

'What … what do you …?'

'What do I want?' he asked in a mocking tone. He shook his head. 'Don't you think that's fucking obvious, Leanne?'

'You said you wanted me to take some things down,' she sobbed.

The old man began to stroke his hand up and down his shaft, all the time looking her, in her rabbit-in-the-headlights eyes.

He noticed she couldn't stop watching what he was doing. There was a dream-like quality to her, like she might have thought this was a dream, or a nightmare.

Again, he liked that. *It's called disassociation,* he laughed, silently. 'Am I really going to have to do this myself?' he snapped.

She swallowed hard. 'I …'

'Suck my dick, Leanne. Do I have to fucking spell it out for you, you dumb bitch.'

'It's … It's not something—'

'I don't fucking care what it isn't in your life. Are you going to suck me off, or not? It's an easy, yes, or no, kind of question.'

'I…' she stuttered.

She didn't get to finish that sentence.

The paperweight that adorned his desk was heavy quartz. It was a beautiful display of deep obsidian with flecks of white dispersed around its centre. Gerard had always looked at it and imagined himself flying through those stars, heading off on adventures on different planets, different universes.

Fucking space aliens. That was right up his alley.

As the heavy piece clattered against Leanne's temple, she crumpled instantly onto his desk, spilling her tea, ruining the coconut rings.

He breathed in, deeply before exhaling shakily.

He looked down at his exposed erection. It wasn't going anywhere soon—*not on its own,* he thought.

He went to work, finishing himself off into the bin next to his desk— not for the first time. *A little something for the cleaners,* he thought as he wiped himself clean.

He looked down at the body of Leanne. She was moaning as much as she was twitching. He pouted and deflated a little.

He picked the quartz paperweight up again. He looked at the blood and hair stuck to it, before bashing it against the back of her head. The feel of the stone cracking her skull, sent another tingle to the tip of his dick, and cursed himself that he had just brought himself off, because that sensation then would have been fantastic. *One for HP and The Master,* he thought.

He made a mental note to not finish before the bashing was over when he took the next sacrifice.

He hit Leanne again, and then once more. *Just for luck,* he laughed before cleaning the paperweight and putting it back on his desk.

He tidied himself up, tucking his shirt back into his trousers and sat down, selecting the only dry coconut ring left on the plate. He crunched into it, savouring the sugary, but totally artificial coconut taste. He closed his eyes as he finished it, imagining himself on some tropical beach filled with dead secretaries, cups of tea, coconut rings, and The Master.

When he was done with his little daydream, he picked up his phone and dialled a four-digit number.

'Hello,' the voice on the other end said.

'Carl, it's your favourite CEO, not to mention co-conspirator. How are things going with that server upgrade?'

'Erm, they're going OK, I think.'

'Good. Well, I seem to have done us a bit of a favour. Could you come to my office immediately? Don't bother knocking; just come straight in.'

'I'm a bit busy here, Gerard. Can you give me ten minutes?'

'I'm afraid I can't, old boy. It's quite simply a matter of life and death if you get my meaning. Straight away, chop-chop, there's a good fellow.'

He put the phone back on the cradle and looked at the dead body of Leanne bleeding over his desk.

He took his laptop from his backpack, careful not to place it down in a puddle of the spilled tea mixed with blood and opened it up. The screen was flashing a message:

TURN HER ON AGAIN!

17.

CARL BURST INTO Gerard's office. His hair was ruffled, and his t-shirt was creased. There was a large stain down the front of it, like he had spilt his lunch or something.

Gerard noticed his hands were shaking, and that, coupled with the wild look in his eyes, made him grin. 'Take a seat!' He beamed, indicating the seat before him.

Carl's eyes went wide as he noticed the occupant of the seat.

'Oh, I'm sorry,' Gerard laughed. 'That one's taken, isn't it!'

The body of Leanne was leaning headfirst on the table. She was facing Carl with wide, sightless eyes that were half submerged in a pool of tea and blood. There were bloated, soggy coconut rings in the ugly mixture. Carl's eyes grew even wider when he saw the large, unsightly gash on her temple. 'Is she …?' he stuttered.

'Dead?' Gerard finished for him. He looked at her, moved his head back, and pouted. 'I do hope so, boy. I wacked her pretty hard over the head a good few times.'

'But …' Carl was having real issues spitting his words out.

Gerard's shoulders raised in a playful shrug. 'But what, Carl?' he asked, raising his eyebrows. 'We need fresh bodies for The Master. You need to hook them up to the network, and I've provided you with the first one. So …' Gerard shooed his hands at him. 'Off you pop. There's a good boy. Plug her in, turn her on again, or whatever it is you do. Just make sure The Master knows it was me who killed her.'

'I've …'

Gerard shook his head and shrugged. 'Are you still here? Go on, get out of my office, and do what you need to do with …' He looked at the body of Leanne with disgust—although Carl had an inkling that if he wasn't there, this dirty old goat would be having a lot more fun with her. 'That,' he finished.

'So, I'm supposed to just carry a dead body from your office to the server room in the hope no one sees me?' Carl asked. 'I'm going to need a hand, Gerard.'

The old man smiled. 'Can you imagine if people saw me, the managing director, shifting stuff with one of the IT help? Ha, we would never hear the end of it.'

'Well, she's not going to the get to Server Room One on her own,' Carl replied, understanding where the boss was coming from.

Gerard clicked his mouth a couple of times as Carl scratched his head.

Gerard's eyes then lit up with a devilish glint that Carl really didn't care for. 'I've got it!' the old man said, picking up his telephone and dialling a number.

Carl heard it ring a couple of times before a woman answered.

'June, it's Gerard Medley.'

Carl heard June, the property manager, suddenly spark to life. He couldn't hear what she was saying, but she was saying it fast.

Gerard laughed. 'Oh, yeah. Well, I'm glad to hear it. Anyway, I need a bit of a favour. Is the young lad still around, what's his name? Robert?' The female voice babbled something incomprehensible. Gerard looked up at Carl and offered him the thumbs-up. 'Excellent. I have something that needs shifting. I've got Carl here from IT, so he'll give him a hand. Brilliant. Five minutes, then. Tell him to bring the trolley; its bloody heavy … Thanks, June.'

Carl was shaking his head. 'So here you go, *Bob*, just carry this dead body into the server room with Carl, will you? There's a good lad,' he said. The sarcasm dripping from his voice was lost on the older man.

'Don't worry. Look what I have here,' he said. He pulled out a large cardboard box from inside a cupboard Carl didn't even know was there. He shuddered as he caught a glimpse inside the cupboard and wondered just what could be in the boxes stored in a secret closet owned by Gerard Medley. The box was large, and it had a large HP emblazoned on the front of it, alongside a picture of a printer. It was the one Carl himself had installed … *before these dark days,* he thought with a bite of nostalgia for the day before yesterday.

'We'll stuff her in this box, then you and Robert can cart her over to the sever room unnoticed. Then we reboot her.'

Carl pouted as he looked at the body and then the box.

He dithered a little as he leaned in to grab her, pulling her back into her chair. He didn't know where to touch her, or even if he wanted to touch her. In the end, he just took a handful of hair and pulled her towards him.

She was heavier than he thought she would be, and some of her hair came away in his hand. 'Eww!' he groaned as he rubbed his hand on his jeans. The hair was coated in cold tea, biscuits, and blood; it took a little while for it come off.

'Don't be such a baby,' Gerard taunted him. 'You've done it before. You did it to your own wife.'

Carl looked at the older man. He knew there must be murder in his eyes as Gerard flinched just a little.

He liked that.

'I'll tell you what. How about I get the tops, and you get the bottoms. Once she's in the box and in the server room, then we'll get rid of Robert and unpack The Master's present, eh? What do you say?'

Gerard was looking at Leanne as if she were a problem that needed solving rather than a young pretty woman who had her whole life ahead of her, a single mother with responsibilities. *Well, she doesn't have them anymore, does she?* 'I say let's just get her inside and get this over with,' Carl snapped, snarling his words, and wiping sweat from his brow.

Gerard moved behind the dead woman and slipped his hands underneath her armpits. To his obvious, and decadent delight, he grabbed the dead woman's breasts in both hands. 'Hmm, I've wanted to do that for ages. What a great set of baps, eh?'

'Cut that shit out, will you?' Carl snapped, hissing his command at the older man.

Gerard laughed, and then, without warning, his face turned stern. 'Watch your mouth, boy. Don't you forget who you're talking to.'

'I know who I'm talking to. A sick perverted bastard with a penchant for dead pussy. Now pick her the fuck up and let's get her in the box.'

Gerard just looked at him. Carl could tell he was sizing him up. *Maybe he just wants to kill me and take all The Master's adulation for himself,* he thought. Deep down, Carl knew he needed him. Yes, he was the only one who knew how to turn *them* on again, but Gerard seemed to have the knack for the *wetter* part of the operation.

Carl sighed as he gripped the woman's ankles, and both men lifted her off the chair.

'Jesus Christ, she's heavy,' Carl strained as Leanne's legs bent and he fell forwards, dropping his half of the body. He lost his balance, and his face ended up between her breasts.

'Hey,' Gerard scolded him. 'You've just shouted at me for that.'

'Fuck you,' Carl cursed as he stood back up.

Gerard was laughing as Carl spasmed, repulsed at what had just happened. He shook his hands, clenching them into fists, before wiping them on his jeans. After a moment, he composed himself, then took hold of the legs again.

'Didn't you think it was a little bit obvious what was going to happen if you grabbed her by the ankles?' Gerard mocked. 'You need to bend your knees, grab her arse, and heft her into the box. Bodies are heavier because there's zero resistance when you lift them.'

'And you'd know all about that, wouldn't you, you sick prick.'

'It's all in The Master's plan, boy. It's all in The Master's plan.'

It took them a few uncomfortable moments to fit Leanne's body into the box. Carl had to lean in and bend her from the waist. Gerard wanted to do this, but Carl didn't trust him. The way he was looking at her, made his skin crawl. He didn't think the old man would be able to keep his hands to himself, so Carl did it.

He stood up, rubbing the small of his back as Gerard fixed the flap of cardboard so the box would stay shut, when there was a knock on the door.

Both men looked at each other.

They both knew it was Robert, the apprentice maintenance worker, but the glaring accusation of their dirty deeds, residing in the box, was weighing heavy between them.

'It's him,' Gerard whispered.

Carl looked towards the door. 'What should we do?' he whispered.

The old man shrugged.

'Mr Medley, are you in there?' the young voice filtered through the door. 'June Keystone sent me. She said you have a box that needs shifting.'

'Erm … yes. Yes, I do. Hang on for a moment, boy,' he replied. 'Is that sealed?' he hissed at Carl. 'We don't want her flopping all over the floor when he gets in here.'

Carl pulled on the carboard flaps. 'Yeah, that should hold until we get to the server room.'

'Right then, here we go,' he whispered. 'Come on in, boy'.

As the young boy entered, pushing a trolley with him, he looked at the two men. One of them was holding his back, the other was full of sweat, both of them shifting their eyes around the room, looking at anything but the box in the middle of the room.

'Is this it?' Robert asked.

'What?' Carl asked, as if he hadn't heard the question.

'The heavy box? Is this it?' the boy asked again.

Gerard nodded and smiled. Carl cursed him for the grin. Not only because he knew it made him look guilty, but also because it must have looked shit-scary. It was all teeth and humourless, cold, reptilian eyes.

'Yes, it is, boy. Do you see any other huge boxes around her?' Gerard spat.

The boy flinched at the scolding. But he was one of those people who just couldn't keep his mouth shut. 'Who's her?' he asked.

Both men looked at each other again.

'What do you mean, who's her?' Carl asked, cocking his head.

'Y—you said, do you see any other boxes around her,' the boy stuttered.

'I said here,' Gerard snarled. 'Do you see any other boxes around *here? Here, I said.*'

'OK.' The boy shrugged, angling the trolley to get the best angle to put the box on it. 'What's all that on your jeans?' he asked, pointing at Carl's crotch.

Carl looked down at the gestured area. There was a large patch of drying blood, Leanne's blood, on the front of his trousers.

His heart began to race. He needed an excuse to have blood on his trousers in the Managing Director's office. But funny enough, absolutely nothing was forthcoming.

'It's red ink!' Gerard said. 'He was fixing the cartridges in the printer, and the ink spilled all over him,' he laughed. 'Funniest thing I've seen all day.'

The boy nodded and smiled.

'I'll give you a hand,' Carl said, shooting a snotty look up at Gerard, who was just watching.

After a few moments of struggling, the box was on the trolley, and they were ready to wheel it to the server room.

'So, what's in it, then?' the boy asked, idly making conversation as the three of them regarded the trolley in almost complete silence. 'A dead body?' he asked, laughing.

Gerard scowled. As his eyebrows came together and his mouth changed into a white line, Carl forced a laugh. The falseness of it would have been evident, even to a deaf person. Carl Riggs' Othello had never been the talk of the town. 'No,' he scoffed. 'What would have given you that idea? Shit, you kids of today have got vivid imaginations; right Gerard?' he laughed, shooting a look back at the boss.

'What? Erm, oh, yeah. I guess so,' he replied, obviously not paying even the slightest bit of attention.

'I blame all those video games you young ones play all the time,' he continued, overcompensating.

Robert smiled and nodded, as if to say, 'Whatever, old man,' before pushing the trolley, loaded with Leanne, out of the office and into the corridor.

~~~

As they turned the corner to the corridor heading towards Server Room One, something dawned on Carl. Something of the utmost importance.

'So, Bob,' he said, trying to push the smaller boy off the trolley he was holding. 'Why don't you go back to your desk now, eh? We can take it from here.'

Gerard looked at him funny. 'What are you saying, Carl? Robert's here to help get the box into the room and off the trolley. Aren't you, Bob?'

The boy looked up at the managing director and shrugged. 'Whatever you say, Mr Medley,' he replied. 'You're the boss.'

'No,' Carl persisted. 'I think we're OK from here. Honestly, Bob. I can get the box off the trolley myself. You can go now,' he said, speaking very slowly, pronouncing every word.

'It's OK. I need to take the trolley back anyway. I'm off out to pick up a delivery. I was on my way to get the van when Jane asked me to come and do this.'

'Leave the boy alone, Carl. What's the matter with you?' Gerard asked as they reached the server room door.

Carl looked hard at the managing director. His eyes were wide and piercing, his teeth gritted. 'I just think it would be better if it was *just me and you in there,*' he said, punctuating the last part of the sentence.

'Listen, if you boys want to be alone,' Robert said, letting go of the trolley and raising his hands in the air.

'No, don't be impertinent, boy. Carl, open the door, please.' It wasn't a request, and Carl knew it.

'I don't want to open the door, Gerard. It's the server room, and I don't think just anyone should have access to what's *inside!*' He emphasised the word inside, but it went over Gerard's head again.

Gerard stood up to his full height. 'Carl Riggs, open that server room door right now,' he ordered.

Carl dropped his head and turned towards the door. He was shaking his head as he keyed the number on the lock.

'You two are weird,' Robert muttered, more to himself than to the people he was talking about.

Carl sighed and pushed the door open.

He looked up just as the trolley was pushed into the cold room.

He didn't see Tasha poke her head around the corner, witnessing the three men and the large box entering into the room.

The fire extinguisher was in his hands the instant the door closed. Robert had his back to him. Both he and Gerard were staring into the once empty server rack.

The same rack that was not empty anymore.

The lifeless body of Jodi was hanging inside it. One eye had been completely gouged, and a thin blue cable was feeding out of it, trailing into the next door cabinet.

'What the—'

CLUNK!

Robert's body crumpled to the floor, clattering against the metal door of the server cabinet.

'Fucking hell,' Gerard gasped as he marvelled at the body inside the cabinet. 'Did you do this?' he asked as Carl slotted the fire extinguisher back into its space behind the door.

Carl exhaled through his nostrils. 'Yes. It was why I was trying to tell you we didn't need the fucking boy coming in here.'

'What happened?' Gerard asked, the awe on his face evident as his eyes crawled over the hanging body.

'I got one of those little daydream vibe things. Have you had one of them?'

'Stinks of fish and you get a feeling like you're under water?'

Carl raised his eyebrows and nodded. 'That's the one. Well, I was in here, hoping to finally upgrade the server, when in marched Jodi. Rod must have asked her to shadow me. She walked in while I was in the middle of one of the dreams, and … well, I hit her with the fire extinguisher.'

Gerard looked on the floor at the twitching body of Robert. 'Just like you did to our young friend here?'

Carl nodded.

'Oh,' Gerard nodded as his eyes fell upon Carl. '*Now* I get it, why you didn't want him to come into the server room.'

Carl rolled his eyes and shook his head slowly. 'Well, now we're going to have to deal with this one too.'

'Maybe not have to *deal* with it, exactly,' Gerard said, looking back at Jodi, his tongue licking his lips in a salacious way that made Carl feel ill.

'What do you mean?'

'Well, didn't you network two bodies together at home?'

Carl's mind flashed back to what was left in the living room at home. The living room where he'd played with his children, where he'd made spontaneous love with his wife, who he had loved beyond everything else. Where *she* had been banged by the other guy whose name he couldn't remember.

'Yeah, so?'

'When you did, on your little broadband connection, were you or were you not able to download two percent of The Master 2.1?'

'Yeah.'

'Well, with the resource we have here, I imagine we would be able to network all of these bodies together, and maybe, just maybe, we can get enough juice to complete the download. The Master can come, Carl; he can come tonight.'

Carl's heart was racing now. He'd had his moment of doubt. He could now see it all clearly. Amy had been a prophet for the old Gods. She had been sent to him, just like the guy who had come to fix his broadband but ended up slipping it into her at every given opportunity, in every given orifice. It was his mission, his quest to expediate the arrival, or the re-emergence, of The Master.

'Gerard, pass me that screwdriver,' he demanded.

The old man didn't even think about it. He bent down and picked up the long-shafted tool Carl had used to gouge Jodi's eye with. He wiped it on his shirt and passed it to his colleague.

Carl pushed the box off the trolley, spilling its contents onto the metal floor.

He looked at the tool, then he looked at Gerard.

He no longer saw his boss. He no longer saw the managing director of the large, multinational company he worked for. He saw this man as an equal. A brother in arms—or tentacles, to be more precise.

They were both murdering deviants.

If the shoe fits, he thought.

He bent down, and without any further ado, he pushed the shaft into the dead secretary's eye.

'Listen to this,' he whispered, calling Gerard down to listen to the sound the screwdriver made as it sunk into the eyeball.

POP!

Gerard giggled like a schoolboy. 'I *love* that sound,' he whispered.

'OMG! What the fuck are you two freaks doing here?'

Both men turned to see Robert lying on the floor looking up at them. All the colour had drained from his face, and he was rubbing the back of his head as his eyes rested on the body of Leanne, her head on Carl's lap and the black and yellow handle of a screwdriver sticking out of her eye.

Carl turned to Gerard. 'Deal with that,' he snapped.

Gerard tipped Carl a wink and then, picking up the fire extinguisher again, he wacked the boy over the head with it.

Robert's last words had been spoken.

The old man put his arm around the young boy's neck, squeezed his nose and clamped his mouth with his other hand. Carl could hear the weakened boy thrashing while being held in a death hold. All of that was of little importance to him now. He had work to do.

Important work.

He had to finish the hole in Leanne's head, thread a network cable into it, and then hook it up through Jodi's other eye. He still had to work out how he was going to make the connection between them and wondered how, or even if, they would be compatible. Then he would have to hang her up before starting on the next one. Bob.

No point in putting it off, he thought as he went to work on the eye sockets. He was growing to enjoy the sound and feel of the eyeballs popping beneath his screwdriver. When he was finished with Leanne, he opened the server cabinet door and went to work on Jodi's face.

Bob had stopped thrashing now, and Carl was pretty sure he was dead. He looked down towards Gerard who was still holding his head in what looked like a tender embrace. He looked a little further down and was only slightly horrified to see the old man was rather obviously sexually aroused.

'You really are a horrible old goat, aren't you?' It was more of a statement than a question as he indicated towards the bulge in the front of the old man's trousers.

Gerard looked where he was indicating, then looked back up at him. He grinned, tipping him the most disgusting wink Carl had ever seen in his life. 'There is nothing quite like the corruption of a young boy, Carl. It's one of my most favourite things.'

'Give me a hand here,' Carl said. He saw that not only was the old man sporting an erection that *he* would have been proud of, but he was also covered in sweat. For a moment Carl worried if the strenuous activities he had just been involved in might have been too much for him, but then he remembered the journals he'd read. The old duffer had been involved in *a lot* more than that.

'What do you need?' Gerard asked, letting go of Robert's head, letting it fall to the floor with a bang.

'Be careful, will you?' Carl scolded as the boy's head hit the metal with a crash.

'Why? He's dead. He's not going to complain to health and safety, is he?'

'But I've got to work on his eyes. I can't do that if they're all puffy and shit.'

Gerard pulled a face as if to tell Carl that he was nagging him and just to get on networking the bodies.

Carl continued his bloody work.

The two men lifted Leanne's body, and Carl hooked it onto the rail, the same way he had Jodi's. He then positioned her so it was facing the other one, making the cabling of the two easier. He thought about Robert.

If Jodi and Leanne were going to be looking at each other, that was going to make Robert harder to network. He bit his top lip thinking about this conundrum, before pushing Jodi's body to the very end of the rail and sliding Leanne's so it was half behind it, like they were standing next to each other but with their shoulders overlapping, both of them facing outwards.

He stood back to admire his work. He nodded. *This way, given both cabinets, we could network maybe ten more bodies in here,* he thought, blissfully unaware of the content of his considerations.

He took a five-meter patch cable and pushed it deep into Jodi's spare eye socket. It squelched like he was inserting it into a jar filled with jam.

He nodded as he felt the plastic clip at the end of the cable snap into place like it did when inserting it into a port on the floor or the switch. He shook his head in wonder at the way things just seemed to be so compatible. He then trailed the sticky cable from Jodi into the eye socket of Leanne. Once again, it clipped into place. As it did, Leanne's body spasmed as the electricity was flowing through her.

True networking, he though with a flash of pride.

He looked at the screen of the main server. After wiping his hands on the back of his trousers, he logged on and checked the network speed. This morning, it had been running at something ridiculous like thirty-three percent. Right now, it was showing nearer forty-five.

He nodded.

'Good work, boy. The Master will be pleased,' Gerard said as he looked over his shoulder regarding the readout on the screen. 'Should we try to download the software now?' he asked, sounding like an over-excited child on Christmas Eve.

'Let's get Robert hooked up first,' he replied.

'Good idea.'

The two men lifted the boy, and Carl attached him to the same rail. He then went to work on his left eye and Leanne's right one.

He took another network cable and hooked the boy and the woman together.

Another spasm ripped through the three hanging bodies as they all interfaced with each other.

He checked the network speed. It was almost fifty percent.

'This is brilliant,' Carl boasted. 'But it's my bet that we're going to need more than fifty percent to download The Master 2.1.'

Gerard's face went dark, and he looked at his partner through sinister eyes. 'Does that mean more killing?' he asked.

Carl held his hands up. 'Jesus, slow down, Hannibal Lecter. Let's see how it goes first. I'll walk around the building and gauge the reception of the faster network. You go and, I don't know, whatever is it you executive types do.'

Gerard looked at his watch. 'Oh, I've got a meeting in ten minutes. I best go and smarten myself up.'

'Right, you do that. If anyone asks, Leanne has gone home sick, Jodi is working in Server Room One, but we have taken the phone offline so she can't be disturbed, and Robert? What did he say about going on a delivery?'

'Yeah, he said he'll be out for the rest of the day,' Gerard remembered.

'Good, then we're good to go,' Carl said, wiping his hands on his jeans.

18.

CARL HAD BEEN acting strange all week.

Tasha liked Carl the most out of the rest of the IT team, he was the most down-to-earth, the most normal out of all of them.

She was well aware that she included herself in that list.

She knew she was a *strange one;* she'd readily admitted it to anyone. But being strange didn't mean she didn't enjoy the reliance on someone who was *normal* from time to time.

Carl was that normality to her, an oasis in a desert of strange.

He was funny, he was irreverent, and, ultimately, he had an empathy Tasha could relate to but, more importantly, needed.

So, when her normality anchor was acting strange, it irked her.

Her anxiety had doubled since yesterday when he'd gone home early. There had been a vibe about him, just a little something she couldn't quite put her finger on but felt like she needed to. She had his personal mobile number and followed him on social media, she liked his comics and loved the idea of the naughty reindeer, but they hadn't really been friends, the kind who messaged each other.

She had written a text to him, a full ten lines of concern; she'd hovered over the send button, deliberating with herself whether to send it or not. In the end, her anxiety increased as the situation got the better of her, and she deleted the message.

This morning's outburst had trigged her again. She was determined to find out what was happening with him. She'd followed him around to the managing director's office and watched him go inside, then pretended to be working on an empty desk in the open plan office when he stormed out and into the server room.

She had observed, from afar, as Gerard Medley, a man she instinctively mistrusted, left his office. Then Jodi had walked around and entered Server Room One.

Tasha left the spare desk after rebooting the machine to make it look like she had done something.

'Where've you been?' Dean asked as she re-entered the department, never taking his head out of the two-monitor set up he was using.

'I had a couple of jobs on desks. Why? Who's asking?' she replied a little too fast for her own liking—she didn't want to sound so defensive.

Dean chuckled. 'No one. I was just wondering, as your phone was ringing, that's all.'

Tasha shook her head. 'Sorry, Dean, I just don't think I'm myself today.'

'Frigging hell, that'll be two of you, then. You and Carl.'

'Have you noticed it too?' she asked, initiating the longest conversation she had ever had with this colleague.

'Yeah, ever since he was fixing Gerard's laptop the other day. He just hasn't been the same.' To Tasha's surprise, Dean turned away from his monitors and looked at her. 'Do you think there was something on there he shouldn't have seen?' he asked. His grin spread right across his whole face—Tasha thought it looked sly.

She looked towards the IT build room. 'Hmm, let's see,' she said.

Dean turned back to his machine; his interest in what was happening in Carl's life had already waned, and his own importance had taken over.

Tasha entered the build room and located the machine that used to belong to Gerard. She closed one eye and flipped the lid, wincing as if expecting something to jump out and bite her.

Nothing did.

She looked at who was logged in. It was still Carl. She snorted. *I'll have to reboot the whole machine.*

She pressed the power button down for ten seconds, and the machine made a quiet meowing noise before the screen went black. She gave it thirty seconds—she didn't know why; she knew it didn't need it, but she thought it best anyway—before pressing the power button again and rebooting the machine. The operating system came up without a hitch, and a few moments later, she was welcomed to the computer and prompted to press the CTRL ALT + DELETE buttons, which she did.

After entering her username and password, she pressed return, and the computer welcomed her by name.

All was well and good. There were a few more icons on the desktop than was normal … *but he is the MD,* she thought.

She was just about to close the lid when a small pop-up box caught her attention. Knowing it couldn't be the log-in script, as her admin account didn't use one, she flicked the lid up again and looked at the wording.

DOWNLOAD IN PROGRESS ...
MASTER V2.1
PROGRESS 10% ....

She moved the machine to one side and checked the network port, knowing already she hadn't plugged one in. Her eyes then moved down to the corner next to the clock. To the network access information.

The machine was showing as connected to a wireless network; there was nothing strange about that, but she didn't recognise the name of it.

MASTERWIFICONNECTION

Masterwificonnection, she thought, then looked at the pop-up command prompt. 'Master V2.1,' she whispered. She pouted her lips in a lopsided grimace. *I'm not sure if I like this.*

Right clicking the network symbol brought up all the available Wi-Fi connections in the area. There were only three: the official work one, the unofficial IT department that flew underneath the firewall, and the one this machine was currently connected to.

Tasha popped her head out the door and addressed the rest of the department. 'Have any of you heard of a Wi-Fi SSID called Master Wi-Fi Connection? It could be something Carl set up.'

'Never hear of it,' Dean shouted.

'If Carl's making his own Wi-Fi connections now, then he's in trouble for sure,' Charles said, there was real excitement in his voice.

Bryan ignored her, still with his earphones in.

'No worries,' she replied and retreated back into the room.

She clicked on the DISCONNECT NETWORK button, and an icon for the network appeared, asking her if she really wanted to do that.

She selected the letter Y and pressed return.

Another pop-up box appeared, overlapping the first.

Download Interrupted ...
MASTER V2.1
PROGRESS 10% (halted) ....

Unsure why, she felt better about that. There was something about Master V2.1 that just didn't sit right for her.

She turned off the computer, took a screwdriver and removed the hard drive and the battery from the slimline machine, she then put them both in her drawer. It just seemed like the correct thing to do.

As she turned back to her own screen, she noticed a message she'd never seen before.

TURN THEM OFF, THEN TURN THEM ON AGAIN!

She looked at the message, squinting. Then she read it again. There was not one word on that screen she liked. She wanted to ask the rest of the team if they had ever seen a message like it before, but she knew none of them would be the least bit helpful, so she closed the message and opened her email.

As she read the first message—a notification of something happening in the company regarding health and safety—her screen began to flicker. The words of the message began to dance around the screen. They jumbled up and became nonsense. She blinked her eyes, shook her head, and looked back at her monitor.

KILL THEM ALL ... PLUG THEM IN.

She sighed and looked around the room. Dean had his head in his monitors, Charles was doing whatever Charles did, and Bryan was ignoring everyone at the back of the room, messing around with scripts. Jodi and Carl were still in Server Room One.

She clicked away from the message and continued to read her emails.

That was when the room darkened around her.

She looked up at the strip lights on the ceiling, thinking they had just gone out, but they were still on. It was just that now there was some kind of green moss growing over them, dimming the illumination. As she looked closer, she saw it looked more like algae than moss.

She turned to Dean to ask him what he thought might be happening but was surprised to see she was alone in the room. Dean and the others had gone. She hadn't seen them leave; they just weren't there anymore.

The room darkened again, and a smell began to seep in, along with a damp chill. There was something about the sea in the feel of the room. She had spent a lot of time around the docks and harbours of Liverpool when she was growing up, so she recognised the smell.

It was high tide.

The door to the department was closed, and it, too, was covered in the odd green algae. The stink was becoming more pronounced and was now reminiscent of rotting fish. Fish that had been dead for a long time, left to deteriorate in stagnant, filthy water.

She gagged as it wafted up her nose and down into her throat. She felt her stomach heave, and she bent over ready to expel whatever she had in her stomach, but seemingly, there was enough in there to banish. Through tear blurred eyes, she looked at her monitor. The email programme she had open was gone; replaced with the strangest screensaver she'd ever seen.

It wasn't one she'd installed. *Why would I? It's horrible,* she thought. The image was of an underwater scene. The water was brown and filthy. Through the murk, she could see the floating bodies of hundreds, if not thousands of humans. Every one of them were dead and decaying. The bodies were torn apart, flayed, impaled, half eaten by the wildlife existing in the grimy depths.

Spiders that could live under the water were crawling over them, eating them, fighting with other deformed sea creatures for the fleshy bounty that was the corpses of the men, women, and, most disturbingly of all, children.

Tasha clicked on the screen, with the sole intention of turning it off, but it wouldn't shut down. The screen felt spongy under her finger, and she had to retract her hand, rapidly rubbing her fingertip with the tips of her other fingers. Reluctantly, she pressed on her second screen, this one felt exactly the same, it also wouldn't shut off. She could feel panic blooming within her. She fumbled around at the back of her monitor to find the power cord; she couldn't deal with the hideous images anymore. Giving the cable a yank, it came away and she expected the screen to go black.

It didn't.

It continued to display the vile images of wherever this submarine catastrophe was supposed to be.

The temperature of the room dropped then, and the chill factor became intense. She pulled the fleece jacket she was wearing around her in an attempt to combat it. She pulled it up and covered her nose, hoping to block the smell, to stop it from making her feel sicker than she already did.

A shadow passed over the window. The mildew coated blinds were closed, so she hadn't been able to see out of them. She stood. Everything in her nature told her she didn't want to look out the window, but whatever the shadow was out there, it was big.

She needed to see it.

Pulling the string, the blinds moved horizontally along the rail, exposing the window.

What she saw caused her to drop her jacket from her face.

It was the same scene from her PC monitor!

Gone were the windows of the other offices that she expected to see. They had been replaced with the decaying bodies of people being devoured by impossible, repugnant sea creatures.

The shadow moved again.

Helpless to look away, Tasha raised her head away from the gruesome scene before her and stared into the murky abyss.

The shadow moved again.

Something hit the window, making her jump.

It was thick, green, and covered in slimy, veined skin. The tentacle hit the window again, as if the thing was trying to break the glass, to get in, to reach the fleshy delights that was her body … *and my soul,* she thought with a shiver.

The shadow, the owner of the thick, vile tentacle, shifted again in the murk. Its bulk, at first, seemed unfathomable to her. But only at first.

The thing was getting closer.

With it came a terrible cold. It encroached over her, chilling her like the air-conditioning units the server rooms did. However, it felt like these ones had been set to at least five hundred percent of their normal output. The stink intensified too. Tasha was having difficulty breathing as the stench assaulted her nose and throat.

Ever nearer it grew, and ever further away from the window Tasha stepped.

Then, through the murk and the dankness, the thing showed itself.

Tasha screamed …

~~~~

'Tasha!'

She felt hands on her, shaking her, waking her from the horrible, ugly daydream she had found herself in.

'Tasha, wake up, you mad cow.'

She raised her head to look up towards the voice, petrified of who, or what she might see there.

It was Dean.

She jumped out of her chair, surprising her colleague, who stepped back out of the mad woman's way.

'Whoa, slow down,' he laughed as he raised his hands, stepping back.

Charles was looking over his screen at what was happening; he, too, had a grin on his face.

Tasha looked all around, her eyes wild, her body defensive. 'What the fuck just happened?' she snapped.

Dean was doing his best not to laugh out loud. She could see it in his face. 'You fell asleep at your desk,' he wheezed. 'You were twitching and shouting. It looked like you were going to vomit a moment or two ago. Then you screamed. That's when I woke you up.'

Ignoring him, she looked at her screens, dismayed to find one of them was off. 'Why is my screen off?' she asked.

Dean shrugged. 'How should I know? You must have knocked it when you jerked back.'

She looked up at the window and rolled her eyes. She was relieved the blinds were still shut.

'What's out there?' she asked, pointing towards the covered window.

'What?' Dean asked. The humour had gone from his face, as if the joke had worn thin. He was now looking at her as if she were a crazy woman who might jump up and attack them at any given moment.

'Out there, behind the blinds. What's out there?'

Dean shook his head as sat back down at his desk. He was mumbling something she couldn't hear and wasn't sure she wanted to anyway.

She could feel Charles's eyes boring into her as she made her way towards the window. Feeling like she was in slow motion, she reached out and flicked one of the vertical slats. She peered out, expecting to see something evil, old, and huge, crashing through the window.

There was nothing out there but the windows of the next offices along.

'What drugs have you been on?' Charles asked from his desk. He looked around, hoping someone might laugh at his little joke. When he saw everyone was ignoring him, he sat back down.

As Tasha let go of the slat, she pondered what it was she had seen and where it had come from. *It was too real to be a dream,* she thought, looking up at the lights. There was absolutely no trace of the algae that had been covering them mere minutes ago.

The IT build room door was still open, and she could see the closed laptop on the bench inside. She put her telephone on forward to her mobile, grabbed the laptop, got the hard drive and battery from her drawer, and made her way out of the department office.

No one challenged her on where she was going.

She was glad about that as she might have snapped at them, and she hated confrontation.

She hurried along the corridor heading towards Server Room One. She needed to see Carl, to tell him about the strange daydream she'd just had after looking at Gerard's laptop. As she turned the corner, she saw him, Gerard, and the young lad who worked in the maintenance department. They were wheeling a trolley, with a huge box on top of it, into the server room. Carl didn't look himself as he keyed the code into to the door lock. *Why would he be going in there with them?* she thought. *And what's in the box?* It was a large printer box, but she knew there were no printer installations happening today, and there was also no need for a printer of that size in a sever room.

She was just about to go after them when something grabbed her shoulder.

In her mind's eye, it was a thick, green, muscular tentacle covered in slime and veins. She turned, sharp, and almost hit the person standing behind her full in the face.

'You're in IT, aren't you?'

It was Alan Bryce. Tasha rolled her eyes internally while beaming a grin externally. 'Yeah, I'm Tasha,' she said. 'How can I help?'

Alan was well-known for moaning. He was also a frequent flyer. Anything, even something small like a flickering monitor, was logged by him. They could always gauge how well the network was running by how often Alan Bryce called.

'Oh, I don't need any help. I just wanted to tell you that the network is working fantastic today. It's faster than it's been in months …' He paused for a moment and smiled—Tasha noticed there was pride in that smile, as if the network belonged to him. 'Maybe even years.'

'That's brilliant. I'll be sure to pass your compliments to the team.'

'No need to. I'm just on my way around to Mr Medley's office now to tell him. Praise where praise is due, young lady,' he beamed as he waltzed past her, towards the managing director's office.

19.

CARL WAS WALKING through the corridors, lost in his own little world of murder, death, computers, and strange daydreams. His t-shirt was stiff and disgusting from the grime that came from the gouging of people's eyes for a returning Master he'd never seen or even heard of before yesterday.

He was cursing the day he ever met Gerard Medley. Without him, he would still have a wife … *albeit a cheating bitch of one,* he thought. He would still have a life, because right now, he knew that once the four poor souls currently hanging in the server room were missed, or when anyone from the IT department wanted to get in there, he and Gerard were going straight to jail. They would not pass GO and they would definitely not collect two hundred pounds.

'There you are.'

Carl instinctively knew the voice was for him.

He also knew who it was.

Alan Bryce.

He was in no mood for this particular *bellend* right now.

'Alan, I'm right in the middle—'

'Carl,' he interrupted. 'I don't know what you've done to this network, but it's running like a dream.'

'What?' Carl asked, cocking his head so his ear pointed at the man, just so he could hear him properly.

'I said the network is running perfectly. Well, maybe not perfectly, but a lot better than it was. Look.' He pointed to his computer, where the screen was displaying a message. The message was telling Carl to turn this man off and then turn him on again.

It wanted him to reboot Bryce.

Carl had to admit that it was a tempting suggestion.

'Just look at that download speed! I don't think we've ever had seven megabytes in the whole time I've been here. Now look, it's over twelve. It's not perfect by any means, but it's not awful either. Whatever you're doing in that server room, I say keep it up.'

Carl looked closer at Alan's screen. All he could see was a large black box with the big white lettering on it.

KILL HIM!
KILL HIM!
KILL HIM!
KILL HIM!

Carl wanted nothing more than to get away from the screen. The obvious fact that no one else could see the message was playing with his head. *I bet Gerard could see it,* he thought with a grimace.

'Wow, that's great. Listen, Alan, I've got to go because what I'm doing isn't finished yet. I'll speak to you later, OK?'

Alan raised his hands and shook his head slowly. 'Do what you need to do, Carl. Because whatever it is, it's working. That's what I told that Tasha one earlier.'

Carl missed this last bit of information as he hurried back off the way he had come. *If the network is running that well, they're going to send someone to the server room to either find me, or to see what I've done.*

This thought made him walk as fast as he could without inciting suspicion. He got to the server room door and entered the code.

It opened.

There was a strong whiff coming from inside. He'd never smelt ozone before, but he thought if he did, it would smell like this.

It was odd. Like copper but with an electric fizzle to it.

It was odd, but he thought it smelt white.

Relieved to see there was no one else in the room—no one living, anyway—he began to change the combination to the lock. He'd send an email to everyone in the department to let them know he had changed it, but he would deliberately give them the wrong code.

Once it was changed, he tested it.

The door opened for him.

Now, Server Room One was his.

Well, his and Gerard's, anyway.

He looked at the screen to his left, expecting to see the black box with the white writing commanding him to kill someone, or to turn someone back on again, but was surprised to see only the small command box informing him The Master V2.1 was fifteen percent downloaded.

He looked at the bodies in the cabinet. All three of them were shaking as if an electrical pulse were passing through them. The eye sockets around where the cables were inserted were pulsing a sickly purple glow.

He stepped back and marvelled at his creation.

'Carl ...' The voice came from everywhere, all at once. 'Congratulations on turning them back on. However, our work has only just begun. The Master is close. Turn them off, then turn them on again!'

The smell of the sea was back, as was the frigid air. This time, he breathed deep of it, taking the stink and the briny moistness deep into his lungs. It was pleasant to him now, and the dampness didn't trouble him; in fact, he embraced it.

There was something about the voice that calmed him, soothed him.; lulled him into a daze. 'We need more, don't we?' he asked, a dreamy look had taken over his face. 'We still need to get The Master closer.'

'That is exactly what we need. Commitment from the disciples. Bring them to me. We will reboot them; we will bring The Master home.'

The smell receded along with the moistness in the air, but Carl hardly noticed; he was too deep in thought.

20.

TASHA WAS WATCHING him like a hawk. Every time he looked up from his computer, she would turn away at the last minute and pretend she was doing something else.

As if I'm not paranoid enough, he thought as he half-heartedly replied to a couple of emails. He was overly aware there was more work to be done in Server Room One, but he wasn't sure he had the heart for it, not tonight.

Every couple of minutes, a large pop-up would flash onto his screen telling him he needed to turn more people off and then turn them on again.

In truth, he was getting a little bored of it.

There was no point in looking around to see if anyone else was getting the messages, as he knew they weren't. It was only him and Gerard. Like it or loathe it, he was stuck with that horrible, dirty old man. They were partners in a crime he knew would eventually take him down. *So why did I do it in the first place?*

He knew the answer to that. He knew when the daydream took over, he was open to susceptibility. He wasn't given an option to say no.

Now he had Tasha looking over at him. He could feel her eyes boring into him. *What does she know? Does she know anything? Has she seen me going into the server room?*

All these questions were running around his head, making a nuisance of themselves, giving him a headache.

He was thinking about the voice from earlier, the one telling him they needed more power. He knew exactly what that meant. It was more sacrifices to The Master, and more bodies hanging in the server room. *Turn them off and then turn them on again!*

Carl turned in his chair and knocked into Charles, who took his mobile phone away from his ear and glared at him. 'Watch what you're doing,'

Charles snapped, mouthing the word *dickhead* as he put the phone back to his ear.

Carl's heart, the one that had been beating in his throat, his ears, his fingertips, *and strangely in the tip of my cock*, dropped back into his chest as he sighed. As he swung back around to his computer and caught Tasha looking at him again.

'Tasha, do you have something you want to say to me?' he whispered, leaning into the space between his monitors, towards her.

The timid woman shook her head and snapped back to whatever job she was working on.

He put his head in his hands and sighed again.

He looked at his screen.

The pop-up was back.

BRING THE MASTER MORE POWER ... TURN THEM OFF, TURN THEM *ALL* OFF ...

THEN TURN THEM ON AGAIN!

TIME IS PRECIOUS.

BRING THE MASTER HOME ...

All this talk of The Master bothered him. He had never been religious. He'd been brought up as a Roman Catholic, with all the guilt that his Irish mother could rain down on him, but he'd lost all interest in religion a long time ago. So, this talk of a Master coming back from the ages, from the Old Gods, should have sounded like a whole load of rubbish to him.

But it didn't.

It kind of made sense, perfect sense, and that was what was scaring him the most.

When he thought about it, the whole scenario was ropey, and he really should have laughed it off. That was until he thought about what he'd already done in preparation for this Master, whoever, or whatever it was. He'd killed two people at home. He'd killed one person in work and had been complicit in the killing of two more. He'd removed people's eyes from their sockets and inserted ethernet cables into their brains. He'd hooked them up—creating a superfast network, by the way—allowing him to download a mysterious piece of software, and he had absolutely no idea what it would do when it was complete.

'Fuck my life,' he sighed as he looked back at his computer screen.

~~~~

Gerard's meeting was the dullest one he had ever been to. He remembered back when he was a much younger man, climbing the executive ladder. The excitement of people coming into the office just to see *you*, the bullying of departments to get *your* request done well before anyone else's. The feeling of being *overly friendly* with the women who wanted to climb the ladder too and were willing to do almost anything to get on that first rung. Back in them days, no one ever went running to HR to complain about lewd advances because they feared losing their jobs.

That was power.

The authority he had over people's lives had been a drug for him. He'd seen grown men breaking down in his office as he fired them from their positions, ruining the nice lives they had built up for themselves and their families. He'd seen them reduced to being on their knees, offering him anything, everything if he gave them one more chance. He'd especially loved the sexual power he had over everyone. He'd used this time and time again. Getting his ruby hands all over them, regardless of age, size, or race. He didn't care.

He got what he wanted, when he wanted, just because he could.

The fun had gone out of the job a few years back when the world went mad, and everything started to become politically correct. He couldn't get his *jollies* on with the women anymore. *It comes to something when even the managing director can't grab a bit of tit in the office,* he thought.

Meetings had become a chore too.

Boring people waffling on about boring things he'd long since ceased to be interested in.

Ordering in vegan buffets in case he offended anyone. He couldn't even get his beloved coconut rings into these meeting in case someone had a nut allergy, or Heaven forbid the hole in the middle of them offended anyone.

It was around about that time that his interests in the delights that the Dark Web could offer had sparked. He'd always been a long-time advocate of pornography. He had forced his wife, the lovely Brenda, *may The Master bless her soul*, to engage in some of his fantasies. He'd forced her into swinging, group sex, filming herself with multiple men for the gratification of others online.

The poor woman, he smiled.

But soon enough, he'd gotten bored of all that too. He longed and yearned for more.

He'd never dabbled in the paedophile pools in the Dark Web; he wasn't that stupid. It wasn't because he didn't want to. The truth of the matter was that he really *did* want to, it was just that he knew they were constantly patrolled by the police, and a man like him, in his position, would make great headlines splashed across the tabloids. He did have a growing interest in bestiality. He had dallied with it a few times; at first, it disgusted him, but he had grown rather fond of it over time. He had often thought about forcing Brenda into making some bestiality videos, just for shits and giggles, but ultimately, it didn't really do it for him, and no matter how much he loved his wife, he loved his dogs too.

He did, however, develop a taste for the more sadistic side of his passions. It was that development, that enjoyment, that led him to exactly where he was today.

With a server room filled with bodies and a Master to bring forth.

There were two men and one woman currently talking at him about some insurances, or was it a merger deal? He'd already forgotten. All he was interested in was thinking of ways of luring them all into Server Room One and getting Carl to patch them into the network. He really wanted to take their eyes out himself—it looked like so much fun. He could feel himself getting hard as he imagined killing both the men and leaving them for later while he took his time on the woman.

He longed to gouge out her eyes and fuck the bloody holes. He wanted to put one of those cables up his rectum while he did it, connect it up there while his cock was connecting with her brain.

He wanted to be part of the network. Why should Carl have all the fun?

'So, what do you think?' the taller of the two men asked. He was a young, annoying looking prick, with a prick's haircut and a prick's smile. All Gerard could think about right then was how he would look with a cable in his eye.

'I think it's all satisfactory,' he replied with a crocodile smile, not caring a jot about anything he'd just agreed to.

The three people looked at each other with confused smiles. 'Satisfactory?' the other male asked. This one was older, shorter, and squat. Gerard put him in his mid-forties. He could also see him in a gym somewhere making animal noises as he tried too hard to keep up with the young people, lifting weights that were far too heavy for him. *He would look good with a screwdriver in his eye too.*

'Yes, satisfactory,' Gerard said standing up.

The three of them followed their host's lead and all stood too.

'So, before you go, and before we sign such a deal, wouldn't you want to have a look around our infrastructure? You know, to see how we tick as a company. Take a peek into the server rooms; what do you Americans call it? Take a look under the hood?' Gerard said the last part with a faux American accent; a bad one.

The older man smiled. 'I don't think we have the time, Mr Medley,' he said, stretching out his hand for the older man to shake.

Gerard accepted the outstretched hand.

As soon as their flesh touched, the room instantly turned dark and damp, and the delicious, intoxicating stink of rotting fish crawled, or slithered up into his nostrils.

A dark shadow passed by outside the window, and Gerard grinned. 'Are you sure you don't have time for the smallest of peeks into Server Room One?' he asked. He hadn't let go of the man's hand yet, and he was squeezing it as tight as he could. He was offering the business equivalent of a hint that the deal they'd just struck hinged on them seeing the contents of the server room.

The man's face twitched as he forced a smile, understanding the nature of the prolonged handshake.

'I'm sure we can fit in a small peek,' the woman piped up as she reached out to shake his hand.

He let go of the man and took the offered hand. He caressed it. As he did, he could see the revulsion on her face and he watched, with a throbbing enjoyment as goosebumps crawled up her arm at his touch. But, to her favour, her face didn't even twitch. *She'll make a great addition to the pack,* he thought. *She has spades of spunk.*

'Excellent,' Gerard replied with a grin!

~~~~

Tasha was having a hard time. The daydreams were becoming more and more realistic, and more frequent too.

She had suffered something similar in her youth.

She could remember it perfectly, as if it was only yesterday.

Reboot: A Cosmic Horror

During school, she would suddenly find herself in a dark, dangerous place. She would be bored in the classroom one minute, and the next, she would be stuck in some depthless darkness, surrounded by sounds she couldn't fathom. She had never been a child who had much of an imagination. Even though she did manage to find herself a few friends, she was considered by the majority of the other children as strange.

She remembered the time a few of them had gotten together to watch a film about a horrible burnt man who haunted kids in their dreams. This imagery had stuck with her. So, when the dreams came, there she would be, stuck in some kind of basement surrounded be strange hissing and rumbling noises. There would always be something else down there with her. Something not hindered by the darkness; something that could see her, smell her, and knew who and where she was.

It would stalk her, coming up behind her, grabbing at her with its claws, or knives, or whatever it had. Its intention was to slice her, to kill her, to drink her blood and eat her flesh.

These dreams had gone when her mother, tired of the bad reports coming from school about her sleeping and daydreaming in class, sent her to a child psychologist. The doctor had helped her with the anxiety and talked her through soothing her fears.

The daydreams mostly went away.

From time to time, there would be night terrors. She would wake up in the small hours of the morning screaming, sweating, freezing cold. An old woman would be sitting on her chest, sucking the very life from her, laughing as she was dying slowly.

When she woke she would be alone, but out of breath.

Thankfully, these were few and far between.

So now that the daydreams were back, although it wasn't a good thing by any stretch of the imagination, it was something she knew she could deal with, something she could understand.

However, these were on a different level from the others. For one, she knew she was still awake during these episodes.

There were smells, and there were colours too. The darkness of the water outside the windows was nothing new, it was akin to the basement, and the menacing figure lurking within the darkness was also familiar; but the stink and the ominous feeling of doom, of an existential dread, they were new.

Also, the messages telling her to kill everyone was new too. She was level-headed enough to know these messages were just episodes and not to act upon them. How could computers be telling her to kill people?

What she was worried about however, was the antics of her rock, the man she had used to anchor herself to reality within the IT department.

He was acting strange. He was somehow in cahoots with the managing director, the loathsome Mr Medley.

Even though right at that very moment, she was sitting in a cold, damp room with green algae growing over the ceiling and lights, while surrounded by deep, filthy water that was filled with decaying human bodies that were being consumed by deformed, alien fish and crustaceans; even the fact that something huge, powerful, and dangerously old was lurking within the shadowy waters, ready to emerge, to return, to destroy and rebuild; that didn't really bother her. She knew it was just her mean brain playing nasty tricks on her.

She closed her eyes and clenched her fists. Her long fingernails dug into the flesh of her palms. As her fingernails were long, they broke the skin and blood began to flow. This was her coping mechanism, one she'd employed in school, and one she knew would work now.

It did.

As she opened her eyes, she was back in her own world, the IT department, surrounded by the normality of her existence. Carl was sitting at his desk, and her hand was bleeding.

Everything was as it should be, except for one small detail: her computer was still telling her to turn people off and turn them on again.

21.

CARL WAS TRYING to deal with what was happening in Server Room One. His brain just couldn't wrap itself around the dead people in there, the ones powering the network. How could he explain what he'd done? He knew it was for some kind of higher authority, that he was serving some sort of old God or other, but he'd killed his wife, her lover, and one of his work colleagues.

What was he going to tell the kids when they got home?

How was he going to explain to them that their mum had been having an affair, and would never be coming home again?

He removed his phone from his pocket and dialled his mother. She answered on the third ring. 'Mum, it's Carl.'

'I know it's you; your number comes up on the screen, soft lad.'

He rolled his eyes. His mother didn't suffer fools. 'Listen, something's come up in work. We're still working on the problem from last night. Amy's still in Scotland, so are the boys OK to stay with you again tonight?'

'Of course they are. You know they're welcome whenever they want. But can you do me a favour next time? Feed them before they come around. The greedy bastards are eating me out of house and home. Also, I need you to have a word with Thomas.'

She had always called him Thomas, never Tommy like the rest of them. 'Why, what's he done now?'

He heard his mother sigh down the other end of the phone. 'Listen, I've seen it all before, right. I mean, I brought you and your brothers up, so I know all about what teenage boys get up to when they are left to their own devices. But Thomas, he's on another level.'

Carl was dreading what she was going to say next, dreading it more than the inevitable police investigation when they found the bodies in the server room.

'What's he done now?'

'Porn Station.'

Those were two words he'd never really associated coming out of his mother's mouth, so when they did, they took him by surprise.

'W—what about it?' he asked, once again dreading the answer.

'I found him, early hours this morning, asleep on the couch, his trousers around his ankles, his socks next to him, with Porn Station on the telly. Now I'm not naïve enough to *not* know what he was doing, but if you could just have a word? Imagine if your father had caught him? It'd be all over the pub by now.'

Carl's shoulders slumped. *First world problems,* he thought. *I miss them.*

'Yes, Mum. I'll have a word when he gets out of school.'

'Good, as long as we don't have another instance of that, then both boys are welcome to stay anytime.'

'Brilliant, thanks, Mum, you're a—' He paused. He was about to say *godsend,* but he didn't think he wanted to now. The silence between them was becoming awkward. He needed to say something, and quick. 'Lifesaver,' he concluded, pleased with himself for thinking on his feet.

'So, are you going to tell me what's really happening?'

Carl's heart fell deep into his stomach.

What does she know? What can I tell her? Well, Mum, this ancient God has been contacting me via the computers, and all I have to do is kill everyone in the office in order for him to break through whatever barriers are keeping him at bay and retake his place as overlord of the earth!

'What's happening with you and Amy? Are you two splitting up?'

'What?' he asked, not fully understanding what she was asking.

'You can't hide it from me; I'm your mother. I've seen it happen a million times before. You know I never *really* liked her, don't you? I always thought you could do better.'

'Erm … well, it's something like that. We've been talking,' he lied. 'I honestly don't know what's going to happen.' At least this bit was the truth.

'I knew it. I knew there was something wrong. I was saying to Helen at the …'

That was when the lights, the computers, and everything electrical turned itself off.

He moved the phone away from his ear and looked around. Everyone else was standing up too. He could still hear his mother babbling on over the phone. 'Mum, listen. The electricity has just gone off. I'll have to go. I'll call you later, and I'll have a word with Tommy tonight. Love you, speak later.' He didn't wait for her reply before pressing the button, severing the connection.

'What's going on?' Dean asked, uncharacteristically looking up from his now blank monitors. He looked like a junkie without his fix, a fish out of water,

Carl shivered at that description. Fish were, right now, his least favourite thing. *Maybe behind squid,* he thought. *I'll never eat calamari ever again.*

'It looks like the electricity has tripped,' Charles replied.

'Stating the obvious since 1979,' Carl mumbled as Rod made his way into the room.

'What's going on?' he asked. 'Has this got anything to do with what's happening in Server Room One?'

Carl shot him a look. 'What do you know about Server Room One?' he asked, his eyes wide, but his brow creased.

'We need to protect the servers,' Bryan interrupted from the back of the room, removing his headphones.

'What?' Rod asked, looking lost.

'The servers, they'll have roughly ten minutes until they shut down. The UPS devices will have kicked in to keep them running, but if you want to avoid data loss, then we need to manually shut them down, one by one.'

There were four server rooms; each room held at least three servers, with the exception of Server Room One. That had nine servers that would all need to be shut down.

Fuck ... Server Room One, Carl thought.

'I'll check Server Room One,' he shouted as he made his way towards the door.

'Hang on,' Rod shouted, halting his run. 'There are nine devices in there. You'll need help shutting them all down. Take Tasha with you.'

Tasha stood up. Carl thought she was looking a little worse for wear but ready to go.

Fuck, Carl thought. 'Erm, no … It'll be OK,' he said, searching his brain for a reason to go on his own. Then one sprung to mind, saving his life. 'Jodi's already in there. She's been monitoring the upgrade for me, watching out for bugs and shit.'

'Right, Bryan, Charles, Tasha, you all spread out around the other server rooms. Carl, you sort out Room One with Jodi, and I'll go and see the maintenance guys, find out what's happened,' Rod said, as if he had the authority in the room. In truth, everyone would be going to do what they needed to do, with or without his say-so.

22.

AS CARL STORMED out of the department on his way around the office towards Server Room One, he was accosted by numerous angry and confused office workers.

'What's going on, Carl?' He could hear the grating voice of Alan Bryce shouting him over the confusion.

'Carl, will I have lost all my data?' That was Carrie from marketing shouting for him. Normally, he'd have stopped and spoken to her, but not today, there were other, bigger fish to fry.

Stop making fish analogies, Carl, he admonished himself.

'Carl, how do you think we'll get on, on Saturday?' He shook his head at this one. *Does that fucking football bore ever think of anything else?*

As he passed the maintenance department, he noticed Jane was nowhere to be seen, leaving Chris, the oldest member of the team, and a handy man to know in a crisis. 'Chris,' Carl shouted. 'Any idea what's happening?'

'None, mate. Jane is heading to the control room. She should be able to diagnose what's caused this from there.'

'Nice. When you find out, can you let me know?'

'Will do, mate,' he shouted as Carl continued towards what he thought of now as *his* server room. 'Hey, Carl?' Chris shouted again. Carl turned. 'Have you seen Bob? He went to help Gerard out with something earlier but hasn't come back.'

Carl shook his head. 'I saw him before; he helped us get a big printer into the server room. He said something about going out on a delivery.'

'Yeah, he's probably just hanging around somewhere making a nuisance of himself.'

'You never know, man. He might be *hanging* around somewhere doing a world of good,' Carl laughed. He laughed because it was funny, and because it was true.

As he turned the corner, Gerard was standing outside the room with three other people. *Who the fuck are they?*

'Ah, Carl, my boy. I was just about to show these three people the intricacies of our main server room, but just as we were going to open the door, the lights went out. Can you let me know what's happening?'

The three people, two men and a woman, all wearing the smart suits that executives liked to wear, were looking at him. He could see that none of them were interested in seeing the server room, but Gerard's face was gesturing as he kept nodding, indicating the door next to him.

Carl knew what he meant. He looked at the three people: a tall young man, a young athletic-looking woman, and a short, squat, muscular man. *How the fuck does he expect to get all three of them? Even if there are two of us, they look like they'd kick our arses.*

Carl shook his head as he walked down the corridor towards the gathering. 'No can do, Mr Medley; no one can go in there right now. There's been a power outage of some kind, we need to get in and fix it.'

'Well, can't my friends just take a peek inside while you do?'

Carl glared at the older man. 'No, Mr Medley. They can't.'

He could see that Gerard was taking offence at the way he was being spoken to, but Carl had to stand his ground.

He could also see that the three executives really didn't give two shits if they saw the server room, or not.

'Well then, the IT department has spoken.' Gerard smiled as he turned towards the group he was accompanying. 'Another day?' he asked, clapping his hands together.

Carl could see the relief on their faces. His face must have looked exactly the same.

As they walked away, Gerard shot a look back over his shoulder that said, *we'll talk later!*

'Yeah, we will,' Carl mumbled as he entered the numbers into the code pad, entering the server room of death. He heard the lock click but held on until the small group had turned the corner. When they were gone, he pushed the door open.

The stench that hit him was intense.

It wasn't the smell of the dead sea or the rotten fish, it was something else, something earthier.

Instantly, he knew what had caused the power outage.

He could have hit himself in the forehead with a facepalm. It was such a schoolboy error. He should have known hanging the dead bodies would cause the corpses' muscles to relax and whatever liquids or even semi-liquids they still contained would drain from them.

The stink of burning excrement and the thick, eye-stinging stench of dehydrated urine mixed with the fish-like reek of wet and burning electrical equipment was almost too much for him.

I suppose it's not as bad as the rotting fish stink when The Master calls, he thought as he closed the door behind him—locking it too, just in case.

He opened the door to the cabinet and shifted the hanging bodies over to the left. He took in a deep breath as he looked at the pile of excrement heaped underneath them. Instantly, he regretted that decision, as the smell, and the taste on the back of his throat was almost physical. He swallowed the saliva building in his mouth, grimacing as he did.

He put his hand over his face to stem the reek, but it wasn't enough. It was probably the worst smell Carl had ever had the misfortune to smell. It was sickly sweet, earthy, and somehow reminded him of the countryside. Despite the nostalgic reminiscent of his youth, driving through the fields with his mum, dad, and brothers, it was making him feel physically sick. He thought was ironic, given the heinous activities he'd recently performed, almost unflinching, to then get sick at a little bit of poop and pee.

Holding in the heaves that were calling from deep within his stomach, he pulled up the metal tile that was slick in human filth. His belly gurgled as he watched the sludge slide off, into the tangle of electrics underneath.

He saw the problem straight away.

There was a ten-socket extension board just below the metal floor tile. Blue smoke was coming from it as wet slime seeped through the narrow spaces between the tiles shlopping onto the board.

Shlopping? This thought sent goosebumps up and down Carl's arms.

The surge of electricity must have tripped the main fuse for the whole floor, maybe even the building.

He reached into the pit of dead human waste and removed the board. He unplugged the other cables before unplugging the main board. He held it by the short wire that led from the four-way to the board and threw it across the room.

There was a knock on the door.

'Carl, Jodi, are you two OK in there?'

It was Rod. He must have tried the lock and, not being able to open it, decided to knock.

'Yeah, we're good. I think I've found the cause of the problem. A power board has blown. It must have been enough to cause a surge.'

'I can't seem to get in; have you locked the door?'

Just fuck off, Rod, he thought. 'Yeah, I locked it just in case anyone tried to get in. I've … I mean we've got the floor up in here. It's a bit dangerous underfoot.'

'You need to open the door, Carl. I need to observe what you're doing. If the health and safety get a whiff of this, they'll hang us,' Rod insisted.

Jesus, good choice of words, Rod!

'OK, I'll open the door. Hang on a sec,' Carl shouted back.

He made his way over to the large cupboard in the corner of the room and pulled out a spare ten-socket plug extension. He held it in his hands, weighing it.

He then looked up towards the door. His shoulders sagged as he exhaled. With the lack of air-conditioning units running and the fans of the servers shut down to conserve the energy that the UPS was pumping, the whistle through his nostrils was the only sound he could hear.

His enjoyment of the small musical note was interrupted by more knocking on the door.

'Jodi? Are you in there? Can you open the door?' It was Rod again.

'Just one second, mate,' Carl replied.

There was a pause.

'Is Jodi OK?' he asked again.

'Hang on, man. I think you'll be OK to come in. I'm just opening the door now.' Carl reached up and clicked the lock.

The door opened with some urgency, and Carl reached out and grabbed Rod by the front of his shirt, surprising the smaller man, forcing him to lose his balance, and therefore dragging him into the server room easier.

Carl popped his head out the door, looking both ways, up and down the corridor, just to make sure no one had seen him drag his boss into the room.

Both ways were clear.

He slammed the door and looked at Rod, lying dazed and confused on the shit-covered metal floor.

Dazed and confused? he thought. *I could really go with listening to some classic rock right about now.*

'What the fuck, Carl?' Rod asked from the floor. 'And what is that smell?'

Carl looked at him, then looked for something to end Big Rod's life with before he found out what was causing the stink.

He saw the metal tile he'd displaced earlier and grimaced as he picked it up. Cold shit rolled over his fingers. Without any further thought or conversation, he bashed Big Rod's head in with the corner of it, silencing him and his fucking stupid, inane questions.

As he lifted the heavy tile, he closed his eyes. He didn't really want to see the damage it had caused to his friend's head, but Rod's curiosity must have been contagious. He opened one eye and peered underneath. The support beams that crisscrossed the tile were bent and buckled and blood was dripping from them.

Carl's heart sank.

He looked at Rod.

For all his faults, he *had* been a good friend.

But now, there was very little left of his face.

Rod had gotten him this job, all those years ago, when he had finished university as a mature student, and no one would take him on because the kids graduating all demanded lower wages.

The force of the attack had broken his nose.

Rod had invited him to his wedding.

The vigour of the hit had caused his eyes to pop from their broken sockets.

He and his wife had been at his and Amy's wedding.

His cheek was broken, and it looked like he had bitten off his own tongue.

Now he was dead, lying at his feet in a shitty-smelling server room.

Life was cruel.

'But not as cruel as I will be,' the voice came again.

Carl dropped the tile as the smell of faeces eroded only to be replaced by the stink of rotted fish. The chill was back in the air, but because there were no air-conditioning units working right then, he embraced the moist decay.

'You know what you need to do now, Carl. Plug him in. Wire him up. Bring The Master ever closer.'

A shrill beep permeated the otherwise silence of the room, and Carl turned to see what it was. It was the UPS screaming its alarm, informing him he only had two more minutes to turn the servers off, otherwise they would lose data.

'Believe me, Carl ...' The voice spoke again. He looked up at the server rack. The letters H and P were glowing in the gloom. 'You do not want to lose that connection to The Master.'

'I need to turn the servers off. I'll get the electricity back on, and The Master will be safe. I promise.' Carl was panicking. He tried to get himself up off the floor but slipped on the slick shit coating the tiles. His face hit the floor, and he felt the vile puddles splatter over his features.

He shook his head as he lay in the cold pool, thankful he'd kept his mouth shut.

He got up slowly and made his way to the console that was the main interface to the servers. He logged on, which was difficult for him to do because his shitty fingers kept slipping off the keys. He selected the main data server and shut it down, before moving on to the other servers and switches. As he reached the last of them, the UPS device that had kept them live during the power outage was screaming. He looked at the black command window that was still on the screen.

Download Interrupted ...
MASTER V2.1
PROGRESS 17% (halted) ....

The machine shut down correctly just as the UPS gave one final whistle before shutting itself off, its battery components drained.

Carl sat on a clean part of the floor and sighed. He had saved the data, and the relief of that was actually staggering. He hadn't realised it all meant so much to him. He looked at the grime over his hands, then the dirt over the floor. His eyes fell on the buckled floor tile before finally resting on the body of his friend and colleague, *Big* Rod Rhoads.

He wanted to rub his hands into his hair, to pull at it, to wake himself up from this horrendous nightmare, this cosmic horror of epic proportions that he'd managed to get himself entrapped in; but he couldn't. His hands were full of shit from the four dead people hanging in the cabinet. The people he'd put there on the say-so of some mystical origin.

Am I psychotic? Has my brain finally snapped?

Whenever he and his brothers were being naughty growing up, their mother had always threatened them with something much more effective than the slipper or the obligatory 'Wait till your father gets home.' She'd threatened them with her brain snapping. This didn't sound very threatening until she added that if her brain did actually snap, then she would run around the streets of their estate completely naked, shouting, ranting and raving.

This always had the desired effect, and got them behaving themselves, no matter what they were up to. The thought of their friends seeing their mum naked was enough to put the fear of God into them.

If my brain has snapped, then why didn't I just run around the streets naked? Why did I end up killing people and networking them.

'Because you're working for a higher good, Carl. Now, you need to clean up this mess, get the servers back on, connect this one to the network, and bring The Master home.'

The last few words of the voice in his head sounded more like a threat than advice.

He realized Jodi was wearing a jacket—as she would have known how cold it would be in the server room—and he struggled to take it off her, careful not to knock to Ethernet cables from her eyes, disrupting the precarious network he had created.

Once it was off, he began to mop up all the human waste that had dripped onto the electrics. When it was dry, he took the replacement extension board and plugged it in, then began to replace the removed plugs, making sure they were all dry.

He made his way to his phone and picked it up. He had three phone calls to make. Glad that the few analogue phones in the business hadn't been affected by the outage, he dialled the internal number for maintenance.

'Maintenance!' Chris almost shouted down the line.

'Chris, it's Carl.'

'We think Jane found the cause of the outage. It's in—'

'Server Room One! I know. I'm there right now. I've isolated the affected extension lead and replaced it. I think it's safe for the power to go back on now.'

'Excellent. What happened?'

'The dead people I have hanging in the server cabinets shit all over the electrics. It's a mess of fried poop and piss in here.'

'Seriously? The air-conditioning units leaked? Fuck, man. Do you need any help cleaning up in there?'

'No, man, I've got it covered. Just go and flick those switches.'

'I'm on it. Power will be back up in five minutes.'

Carl thanked him and hung up the phone. His next call was to the IT department.

'Dean, Rod's gone.'

'What do you mean he's gone?'

'He's gone home. He slipped on the water coming from the air con units and banged his head. He's signed the accident book, but he was a little bit dazed. I offered to take him, but he called his wife and she picked him up. The power will be back on in five minutes. Me and Jodi will bring all the servers in Room One back up. Can you and the guys go around and start to tell people what's happened? I'll join you as soon as we get this sorted in here.'

'No worries. Bad news about Rod, though. We could have done with him to appease the top brass. I can see Medley kicking up a fuss about this.'

'I'll deal with him; you just get everyone back up again.'

'We're on it.'

Finally, he rang Gerard's office—as the CEO, he would have an analogue phone too.

He had an idea this would ring out, as Leanne, Gerard's secretary and PA, was currently hanging in the server cabinet next to him. Her shit was currently all over his face, hands, and clothes.

He was surprised when the phone answered on the third ring. 'Gerard Medley.'

'Gerard, it's Carl. I'm in Server Room One. The power will be back up in five minutes. But we've got a problem. Actually, we've got two …'

'I'd say three problems, mister. The way you spoke to me before, outside the server room. I should fire you for that kind of insubordination.'

'Gerard, between us, we've killed a shed load people ... I don't think you're going to fire me any time soon, do you?'

The silence on the other end answered his question.

'I need you to get over here as soon as you can. I'm covered in shit. I need clothes and something to wash this off with. Oh, and I've killed Rod. So, I'm going to need your help to get him onto the rail.'

'You're covered in shit?' the older man asked; Carl thought there was a hint of excitement in his voice.

'Yeah, no time to explain. Can you also bring a bucket? The outage was caused by all this shit and piss getting into the electrics. We can't have that happening again.'

'It sounds like you're having a whale of a time. I'll be there in a moment.'

~~~~

Within the next fifteen minutes, the power had been restored. Carl had changed from his stinking clothes into a shirt and trousers that Gerard supplied and didn't quite fit him properly.

However, he'd successfully brought up all of the servers in the room. The readout on the command prompt still said they were at seventeen percent of The Master V2.1 download.

Carl was now working on the eye sockets of Rod and Robert, making them compatible to the network.

'I really want to have a go of that,' Gerard said as he watched Carl work from over his shoulder.

'Can you just back the fuck away from me? You're putting me off,' Carl snapped as Rod's eyeball popped. This time, he'd anticipated the juice to fly and caught the spatter in the clothing they had taken off the victims.

'Let's get him up on the rail, plug him in, and then I'm going to get washed. I fucking stink.'

'I quite like it,' Gerard said, sniffing him. 'It reminds me of Brenda, just after she ... expired.'

Carl pushed the older man away from him. 'You are nothing more than a fucking deviant,' he snapped.

Gerard laughed. 'Oh, that's rich coming from the man who has just pushed a network cable into the eye socket of one of his best friends.'

Carl looked at Rod, lying on the floor, one eye staring blindly up towards the ceiling, the other nothing more than a bloody, red-raw hole in his head. He rubbed his hands over his forehead.

He removed them when he was reminded about the stink.

'Come on. Let's get him up, then I'm going to get a shower downstairs.'

The two men heaved the small body of 'Big' Rod Roads up onto the server rack, where Carl attached the network cable from Robert into his head.

Almost immediately after feeling the satisfying click of the cable connecting, the server beeped.

Both men looked at the screen.

Download continued ...
MASTER V2.1
PROGRESS 22% ....

Carl looked at the man beside him. 'I'm going to get a shower! Can you make sure that doesn't get full?' he asked, pointing to the bucket Gerard had brought, that had been placed underneath the hanging bodies, over where the electrics were.

He was expecting some level of resistance from Gerard, but there was none. He actually looked excited by the prospect of being left in this server room on his own.

Carl shuddered as he left.

Reboot: A Cosmic Horror

23.

TASHA WAS WATCHING as Carl exited the sever room. Her brow creased and mouth skewed when she saw he was wearing different clothes to what he'd been wearing earlier.

He was sniffing his hands and grimacing as he walked off towards the reception. She waited until he'd turned the corner before following him. She wanted to tell him about the voices in her head and what they were telling her to do. She didn't know how she was going to go about that exactly, but they were becoming more and more intense and frequent, and she was worrying about their message.

As she walked down the corridor, there was an awful smell in Carl's wake. It wasn't like the smell of her dreams, to her relief, it smelt like the toilets had overflowed or something. She spared a glance at Server Room One as she walked past it. The smell seemed to intensify the closer she got to it, but then she remembered it was located next to the men's toilets, and she knew how mucky engineers could be.

A noise from inside the server room caught her attention. It was a muffled groan, like someone trying to lift something off a high shelf and having a difficult time doing it.

She was about to let herself in, to see who could be having difficulties inside, when she remembered Jodi was inside. She'd been helping Carl do the server upgrade. The grunt had sounded masculine to her ears, but then, when trying to lift heavy stuff, even the most girlie girl could sound mannish.

She decided against going inside—Jodi needed to start doing things for herself—and she followed Carl instead.

'Did Carl go this way?' she asked Margaret and Cheryl on reception.

'You mean stinky Carl?' Cheryl asked.

Tasha didn't get the reference.

'He went that way, hun. I think he was heading for the shower's downstairs. He was stinking quite a bit. What's he been doing?'

'Upgrading the servers in Room One,' Tasha replied.

'So, he was to blame for the 'lekky going off then?' Cheryl asked, laughing. 'Thank him from me, will you. We had a great twenty minutes or so then. No phones, no computers … just me, a chocolate bar, and my book.'

'Was he upgrading the toilets as well?' Margaret asked. 'He didn't half whiff,' she whispered.

Tasha just looked at her. *So, the stink* was *him and not the toilets. What could him and Jodi have been doing for him to stink like that?*

She thanked the receptionists and made her way down the stairs towards the shower rooms. As it was past dinnertime, she guessed they would have been pretty empty right about then. She put her ear against the door and listened.

One of the showers was on.

Someone was in there. She guessed it was Carl.

Looking both ways, she pushed the door open and slipped inside. There was something going on here, and she had a hunch Carl was right in the middle of it.

The room was deserted and steamy, but there were clothes hanging on one of the pegs, the same ones Carl had been wearing when she saw him leaving the server room.

She picked up the trousers off the peg and looked at them. In all the years she'd known Carl, he had never once worn a pair of trousers like this. The smell she'd encountered in the corridor was coming from this clothing. It was hideous, and she gagged, making a sickish noise. It was shit. She was certain about this. She had been in one of the cubicles in the women's toilets many a time after Annie from accounting had been in there.

She knew what that smell was like.

But why would it be on these clothes?

Right then, she feared for Jodi's life.

She remembered the noise in the server room, the grunt, *or was it a moan?*

The shower turned off, and she suddenly realised where she was. She put the trousers back on the peg and retreated out of the steamy room.

'What have you been doing in there?' a female voice asked from behind.

Tasha didn't even try to defend herself, just walked away from her accuser, hoping she hadn't seen her face.

She decided to investigate the server room. *The stink in there can't be any worse than I'm smelling in those horrible daydreams.*

She made her way back into the office.

'Did you find him, love?' Cheryl asked.

Tasha smiled. 'Yeah, I saw him as he slipped into the shower room. Whatever he was doing, you were right about the smell.'

'Stinky bastard,' Margaret laughed.

Tasha smiled and walked off towards Server Room One.

As she got there, Mr Medley was walking out, fixing his trousers as if his fly had been down.

Has he been in there with Jodi?

There was something wrong, and she needed to get to the bottom of it, even if it was just for her own state of mind. She reached Server Room One and punched in the code in the key-lock pad. She turned the knob and pushed the door.

It didn't move.

She pressed the buttons again, thinking she'd gotten them wrong. But the door still didn't budge.

She stepped back and looked at it. She cocked her head, and bit her lip. It was the right number; she was sure of this. She had been using it for the last five years at least.

She gave it one more go.

Nothing.

She knocked on the wood. 'Jodi? Jodi, are you in there?'

She was greeted with silence. Nothing more than the roar of the air conditioners and the hum of the servers still in their reboot cycle. The ugly stench was clearly coming from inside this room, and Tasha was fearing for Jodi, being stuck inside there with that stink. *Not to mention Gerard Medley walking out fixing his fly.*

When there was no answer from her next knock, and her call through the door, she turned on her heels and set off towards the IT department. 'Rod'll know the number,' she mumbled, ignoring all the calls for IT help while walking through the open-plan office.

There was no one in the department when she got back, and the phones were ringing on every desk. Ignoring them, she logged on to her PC and looked through her emails. There was nothing from anyone else.

What the fuck is going on here? she thought.

That was when the room began to spin.

She was glad she'd sat down, as the monitors on her desk tilted the same way the room was spinning. The floor shifted, and she felt the wheels on her chair begin to roll. Looking around at the other desks, she saw them all doing the same thing. She grabbed the desk and held on for dear life. It brought back bad memories of being a young girl at the funfair and the boys spinning the carriages on the waltzes. Faster and faster, they spun, even though, or maybe because, she and her best friends were screaming the loudest. Whether they thought they were having a good time or whether they were just being horrible Tasha would never know, but she had never, ever ventured on that ride again.

Until now.

The lights dimmed. It added to the claustrophobia she was feeling in the spinning room. It was difficult for her to catch her breath. She looked towards the windows and was not surprised to see the deep, dark water and underground wreckages, and the decaying bodies were back. They were all swaying the other way than the room was spinning.

She felt as if her brain was acting at least a couple of seconds behind the rest of her body. The dizziness was making her woozy, and she had time to wonder why that would mess with her stomach so much, making her feel sick. Her insides felt like a beach, with her vomit rising and falling with the rhythm of the tides.

She was on a ship. It was listing as it was caught in quite a storm. As she looked out the window at the sub-aqua scene, she knew the boat was sinking, or maybe it had already sunk.

'The Master is displeased with you,' the voice in her head spoke as the spin of the room picked up speed. 'He needs you to turn them off, then turn them on again!'

Tasha wanted to speak, but the bile rising from her stomach was stopping her.

'The Master is near, Tasha. He is not pleased with your lack of devotion.'

'You're not real,' she screamed, swallowing hard to repel the bile rising in her throat. 'This is the waltzes! I don't want to go faster. I just want to get off.'

Something thudded against the window as it spun past her. She caught a brief glimpse of it as it passed. It was the same long, slimy tentacle she'd seen before. It slammed against the window, this time cracking the glass. Water seeping into the room through the spiderweb fissures in the pane.

The stink of the dirty water reminded her of the smell of death. She had never smelt death herself but had been told what it smelt like entering a room with a month-old corpse in it by her uncle, who was a fireman.

That had been a nice conversation. Him drunk, sitting on his chair with a bottle of whisky next to him, her playing with her dolls, who all seemed to hate her.

She closed her eyes, hating her childhood.

The stink was sweet but in a heavy, cloying way. It assaulted her nostrils in a way the fish stink hadn't. It felt like a physical attack. Like a slimy monster was crawling up her nose and through her mouth. She could smell it, taste it, feel it. She felt like she could close her mouth and take a bite out of it if she so desired.

She didn't desire.

'Turn them off, Tasha, then turn them on again. The Master will only wait so long.'

She put her hands over her face and screamed.

The room stopped its spin, and the stink abated.

It was moment or two before she realised she was still screaming.

She opened her eyes, expecting the room to be back to normal, like everything she had just witnessed was nothing more than a bad dream.

She wasn't disappointed.

The room was exactly how it was before the smell, before the spinning, before the …

She looked at the window.

There was a crack right across it, she knew it hadn't been there before.

A flash of the thick, ugly tentacle pierced her mind like a lightning bolt, causing pain akin to an ice-cream induced severe brain-freeze.

'What's happening? Are you OK?' One of the engineers from the open-plan office ran into the department. He must have heard her screaming and had come to investigate.

Tasha was sat at her desk, her head in her hands.

'Are you OK?' he reiterated as she didn't answer. He moved in and put his hand on her shoulder.

She jerked at his touch, surprising him enough to make him step backwards, away from her.

She lifted her head and looked at him. Her eyes roamed around the room. Every screen was displaying the same message:

KILL HIM
KILL HIM
KILL HIM

She blinked, and the message changed.

TURN HIM OFF AND TURN HIM ON AGAIN …
TURN HIM OFF AND TURN HIM ON AGAIN …
TURN HIM OFF AND TURN HIM ON AGAIN …

The man—Tasha couldn't remember his name, if she even knew it in the first place—stepped further away from her. The abject horror etched into his features, blossomed. The comedy of his look almost made her laugh.

She watched as he fell to his knees. She opened her mouth as the spray of blood from the deep gash in his neck gushed over her. The warmth of it was strangely comforting as it covered her face. She licked her lips, savouring the salty, coppery, warmth.

His wild eyes looked at her as the arterial spray slowed yet continued to flow from his injury. His hands were at his neck. Bizarrely, they looked like they were attempting to stem the torrent of his life slipping away from him, by fixing the edges of the hole back together.

The screens, now with a pink tinge to them, as their illumination eased through the coating of blood, read another message.

NOW TURN HIM ON AGAIN …
NOW TURN HIM ON AGAIN …
NOW TURN HIM ON AGAIN …

She blinked.

The man was back standing before her, staring at her with eyes that might be beholding a hungry, crouching tiger. 'You... you don't look good,' he mumbled. 'Do you want me to call first aid?'

'Can you see a crack in that window?' she croaked.

The man looked to where she was pointing. His eyes creased a little. 'Yeah. What happened? Did you fall into it or something?' he asked.

Tasha stood and pushed him away from her and stormed from the office.

'All right then,' he called after her. 'Maybe not first aid ... Maybe a fucking psycho hospital instead.'

Tasha heard these final comment as she rushed out of the office but thought nothing of them. She felt they were rather inconsequential with what was happening in her head.

She burst into the bathroom. There were two other women in there who stopped what they were doing as the madwoman careened in.

Tasha saw them. They both looked already dead. Their pale skin, dark eyes, and rotting flesh around their mouths were stark against the makeup they had been touching up. There were holes gouged into both of their heads where their eyes should have been.

A green cable trailed between them, connected by the eye sockets.

'Turn us on again,' one of them demanded.

'Do it NOW, Tasha. You've turned us off, now turn us on again.'

'Add us to the network, Tasha,' the first one demanded again.

'Bring The Master home. Bring HIM home, Tasha.'

She didn't like any of this, so she turned, opened the door, and fell out of the bathroom, into the main office. A number of engineers and staff stood from their desks at the clatter, hoping to see what was occurring on this strange day. A man and a woman ran towards her, offering help.

Tasha could see both of them.

She could see everyone in the room—there must have been fifty or so people—and every one of them were looking at her.

All of them looked dead.

Every screen on every desk was displaying the same message.

KILL THEM ALL ...
KILL THEM ALL ...
KILL THEM ALL ...

She looked at the two closest, who were now kneeling beside her. They weren't helping her; they were praying. Blood was pouring from their faces, from holes where their eyes should have been. They looked to her like bloody network ports. 'You need to plug us in,' the woman whispered, her joined hands raised in praise to someone, or something Tasha couldn't see.

'Do us before the others,' the man whispered. 'Take us to Server Room One,' he demanded. He offered her a salacious wink, causing the hole, that used to be his eye, to leak filthy, bloody seawater.

There was something inside the hole. Something wriggling and jiggling inside. It was something that shouldn't have been there, it had no business being in there. It was thin and green, and it was slimy.

'What?' Tasha asked, shuffling on her backside away from him.

'Take us to Server Room One and plug us in. We want to help The Master return. You need to do it, Tasha; turn us on again.'

'Please,' the man moaned.

Tasha closed her eyes.

When she opened them, everyone was still looking at her, but they were all alive and well. There were no holes in their faces, and there were no tentacles sprouting from their eyes.

What the fuck is happening to me?

She looked at the screens. They were *still* displayed the same message.

She stood, pushing the helpers away from her. They retreated as if she might just bite them at any moment.

'I need to find Carl,' she spat.

The helpers looked at each other. She watched the questions form in their eyes as they backed away. She didn't care.

The women exited the toilets. Neither of them dead, but very much alive and healthy. They looked down their noses as they passed her. Tasha could deal with that. She didn't care about anyone else; she needed to find Carl and find out what was happening in Server Room One.

24.

THERE WAS SOMEONE in the shower room with him. He heard the door open and close. He removed his head from the gush of the hot water that was cleansing him—his body at least, if not his soul.

He listened. Whoever it was, they were sneaking around in the changing area. *I don't have any valuables in Gerard's clothes*, he thought.

Then a horrible thought occurred to him.

What if it *was* Gerard. The old man could be creeping up on him, trying to catch a glimpse of him in the shower? *It wouldn't surprise me, the dirty old bastard.*

Then another, worse thought occurred to him.

Is he trying to add me to the network?

Carl stepped out from under the hot flow and looked back into the changing room. All he saw was the door closing behind whoever it had been. He grabbed a towel, stepped out of the cubicle, and checked that his clothes were still there. Whoever it had been hadn't been there to rob him, that much was certain.

He dried himself off and began to dress when the world flipped.

The room tilted, and he found himself at the precipice of a steep hill of wet tiles. He began to slide, slowly at first, then as the darkness and the stench of death and decay made a reappearance, it got faster.

He fell onto his back and scrabbled at the tiles as the camber steepened, and he slipped faster. He was heading for a dark vortex that had appeared at the bottom of the hill he was stumbling down. It was blacker than black, it was the darkness that plagued every single child's dreams, or nightmares. He was sliding into...

...nothing!

As he continued towards the obscurity before him, and even before the scream that was welling within him could make itself bloom, the obsidian inside the abyss began to clear.

To his relief, yet still to his fear, he could see something, or more precisely, somewhere open up before him.

He was heading for Server Room One.

There was no way he could stop himself, there was no grip on the wet tiles he was sliding on, and all he could do was surrender to whatever fate this tear in the space/time fabric had planned for him.

He fell through the hole.

He landed on the shit puddled metal tiles that he'd hoped Gerard might have cleaned, with a thump and a splat. Through dazed, unfocused eyes he could just about make out the large cabinet with the dead bodies hanging within it. *Is this just another episode?* he asked himself. *Another dream?*.

But his reason brought him back with a stinky gargle, as the taste of metallic shit entered his mouth. *If I'm dreaming, then why can I taste this shit and blood?*

He closed his eyes and counted to ten, hoping the bang on his head might knock some sense into him, and he would wake up back at home, with Amy, who was his loyal wife, with no thoughts of sleeping around with Malcolm, or whatever his name had been.

When he opened them again, he was still on the floor in Server Room One. He was still wearing Gerard's clothes; the room still stank of human waste.

The dead bodies were still hanging in the cabinets; all of them except one. Rod's body was on the floor. The eye that Carl had gouged and connected to the network was now empty, and the other eye was nothing more than a raw, empty hole. There was a pearlescent residue over his recently deceased friend's face.

It was a residue he recognised straight away.

He'd been overly familiar with the off-white substance ever since he was about twelve, or maybe thirteen, and had found out about the late-night films on TV.

'Holy fuck, Gerard,' he cursed. 'How the hell did I end up getting involved with a twat like you?'

He was seething.

Without giving even a moment's thought to how he'd gotten into this room from the shower room, he bent down to pick up his friend. He needed him attached to the network if they were ever going to be able to download The Master's software.

As he picked him up, Rod's head lolled forward, headbutting him. He stepped back, still holding the body in an upright, ugly parody of a dance.

Something cold dripped from Rod's face onto his face.

He was too busy stopping Rod from falling to be able to stop whatever it was dribbling slowly into his open mouth.

He knew exactly what it was; he could tell by the smell. He used to joke that it smelt like the public swimming baths, but as it slowly trickled into his mouth, he realised it tasted nothing like water that had too much pee, and too much chlorine in it.

It was salty, and it was grim!

Gerard must never have heard about the pineapple trick, he thought, retching at what was on his tongue.

Trying to stop himself baulking about what he was currently swallowing, and how many sexually related infections he had just consumed, he heaved Rod up onto the rails and attached the network cable.

The server beeped once, and the fans kicked in, overpowering the roar of the air-con units.

He looked at the screen, and the command prompt box informed him the download was continuing. It was now up to twenty-six percent.

They needed more power.

He thought about going home and bringing in the bodies of Amy and whatever her friend's name had been. Then he thought against it; that would be a bigger risk than just getting what he needed from the pool of power he was currently surrounded by. *Anyway,* he thought, w*asn't it those two who got me to two percent in the first place?*

He picked up the phone and called Gerard.

The old man answered on the third ring.

'Carl? What can I do for you, my boy?'

Carl shook his head. After everything they had been through today, he would have thought Gerard would know what he was ringing for.

'What the fuck did you do to Rod?' was the first question to come out of his mouth. *Or should that be come into my mouth?* he thought with revulsion, and another gag.

'Nothing he didn't mind me doing. The man's dead; he wasn't going to complain about a little skull fuckery going on.'

Carl made his hand into a fist, his knuckles turning pure white, before he put it to his mouth. He wanted to bite down into his flesh, to wake himself up from this excruciating nightmare where he'd killed his wife, his friends, where he'd teleported from one room into another, and swallowed his boss's cum.

It all sounded like a bad horror novel, written by a hack with no grasp on reality, physics, or even morals.

'We need more power. We're on twenty-six percent. The Master is not going to be happy with this. You need to get your arse over here and help me out.'

He slammed the phone down, almost knocking it off the desk. He rubbed his eyes and sighed before looking at his watch. It was just after three-thirty. People would be thinking about leaving for the day.

That's not a bad thing. Maybe we can snatch a few stragglers.

His thoughts were disrupted as a sound like someone snapping their fingers next his ear caused him to spin. He was just in time to see Gerard appear out of nowhere, in front of the cabinet. The old man had a huge grin on his face. 'What in damnation?' he asked as his grin levelled on Carl. 'Did you see that? I think The Master is getting stronger.'

Carl's eyes were still trying to convey to his brain what he'd just seen. He tried to swallow, but it was difficult with his dry throat and the taste of Gerard's love still on the back of his tongue.

'I see you put Rod up, then. Good lad. Didn't want the old Master to get his knickers in a twist just because I forgot to clean up after myself, eh?' The old man laughed as he made sure his zip was in place. 'Anyway, I saved you some time. I already did the eye for you.' He winked at Carl as he leaned in. 'Although, I didn't use the screwdriver, if you know what I mean.'

Carl licked his teeth as the corners of his mouth registered his disgust. 'I think I do know what you mean,' he replied. 'We need to get more power to this thing. We need more bodies. I can't actually believe I'm saying this, but we do.'

'Can we do that *Star Trek* thing all the time? If we can, then it really would help with getting bodies in here without having to drag them through the office. It would stop with the awkward questions, wouldn't it?'

'Do we have any way of contacting HP?' Carl asked.

Gerard pointed towards the server screen with the command prompt on it. 'Can't we use that to message him?'

Carl's eyes followed to where the old man was indicating, then back to the bodies in the cabinet. It was a good idea, but he didn't want to give this old pervert the satisfaction of knowing he could be right.

'Yeah, of course,' he said as he clicked on the desktop.

There was a new icon, one he was sure he had never seen before, ever. It looked like a bloody handprint with blood dripping from it. The word MESSAGES was written underneath it in bold white letters.

'Have you ever seen that icon before?' he asked the old man.

Gerard looked at it and shrugged. 'It says messages on it. So, I suppose you must just click on it. What's the worst that can happen now?'

Carl did just that.

A familiar screen opened before him. It was a generic messaging screen, split in FROM and TO sections.

There was only one person on his list of contacts.

HP is ONLINE!

'There you go!' Gerard said, pointing at the screen. 'Message him.'

Carl's hands were shaking. Up till now, HP had been doing all the talking. They'd had to wait for him to contact them, either by the messages on the machines or by the strange dream-like nightmares he'd been experiencing. He clicked on the MESSAGE NOW button, and a box appeared for him to write in. He didn't have a clue what to say.

'Hey HP, how's things?' he typed, then clicked SEND.

'How's things?' Gerard asked. 'What kind of question is that for a prophet of an old God?'

'Well, what the fuck would you have written?' Carl spat.

'Move over,' he ordered, barging Carl away from the screen.

Hello HP, this is Gerard. We met online a few nights back. Things are developing at pace down here, but we have hit a bit of a lull. We noticed that you, or The Master, were able to teleport us from one room to the next a few moments ago. Is this something that we can use to obtain more bodies?

'There you go. What's wrong with that?' Gerard asked, smiling at the screen with his arms crossed.

'Look … he's replying,' Carl shouted, pointing at the graphic of the circle spinning.

'Fuck!' Gerard said, staring at the screen, his eyes as wide as they could go.

> The Master is not happy with your progress. We need more power. Turn them off and then turn them on again. Do it before The Master loses his patience. You will have limited use of teleportation …
> Kill them all …

Carl just looked at the screen. 'The Master is not happy?' he read. He turned to Gerard, whose face was akin to a child who had been told he can have anything he wants in the toy shop.

'Limited use of teleportation?' Gerard read. 'How do we use it?'

'Ask,' Carl replied.

> Thanks HP. We understand the message about The Master. How do we use the teleportation?

Gerard looked at Carl as if for approval before clicking SEND. A short while later, another reply came through.

> Cut your wrist and drip your blood onto the network connection. This will give you a link back to the main server. The more you use it, the more blood it will require. Use it sparingly. The Master will NOT be let down!

'I think we had better up our game. It's nearly four o'clock. People will be going home. Do you think we can knab the late stayers?' Gerard asked, looking at his expensive watch.

'Maybe you can. But I'm stuck in here until everyone's gone. Have you seen these clothes?' He raised up his knee so the older man could see the ridiculous trousers he was wearing.

'Don't be stupid, boy. They are my best golfing strides. Be careful with them; they cost over a month of your wages.'

'A month? I bet you paid for them on the company credit card, though, didn't you?'

Ignoring the question, Gerard made his way to the server. 'Pass me that screwdriver, will you? I'm going to bleed on the server.'

Carl picked up the gore-covered tool and tossed it across the room.

Gerard wasted no time slashing his wrist with it and allowing his blood to drip onto the server. 'There you go. I'm now connected. That sounds like one of your young hip-hop songs, doesn't it?' the old man said, grinning as he flexed his fingers, allowing the drips of crimson to fall.

'Not really,' Carl answered, deadpan. 'Can you go and get us some fresh power for this, please. I do want to go home at some point tonight.'

Gerard just looked at him. His head was ever so slightly cocked. 'Why? What do you have to go home to?' he asked as he opened the server room door and walked out.

As Carl turned back to face the screen, he sighed.

~~~~

As Gerard walked along the corridor towards his office, he noticed the delightful young brunette who worked in one of the departments, he had no idea what she did, other than give him a twinge each time she strolled past, walking towards him. She had her jacket on, and a bag slung over her shoulder. He didn't know her name, but he recognised her face from emails sent to the company, *not to mention the swagger of that delectable ass.*

If he remembered rightly, and he knew he did, the emails she sent were all regarding first aid. *A stroke of luck,* he thought with an internal smile.

'Ow! Ow ... bloody hell!' he shouted along the corridor.

The first aider in the girl kicked in, and she sprang to action. 'Mr Medley, what have you done?'

If only you knew, young lady, if only you knew.

'I caught my hand on the back of the printer while retrieving my print. Normally, Leanne would get them for me, but she went home early, sick.'

The girl sucked in a breath through her teeth as she looked at his hand. 'That looks nasty, Mr Medley. Maybe you should sit down somewhere, and I'll go and get my first-aid kit.'

'I have one in my office. It's just there. I think it just needs a plaster or something,' he said, looking at the blood dripping onto the carpet.

'Right, well, let's get you in and see how deep this cut is. It's going to need to cleaned, you may even need stitches.'

As they walked into the office, Gerard pointed to Leanne's desk. 'It's in one of her drawers,' he said.

The instant she turned her back on him, he grabbed her, putting his bloody hand over her mouth, stifling her scream. Not knowing how this was meant to work, he thought about the blood on the server, and as if by magic—well, not as if by magic, but with actual, real life magic; dark, mystical, dangerous magic—a portal to Server Room One appeared. He dragged the struggling girl backwards and into the hole in time and space.

~~~~

Gerard and the girl fell backwards onto the metal floor of the server room.

All three people present were shocked at what had just occurred.

'What the fuck?' Carl spat as he saw Gillian rolling on her side, now covered in shit, and confused as to where she was.

'Hit her,' Gerard shouted.

'With what?' Carl shouted back.

Gerard looked around the room and saw the fire extinguisher. 'This,' he shouted, passing it to the younger man.'

Carl caught the heavy red tube and swung it around to contact with the skull of the confused woman, who was still lying on the floor.

There were two thuds—one from the connection of the metal to her head and the other from her face hitting the metal tiles of the floor.

'Hit her again,' Gerard goaded. 'Go on, twat the little bitch right in the back of her fucking head.'

Carl turned, he couldn't stifle his laugh when he saw the old man jumping up and down, grabbing his crotch, holding on to his obviously excited member. He looked like a monkey in a zoo, a very horny monkey. 'Hit her again; look, she's still moving. Fucking hit her.'

'Turn her off, Carl,' the voice in his head spoke.

Gerard turned his head to listen to it.

So, I'm not the only one who can hear it, Carl thought. This cheered him up a little. Maybe he wasn't going mad.

Reboot: A Cosmic Horror

What? You're in a server room with a perverted psychopath, surrounded by dead people hooked up to a network, with a half-conscious first aider laying on the floor beneath you, her brain bashed in by the fire extinguisher you're holding, while being talked to by someone called The Master, via computer screens, while your wife and her lover are lying dead in your living room... and you think that you're not mad!

It was a depressing thought, yet it did make him laugh.

With a chuckle, he brought the extinguisher down again onto Gillian's head. Her body flopped on the tiles … and other than a few twitches, she stopped moving.

'One more time! One more time!' Gerard shouted, looking like an avid football supporter after his team had just scored.

Carl obliged.

He had to admit that he was getting pretty good at this.

'Great, now hook her up. I'll get us another one. This is the most fun I've had in years.'

The two men lifted the dead girl up onto the rail.

'I think we're going to need another bucket,' Carl said.

'Not to worry. I'll get one on my next jaunt,' Gerard replied, obviously pleased with his new ability.

As Carl began to work on the new girl's eye, Gerard left the room.

Just as he had fitted the ethernet cable into Gillian and scraped out the scum that Gerard had left in Rod's other socket, the old man returned with another shocked addition to what Carl had come to think of as the team.

This time, it was the football bore. This man was tall and skinny, with a long, crooked nose. 'Wha …' he began but stopped as Carl jabbed the screwdriver he was holding into his eye.

Gerard grabbed the man from behind, stifling his burgeoning scream. As he fell backwards, he knocked Gerard over, banging his head against the wall.

'Oh, for fuck's sake,' Gerard swore.

Carl laughed. He liked the way posh people swore; there was something deliciously decadent about it.

The football bore was still struggling, so Gerard pulled the screwdriver from his eye and plunged it into his other eye.

He didn't struggle for long after that.

Carl, aided by Gerard pulled him to an upright position and hung him on the rail. Carl has pleasantly surprised that he didn't have to do much work on this one, his eyes were almost gone already.

'Why don't you go and hunt? I'll take care of this,' Gerard said, gripping the screwdriver that was still sticking out of the football bore's eye. He gave it a wiggle, and Carl was not surprised to hear the CEO giggle like a child.

'I hope I get you in the Secret Santa this year,' Carl laughed. 'Please refrain from fucking this one's head while I'm gone.'

Gerard shot him a sullen look.

Carl took another screwdriver; he didn't want to infect himself with whatever Gerard might be riddled with and cut his hand. He allowed it to drip onto the server.

He then walked out of the room, bumping straight into Tasha.

~~~~

'Tasha, what are you still doing in work?' he asked, trying his best to look and sound as if he were still completely sane and not at all out stalking for victims to teleport back into the server room to kill, and hook up to the network.

Tasha's wild eyes regarded him as if he were something she should be afraid of. 'I could ask you the same thing,' she replied.

'I was, erm … just going back to my desk to get my, erm, I mean Mr Medley's laptop.'

'Well, you needn't worry. I've wiped it. The hard drive has been rebuilt. It's a brand-new machine right now.'

'Oh, right,' he replied as if that didn't mean a thing to him. 'Well, that's OK. Did you … erm, log on to it at all? Before you wiped it, I mean.'

He could hear himself stuttering, and he cursed each time he did. He hoped she hadn't logged on and seen the files on there. He hoped she was as innocent in this shitstorm as he had been prior to getting involved with The Master and Gerard *fucking* Medley.

Her eyes went wide, and her eyebrows knitted together in the centre of her forehead. 'No.'

He knew she was lying.

Inside, he died a little more than he already was. *She knows,* he told himself. *She knows about The Master. She knows about The Master and what's happening in Server Room One. Fuck! I'm going to have to kill her now. Aw Jesus, Tasha, why did you have to log on to the machine?*

'What's going on in Server Room One?' she asked as if it was a general question, and she wasn't really interested.

Carl shook his head, turning the corners of his mouth down in a non-committal grimace. 'Nothing, just a server upgrade, you know that.'

'And is Jodi still in there with you?'

Carl shook his head. 'No. She went home about half an hour ago. She'd been in on the early shift, so I let her go. She was next to useless anyway, just hanging around and getting on my tits.'

Tasha nodded taking out her mobile phone. 'I need to ring her and ask her a quick question. What have you done to your hand?' she asked as she held her phone to her ear.

Carl looked at the deep gash in his palm. He shook his head, not even bothering with an explanation. He was licking his lips as she dialled the number. He stopped as the call rang out.

'She's not answering.'

There sounded like accusation in Tasha's voice, and Carl marvelled at it. *Of all the time in the world to start standing up for yourself, it* had *to be now, didn't it?* He shrugged. 'Maybe she's on the bus,' he offered.

'Are you sure there's nothing happening in Server Room One?'

Carl smiled and laughed; it was a humourless laugh. 'There's nothing going on in Server Room One, I promise you. You can come and have a look for yourself if you want.' He hoped she didn't want to.

Her phone buzzed, and she looked at the screen. Her eyebrows knitted together again, briefly this time, and she looked up at him. 'I can't. I'll have to answer this message. Listen, Carl, we need to talk. Tomorrow, OK?' She was already walking away as she asked the question.

'Yeah, no worries. Listen, have a good evening,' he shouted as she walked off. 'Enjoy it,' he continued, lowering his voice so only he could hear it. 'It's quite possibly going to be your last!'

He watched her go as two engineers, young apprentices, walked into the toilets together. His eyes shifted as he watched them. *Could we take out two of them?* he asked himself.

He followed them into the toilets to find out.

~~~~~

KILL THEM ALL, TASHA …

That was the message on her mobile phone as she spoke to Carl. As she hurried away from him, she pondered what it meant. *Who the hell wants me to kill people?* she thought, then she remembered the cracked window in the IT department, it gave her a shiver.

Is Carl getting these messages too? If he is … Oh SHIT!

The realisation of what might be going on in Server Room One dawned on her. 'Carl is killing them all,' she whispered.

She passed the deserted IT department and couldn't help a quick peep inside. The crack in the window was still there. She felt it was an accusation of something she hadn't done. *Not yet anyway.*

She wondered when she would succumb to the messages that were plaguing her at every given opportunity. She honestly didn't think she had that much resolve within her. With that horrible thought lingering in her head, and with a shaking hand, she put her phone back into her pocket and left the building, heading home.

Her bus stop was only a few yards from the office, and the buses were usually frequent. Sometimes she liked to walk the mile or so home, letting the worries and frustrations of the day wash away from her, but today had been too strange. She felt like she didn't have the energy to pound the pavement all that way.

She paid the driver and got on.

The bus was filled with familiar faces; the same faces she would see almost every day. They were either reading, chatting, listening to music, or staring vacantly about them. There were a few nods her way but nothing she would call comradery.

As she sat down, she felt her phone buzzing in her handbag.

She hoped it was Jodi calling her back, asking her what she had wanted, seeing if she fancied going out for a drink, maybe even something to eat … *then back to my place for a nightcap and a chat, and … who knows where it could lead?*

As the small fantasy played out in her head, her phone buzzed again, reminding her to read the text she had been sent.

She took the phone out of her bag and clicked it.

The screen read HP!

She knew for a fact she didn't have any contacts on her phone called HP. They had a lot of dealing with the computer company with the same name, but they wouldn't be sending her messages, not at—she looked at the time it was sent—five forty-seven.

Against her better judgement, she opened the message.

LOOK AROUND YOU, TASHA. THEY ALL NEED TO BE TURNED OFF AND TURNED ON AGAIN. BRING THE MASTER HOME. COMPLETE WHAT YOU HAVE STARTED. THE MASTER DOES NOT FORGET. REBOOT REBOOT REBOOT!

She closed her eyes as the stink she'd first encountered in the office seeped back into her nose. The already rank air on the bus began to thicken. She could smell the sweat and grease coming from the other passengers.

She could smell their deaths.

Outside the comfort of her closed eyes, she could feel the bus, and the daylight outside had darkened. She knew she would be surrounded by dirty water, water filled with the decaying bodies of people—women and children—being torn apart by the ebb and flow of the stinking filth around them. They would be being eaten by the disgusting, and deformed wildlife that lurked around them.

She didn't want to open her eyes but knew she had to.

When she did, she regretted it.

Outside was indeed the underwater graveyard she'd been expecting. It was a watery Hell. Hundreds, if not thousands of corpses, all of them screaming silently at her as ravenous deformed oddities devoured their flesh. Chunks of decaying meat floated off in the current as the demons with their dangerous, fishy mouths feasted on them.

Panicking, she turned her attention to the others on the bus.

Everyone was dead.

Each person she had passed on her way to her seat was now a rotting corpse. Some were sitting in their seats, heads back, mouths wide open in silent death screams; others were still animated, twitching, gagging, trying to speak, to accuse, to screech.

She looked at her arm, half expecting to see green, flaking, oozing flesh; but it was normal.

'Turn us on again …' came the whisper from behind her.

She turned to see an overweight woman, half naked, her clammy skin was dripping from her body. The wounds in her sliding flesh were infested and stinking, as smaller versions of the ugly fish outside feasted on her decay.

As Tasha looked closer, she saw they were eating her from the inside out. 'Turn us on again ...' the large woman whispered; pink froth, tinged green with algae, bubbled from her mouth as she hissed. 'Bring The Master home. Bring Him back to where He belongs ...'

There was thud, and the bus shuddered.

Something had wrapped itself around the windows on the opposite side of her. It was huge. It was a sickly pink, with purple veins running through it. There were suckers running the length of it, making it look like a gigantic octopus tentacle.

It gripped the bus windows. Tasha could see the stress it was causing on the glass. She knew at any moment, the glass would crack and shatter, then the filthy, stagnant, and corrupt waters would cascade through the bus, drowning her in the grime.

'Turn us on again ...'

The whisper was coming from everywhere now. Frantically, she looked around to see all the other passengers had become reanimated. They were all leaning forwards, reaching for her, accusing her, goading her. Blood mixed with filthy water gushed from their wounds, from their mouths, from the empty holes where their eyes should have been.

'Turn us on again,' a rotting old man hissed.

'You know what to do ...' a young boy said, his dead hand reaching towards her. His fingernails long and black.

'Turn us on again. Bring The Master home.'

She stood up, her eyes were wild, and her heart was racing. Her head whipped around, backwards and forwards. She couldn't fathom the depravity she was witnessing. She'd had the daydreams—waking nightmares—before, many times, but they had never been this intense.

As she staggered along the bus towards the front doors, dead and dying corpses reached their claws out to scratch at her, to prevent her from leaving them.

She brushed them away as she ran to the front.

'Where do you think you're going, love?' the driver asked.

She looked at him. He was dead too, his face a rictus of a smile, a rotten, too-real Halloween mask. He leaned out and grabbed her arm.

The thing outside flexed, and the windows cracked. Water began to seep in; the stink worsened.

'The Master needs you,' the driver hissed as his slimy grip tightened and the water began to slosh around her feet. 'He needs you. He is counting on you to bring Him back. You need to turn us off, then turn us on again. Do it, you fucking bitch, DO IT!'

As the driver shouted, reality sprung back and hit her full in the face. She found herself at the front of the bus. The driver was holding her arm, and all the passengers were glaring at her.

Only this time, none of them were dead. None of them were reanimated zombies, calling to her, hissing at her. They were all just regular human beings, and they were looking at her as if she had two heads.

'This isn't a designated stop, missy. You can't get off here,' the driver scolded. 'The next stop is about five hundred yards further up. I could lose my licence for letting you off here.'

She looked at the man. Her head was shaking, and her skin was clammy and far too hot.

'Are you all right?' he asked.

'No ... I'm not,' she said, shaking off the driver's grip and pulling at the doors.

She got them open and jumped off the slow moving vehicle.

She landed in a run, with the cool of the evening air relieving her skin.

She looked back at the bus and saw the passengers staring out the windows at her. For a brief moment, they all changed into zombies ... all of them clawing at the glass, trying to get at her.

But it was only for a moment.

25.

WITH BLOOD STILL dripping from his hand, Carl entered the toilets after the two apprentices.

The pair were standing at the urinals.

There were three units; one was standing at one end, and the other was at the other end. The only one left for Carl to use was the one in the middle. It served his purposes rather well.

He walked in between them as if he was going to relieve himself. 'Jesus, have you seen my hand?' he said, holding his bleeding hand up for them to see. Both boys looked at it, both uncomfortable at the conversation from the older man at the urinal. 'I cut it on that knife in the kitchen, you know the one people use to cut the bread. Just sliced right through it.'

Both boys finished what they were doing and zipped up their trousers in unison, then stepped away from him.

Carl zipped up his trousers too and turned towards the sinks.

He closed his eyes and thought about Server Room One. When he opened them, the portal was there, hanging in the air.

'So, what do you say, boys?' he said, breaking the uncomfortable silence.

'About what?' one of them asked as they turned to face him.

'About this,' he shouted and ran at them.

They didn't know what hit them as the IT engineer careened into them, pushing them both backwards. They would have assumed the mad man would be pushing them into the mirrors, but that wasn't the case.

As he rushed them, they fell backwards … and kept on falling.

As their heads bashed onto the metal plates of the server room, Gerard was ready.

He grabbed the t-shirt Carl had taken off because of the excrement that was all over it and wrapped it around the first boy's head. As the lad struggled, he climbed on top of him. Using this element of surprise, he easily controlled the boy's undulations, and before long, his struggles began to wane.

Carl wasn't so quick off the mark with his victim.

The lad was up and on his feet in no time and backed up against the wall. His eyes were drinking in everything, all the horrors that the server room had to offer.

Dead people were hanging in the cabinet, there was blood and shit on the floor tiles, one of the tiles was buckled and covered in blood, there was a bucket that was filling up with human excrement, and his friend was lying on the floor, being smothered by someone who looked suspiciously like the managing director.

'What the fuck?' he asked. His voice came out at least three octaves higher than it should have.

The poor kid is petrified, Carl thought as he looked at him. 'Look. This isn't at all what it seems. This is all a dream. You've blacked out and are currently lying on the toilet floor. Can you smell that stink?'

The boy took a moment to sniff the air before nodding.

'That's because you've slipped on a leak and you're now lying in a pool of shit.'

The boy's eyes kept flicking between Carl and Gerard. 'I am?' he asked. His eyes lit up with the realisation. 'Is that how I got here?'

'Yeah, it is. You'll wake up in a moment and laugh to your mate about what you saw.'

'Will I?'

Carl didn't like the pleading in his voice. He sounded like his son, Tommy. Young, scared, naïve. He felt sorry for him. This fella had his whole life ahead of him. *Shit, his mum probably made him a packed lunch before he came to work this morning.*

'Can I go now, then?' he asked, or, more precisely, pleaded.

Carl nodded. 'Yeah, mate. You just need to do this one thing first.'

'What?'

Carl reached behind him, wrapped his hands around a keyboard on the small desk, and brought it around in a violent swing. 'I just need you to die,' he shouted, bringing the makeshift weapon around and crashing it with an explosion of letters into the boy's face.

D E McCluskey

The lad fell, holding his wounded head. 'What the fuck?' he muttered.

For some reason, Carl's mind asked him a question. Was the boy's utterance of *what the fuck* a question or an exclamation? He didn't have time to answer, as the boy was back on his feet. His face was cut to ribbons. Carl was bemused to see a letter H and a letter P stuck to his bleeding cheek. But most of all he could see the boy wasn't seriously hurt.

'I'm not fucking dreaming, am I?' he growled.

I'm in trouble here, Carl thought as the boy stood to his full height, looking ready to attack his attacker.

That was when Gerard appeared behind him, wrapping a power cable around the boy's neck and pulling him down.

'No, you're not,' Gerard whispered as he pulled the cable tighter,, knocking the letters from the boy's face.

Carl watched as Gerard's face grew purple with the effort he was exerting killing the boy. He was worried he might not survive the murder himself.

The boy's eyes were almost popping out of his head as he slid down onto the metal tiles of the room. His face was purple, and a thick, bloated tongue lolled out of his mouth.

Gerard looked almost exactly the same.

Carl wanted to help. He moved to give the older man a hand, then a thought occurred to him. *He's an old man anyway. He won't last long in the new reign of The Master. What if I let him die here and hook him up too? I bet we'd get a huge boost from that dirty old goat.*

As the thought passed through his head, the boy stopped struggling. His foot tapped on the metal tile a few times, beating out the erratic rhythm of his death.

Gerard eventually let go of the cable, and the boy's lifeless form crumpled to the floor. A moment later, Gerard did too.

'Are you OK?' Carl asked, looking at the old man as he gasped for breath on the floor.

Gerard wafted himself with his hands as he tried to talk. 'I … will … be …' he gasped. 'Who … knew … how much effort … it took … to … strangle someone … with a … power … cable?'

Carl didn't want to tell him that he kind of knew it would take quite a bit of effort, even if the person being strangled wasn't expecting it. He had to give the old man kudos for the feat he had just performed.

'You can get them... onto the rail... yourself,' Gerard panted, pointing to the two dead boys.

Carl rolled his eyes. 'I have to fucking do everything around here,' he grumbled as he pulled the first body closer to the rail.

~~~~

Ten minutes of lifting, huffing, and puffing, gouging, and scraping, inserting, and clipping, and another two bodies were hanging in the cabinet. They were both hooked up and quivering with the network passing through them.

'It's up to fifty-seven percent,' Gerard said, the glow of the monitor illuminating the fact that his face had returned to a semi-healthy pink. He looked at his watch. 'It's nearly seven o'clock. We could stay on and get some of the cleaners. What do you say?'

Carl was physically tired and emotionally drained.

His arms were aching, his back was aching, his head was aching, but he thought about what the old man had said to him earlier. He had nothing to go home to. Just a couple of stiffs on his couch, powering his Wi-Fi connection. The kids were staying at his mum's; they wouldn't miss him. He walked over and looked at the command prompt on the screen. 'Fifty-seven percent,' he mused. 'How many more do you think?'

The two men looked at their trophy cabinet.

Jodi, Leanne, Bob, Rod, Gillian the first aider, the football bore, the two apprentices ...

Gerard shrugged. 'Another five?' he said.

Carl rolled his eyes, but his smile gave him away. 'Another five,' he agreed.

~~~~

Tasha was sitting in the corner of her living room. The television was off, as were the lights. She didn't need any entertainment tonight. Her mind was doing it all for her.

The tentacled monstrosity was outside her window, lurking in the shadows of the deep murky water that her street had become. She could feel it slithering over her roof. She could hear it pressing its hideousness against her windows. She fancied its stomach was growling and grumbling. Like it was hungry.

She knew instinctively that the thing wanted more than just to eat her. It wanted her soul; it wanted her devotion.

It desired her sacrifice.

'I won't give in to it,' she whispered in the semi-dark, her breath pluming around her in testament to the uncharacteristic cold of the room.

Even though her television was not turned on, it didn't stop it from flashing up messages. They were corrupting her brain, destroying her will, weakening her resolve.

KILL THEM ALL …
TURN THEM OFF AND TURN THEM ON AGAIN …
KILL THEM ALL …
TURN THEM OFF AND TURN THEM ON AGAIN …
BRING THE MASTER HOME …
TURN THEM OFF AND TURN THEM ON AGAIN …

It was like the repeated chorus of a very bad pop song. They were coming hard and fast, strobing into her head. Images of dead bodies being eaten by fish with razor sharp teeth. Torsos being torn apart by the flow and currents of the water. Images of hundreds of thousands of people—men, women, and children—killing themselves, slaughtering each other, all in the shadow of something … something with thick tentacles, something monstrous, hideous, evil, alien … something old!

She held her hands to her eyes, attempting to block out the sights and sounds of death and blind worship. Fornication, bestiality, suicide … mutilation, death, death, death, DEATH!

She screamed.

As she lived alone, there was no one to hear her scream.

Except whatever it was outside her house.

The shrill noise excited the beast. She could hear the rhythmic beating of a heart. As she shouted and raved, the beating thrashed faster and faster.

She stopped yelling.

She didn't want to bring the thing to a frenzy; she didn't know what that might mean for her, or for the world.

What was outside the house was only in her imagination; she knew this. She wanted to believe her house wasn't submerged in some kind of dead sea and that she was imprisoned in a deep watery grave, about to give up her soul, her very being, to something wicked and malevolent.

'Kill them, Tasha … kill them all. They are but ants to be crushed underfoot. They are nothing compared to the Olde Ones. Commit yourself to the rise of the Gods. Take your place at their side. The Master needs power … give it to him.'

'HOW?' she screamed into the empty room. 'HOW do I give him power?'

The voice, the one she'd assumed was buried deep in the psychosis of her own metal state, whispered.

It was only three words.

'Server Room One!'

26.

BETWEEN THEM, THEY bagged, captured, killed, and attached three of the evening cleaning staff to the network. They had been relatively easy pickings, as they had not been expecting anyone to be in the building, so they all worked wearing earphones, listening to music.

The surprise on their faces as either Carl or Gerard jumped out of nowhere and dragged them through a portal back to the server room might have been comical if it hadn't been so fatal.

They passed through the portal, from a place where they knew and worked every weeknight of their lives, into a place of cold winds, metal floors, flashing screens, and certain death. Carl had considered the unfortunate cleaners must have thought they had been dragged into some kind of dystopian alternative reality where technology and death went hand in hand.

Then he realised that was exactly where they'd been taken.

Each cleaner had been dispatched effectively, keeping as much of the blood as they could inside the body. They had been offed, usually with one of the tiles from the floor or with the trusted old fire extinguisher.

The screwdriver had also done its work, and each member of the cleaning staff had been added to the network.

The command prompt was now reading sixty-eight percent.

'I don't think we're going to get this working tonight,' Carl said as he checked the cables in the eyes of all the bodies. 'It's not even seventy percent, and the rest of the cleaning staff will be leaving soon.'

'Then we need to get out there and get more of them before they do.' Gerard shrugged as if it was the most natural thing in the world to off a whole shift compliment to bring forth the return of The Master.

'Are you not getting tired?' Carl asked the old man. He looked at his watch. It was nearly half past eight. 'We've been at this for twelve hours straight.'

As he spoke the word tiredness, a lethargy spilled over him, one that he could feel in his bones, that threatened to consume him, to drag him kicking and screaming down into the land of Orpheus. He had an idea that falling asleep with Gerard lurking in the vicinity might not be the best of ideas. *The dirty old fuck would either kill me or bum me.* Another thought occurred to him that almost made him laugh, but it didn't … it was all too real: *Or kill me* by *bumming me.* A shudder ripped through him at the thought of that filthy old bugger getting his rocks off inside him.

He snapped out of this reverie of madness to see the old man leering at him. Carl did not like the look he was giving him in the least. His head was lowered, and he was looking up at him through hooded eyes. His sinister grin was shadowed in his dark demeanour.

'Why are you looking at me like that?' Carl asked, the chill he'd felt moments ago now more pronounced.

'Are you tired?' the old man asked.

Carl sat up in the tall stool he was slumped on. His eyes widened, and he straightened his back. 'No, I'm not tired at all. Are you?' He wished he hadn't started this line of enquiry.

The old man's look didn't waver. He shook his head. 'No. I'm really not. Do you want to know why a sixty-four-year-old man can kill for the whole day and not get tired?'

Deep down, Carl really didn't want to know, but he knew he was going to say yes to the question. He blinked his eyes and fought them to open again. They didn't want to, and he struggled to conceal his tired, dry, pink eyeballs from the world, from the horrid old man sat before him. He ended up shrugging. 'Yeah,' he replied, cursing himself as he did.

The old man didn't say anything. He just stood up and began to unbuckle his trousers.

Carl was horrified at what he was doing. He wanted him to stop but was far too tired to even speak.

'I did this. I think it might have taken a little bit of juice from the download, but I'm sure The Master will let me off if it gets him here faster.' The old man dropped his trousers. To Carl's horror, the front of the man's underwear was stained in a spreading, wet, deep-red blotch.

'The Master, or rather HP, told me what to do. It only hurt for a moment. Well, a bit longer than a moment, but once I plugged myself in, I was as right as rain.'

Carl's eyes were drawn when Gerard pulled down his wet underwear. He wanted to look away but that was simply impossible, he couldn't. He was instantly reminded of an accident he'd seen not so long ago on the motorway. The traffic had been stopped on both sides of the carriageway because a car had smashed into a motorbike, before running up an embankment. The motorbike was smashed to bits, and he, just like all the others on the road, had not been able to take their eyes off the carnage all around them.

It reminded him of the motorbike rider, the one whose head had been cracked, smashed, flattened by the wheels of the car.

He didn't know why, but it reminded him of the pool of blood the poor rider had been lying in. As it spread around him, sinking into the asphalt of the road, while everyone watched.

What has he done that for? More importantly, what's he done that with? Carl could only hazard a guess. He hadn't seen him with anything more lethal than the screwdriver they'd used to remove their co-worker's eyes.

What was left of between Gerard's legs was akin to a butcher's shop floor. It was pink, raw, and full of limp gristle. Carl had another flashback to the motorbike rider. What had once, presumably, been a healthy, if somewhat overused, penis was nothing but a dripping, gaping chasm. Carl could see the bloody urethra, the tube that ran up the length of the appendage flopping around and dripping as it dangled between his legs. His balls were hanging limply below the tube, they were completely slathered red in drying blood.

From out of the hole trailed a cable. It might have once been blue, but it was now so covered in meat and gore that there was no real way of telling, unless it was wiped. There was no way on this Earth that Carl was going to perform that duty.

'I plugged this into the last body, and then into me, and a few minutes later, bingo, I was good to go.' The old man was smiling as he held out his hands towards him. He pointed to the corner of the room.

Carl's eyes didn't want to go there, but there was some unstoppable force that made him look. He simply had no choice.

There, nestled in the corner of the room, was a small clump of meat.

Carl felt his stomach churn as he realised what it was.

'HP told me that when The Master returns, I won't be needing that anymore. Life itself will be sexual in nature. He told me to clip it off and plug myself in. He told me everything would be all right … and do you know what, Carl? It is.'

As he reached down to his trousers on the floor a small squirt of blood shot forth from the tube and splashed on the already soiled metal tiles.

I'll have to wipe that up, Carl thought. *I don't want to slip on it.* The fact he'd become so desensitised to the horrific nature of what was happening around him, to him, in just one day, scared and disgusted him in equal measures.

The old man was handing him over a filthy pair of scissors he'd retrieved from his trousers.

Carl found himself reaching for them.

He snapped his hand back when he realised what he was doing. 'What the fuck? Why would I want to cut my …' He didn't know what to call it. To Amy, he used to call it Mr Knish, but he didn't think he'd ever had a serious conversation about his penis to another man, especially the managing director of the company he worked for. '… thingus off?' he finished, feeling more than a little bit silly for calling it that, but it was as good a word as anything else.

'That's what I thought, but HP told me that there's no point having one. Once The Master returns, sensuality will be the order of the day. There'll be no need for the more carnal nature of us humans. It'll become redundant.'

Mine's been redundant for years, he thought with a dazed smile.

Gerard unplugged himself from the network, pulled up his trousers, and retracted the offer of the scissors. 'Suit yourself,' he said as he buckled his trousers. 'But it's done wonders for me. I also think it's brought me closer to The Master.'

How did I not see the red stain at the front of his trousers? Carl thought as he watched the old man drip some more of his blood on the server.

'I'm going to find us some more cleaners to plug in.' With that, the old man opened the server door and walked out.

Carl's eyes were instantly drawn towards the small mound of meat in the corner. Without thinking about it, he grabbed at his own crotch, reassured that it was still there.

D E McCluskey

Is he now closer to The Master than me?

27.

THE SHAKING, SLITHERING, and thumping continued. The voices in her head were draining her. She could feel the tentacles wrapping themselves around her house and piercing into her brain at the same time. They were slinking into her ears, and up her nose. They were creeping around her eyes, and probing her mouth, making her want to vomit.

She scratched and tore at the sensations as the voices continued to taunt and cajole.

'You should see what is happening in Server Room One. They are summoning The Master. You're going to want to help them. You have been chosen. You really cannot resist.'

Over and over again, the voices whispered at her. The vile tentacle that had been chasing her all day was thrashing at her double-glazing. Spider-web cracks had bloomed over them where the hideous thing battered against them. Stinking water was seeping through the cracks, dripping down the glass, and pooling on her carpets. She could see the deformed silhouettes of the impossible fish swimming backwards and forwards along the fissures in the windows. It made her wonder where she got the word fissure from, as it was rather fitting for the situation. They were either keeping sentinel for whatever depravity the tentacle belonged to or simply waiting for the windows to smash so they could swarm in, gnashing their sharp razor-like teeth, ready to tear her to pieces, into bite sized chunks of chum.

'Turn them off, Tasha, then turn them on again. The Master awaits, and he has such delights to offer you.'

Tasha was crouched in the corner of the room where she had been since she got home. Her face was scratched and bleeding where her nails had raked her flesh, attempting to claw away the disgusting things trying to penetrate her.

Her screams were unnoticed, unheard. She could feel the dryness in her throat where the yelling caused it to turn raw, sore, and broken. From the corner of her eye, she saw something shift in the darkness of the algae filled room. The shadows were moving, slowly creeping towards her.

'Turn them off, Tasha, then turn them on again. Reboot the system. Begin again from factory defaults. Usher in the new world order. Sit at the right hand of The Master. Succumb to his will. KILL THEM ALL! Your destiny awaits you in Server Room One.'

'Carl,' she croaked.

'Yes … Carl is there. He's assisting. He is a willing volunteer. Join Carl and bring The Master home.'

A drop of blood fell from her cheek, from one of the deep scratches she'd ploughed through her skin. It clung onto the line of her chin before finally succumbing to the will of gravity. It fell. She watched it land on the thick carpet of her living room and soak into the shag pile.

A portal opened before her.

She was unfazed by this. *What's he showing me now?* she thought as she looked into the phenomenon before her.

She recognised the walls, the desks, and the open plan office of work.

'Why are you showing me this?' she asked.

'Pass through the portal, Tasha. Join your colleagues. Bring The Master home.'

Tasha leaned forward, outstretching her arm to touch the image that was floating in her living room. Her fingers passed straight through, into the portal. She had been expecting to touch a cold glass-like surface, so as her hand passed through, she snatched it back again.

Staring at her fingers, she wriggled them, making sure that they were still there.

They were.

'This will take you to where you need to be. All you need to do is step through and you will be where you need to be. Where The Master needs you to be.'

She looked up from her fingers just in time to see Carl. He was walking past the portal, not noticing she was there, watching him.

'Carl,' she shouted, but he didn't seem to be able to hear her. 'Carl, it's me … Tasha.'

Carl continued walking away from the portal.

'He can't hear you. You're miles away from him. But one small step through and you can join him. You can both usher forth the new age. Carl and Gerard are already working towards it, but they need your help, Tasha. Are you ready to give your all for the return of The Master?'

Tasha looked around her living room.

It was still dark, and the dank water was still rolling past her windows, trickling in through the cracks. *Fishers,* she thought, supressing a giggle. She knew something was out there, lurking within that dark water, ready to get her, to destroy her, perhaps destroy all of humanity.

The small, ugly fish were snapping at the thick, ugly tentacle that was resting against the windowpanes, its thrashings had ceased.

'You know you can't go out there, don't you?' the voice said to her.

'I can't?'

'You wouldn't last a minute in that freezing cold water, that is if you even survived The Master's little pets.'

Tasha could hear humour in the disembodied voice. Dark humour that chilled her to the bone.

'Your only way out of here is through that portal. Take the offer, bring The Master home, and take your seat at his table. He needs you.'

Tasha watched as Carl began to walk back towards her. He looked tired; his eyes looked older than they should. She decided then, that she would indeed help her friend, *in whatever it is he is doing.*

She stood from the couch, her knees cracking as they stretched, and without thinking too much about it, she stepped into the portal.

As she did, she thought she could hear a slow, maniacal laugh!

28.

CARL TURNED. HE had a nasty feeling of being watched.

The office was empty. In this wing, there was not even a cleaner—mainly because he and Gerard had disposed of them all. He shook the odd feeling off as he continued around the building, looking for someone else to help bring The Master's download over the seventy-percent mark.

Everyone was either dead or they'd gone home.

He wondered what the hell they were going to do now to get this download up to the one-hundred-percent mark.

A noise caught his attention. It was only a small one, but it brought his heartrate back up again in an instant.

An ugly thought rose in his disturbed brain.

It's Gerard. He's trying to kill me. The idea was indeed plausible. Anything was with that man. He'd mutilated himself for the cause. Cutting off his own penis and inserting a network cable into himself. *If he's capable of doing that, to the one part of his anatomy that he worshipped above all else, then he's not even going to hesitate killing me, is he?*

The noise came again, and Carl decided to hide in one of the bays. He didn't want the old man creeping up on him, at least not until he was ready to be found. If he could get the jump on him, then maybe *Gerard* could be the final push needed to bring this whole thing, all this madness and death, to a halt.

He stepped into the bay as the noise came again. It was a whistle. He saw the flashlight beam from the other part of the office, the part where the cleaners had turned off the lights. *A security guard*, he thought. *Oh, happy days*. He realised he wouldn't have to save himself from Gerard's advances if there were still fresh bodies to be had.

He snuck out of the bay and made his way back the way he'd come. Again, he had the strange feeling of being watched as he ducked into the last bay before the corner to the corridor where Server Room One was located. He crouched low behind a chair and opened the door to one of the small chests underneath the desks. He opened the first drawer and searched for something, anything he could use to take the security guard down with. All he could find was a load of paper and several books. He considered using a book, hitting the man on the head with the spine of it.

That's not going to do it, he thought, closing the drawer. *I might as well fucking read it to him if I was going to do that.*

He opened the next one and found a cup, a knife, fork, and spoon. The knife was a butter knife and would have been useless. The fork, however—*Right in the eye,* he thought, causing a chill to run up his spine at the fact he could be so cold about killing an innocent man.

It's for The Master, he told himself.

That thought didn't comfort him one bit.

He opened the next drawer and found a pair of scissors. *Perfect.* He smiled as he grasped them.

The light, and therefore the man was getting closer. Carl popped his head out of the bay and watched his progress. He was mooching on the individual desks, picking up pictures and looking at them, helping himself to sweets and biscuits; in some cases, picking up the small change the people had left on their desks, and putting it in his pockets.

'Come on, come on,' he urged as the guard took his time getting towards him. 'Stop eating the biscuits, you fat bastard,' he whispered as the man walked into the bay opposite.

He picked up a photograph of a group of young girls dressed in party wear, looking a little worse for the drink but all smiles at the camera. Carl scowled as the man licked the image, then touched himself before putting the picture back on the desk.

This gave Carl all he needed to *not* feel sorry for this man, for what he was about to do to him. 'Fucking wierdo,' he whispered.

The man began to exit the bay when Carl stood. He moved a little too fast for his head, and suddenly felt a little woozy. His knees also cracked, shooting pain through his legs. *Getting old was not convivial to multiple murders,* he thought. He lunged at the surprised guard, attacking him first with the scissors, and then with the fork.

Both attacks missed their targets by a long way.

As he realised, too late, that he hadn't moved the desk chair away from the table he was crouching under. So, as he attacked, shouting, screaming, all guns blazing, the element of surprise was gone, as he himself went sprawling over the chair. He thrust the scissors, and then the fork, towards the startled man's face. His aim was for the eyes, but only managed to cut his jacket a little on the sleeve and fork him in one of his man-boobs.

'What the shitting hell?' the guard spat as Carl barged into him.

It was then Carl realised how big the man was. He was almost twice his size, and it wasn't just fat either; there was muscle too.

'What the fuck are you doing with that fork?' the guard shouted as the makeshift weapon bounced off him.

As the guard stepped back, away from the pathetic attack, Carl fell with him, but the guard was more robust than he was and found his feet quicker.

He was in trouble now.

'Who the fuck are you?' the big man asked as he recovered, grabbing Carl by the scruff of his t-shirt with his hand not holding his flashlight. He looked at the cut on the sleeve of his jacket and then back at Carl. His face was red and getting redder by the second. His mouth was an angry little white O in the middle of his face.

The strong grip on the back of his neck, pushed and Carl's head hit the floor. 'Did you just try to stab me, you little prick?' the man asked. Carl noticed a cockney twang in his voice. Whether it was real, or not, he couldn't tell, but he'd seen a lot of London gangster films and had maybe just imagined it.

'I'm calling the cops, mate. You're fucked.' The word came out *fact*, so he surmised the man was from London. Although, why any of it mattered while his head was being pushed into the hard-wearing grey carpet of the office, he just didn't know.

The big man, still holding Carl, bent, and proceeded to hit Carl with his flashlight. The force of the blows sent his head reeling.

'You do not simply go around sneaking up on people and attacking them with scissors,' the guard spat, accentuating every word with another smack with the torch. 'Especially the likes of me,' he continued. 'By that, I mean someone who takes great pleasure in twatting people.'—*Peepow;* he was one hundred percent from London, or at least the surrounding areas. 'As sometimes I *facking* forget to stop. Do you 'ear me?'

Carl felt every blow of the torch, although the pain had already started abating, mainly due to his face going numb.

'I—I …' he stuttered, hearing the almost nonsensical word jibber from his swollen lips. He could see a small pool of blood underneath him as the man continued to push his face into the carpet. Even though his eyesight was becoming fuzzy, he could see the scissors, they were just out of his reach. The security guard laughed as Carl's shaky hand reached out towards the potential weapon.

'All I need to do is say that I caught you stealing, and you attacked me. Then I can do anything I want to you, you facking scumbag,' the big man growled.

Carl closed his eyes and envisioned Server Room One. He thought about the blood on the server that had created the portal earlier.

Nothing happened.

He felt the man's boot come down into his ribs and almost blacked out from the shooting agony.

The guard leaned down, putting his face next to his. Carl could smell coffee, alcohol, cigarettes, and a vile, greasy garlic stink blow into his face as he whispered. 'I have a special place for scum like you. A place where no one will ever think to look for a body.'

Carl wanted to reply, he wanted to ask him to let him go. He wanted to tell him that he was working for The Master and if he knew what was good for him, he would let him go, drop to his knees, and allow him to sacrifice him cleanly.

But he could hardly talk.

His lips were swollen, and he was drooling blood.

He felt rough hands on the scruff of his neck and himself being dragged, unceremoniously, out of the bay and into the corridor.

Is this how I die? he thought as he felt the carpet burn through Gerard's trousers. *All the fucking things I've done for The Master, and I get murdered by this fat tub of lard!* He could see the irony in it, and in a strange way, he accepted it; he welcomed it even.

The things that he'd done today, and last night, were unforgivable. His soul was tainted, and even if he got away from this big galoot, and The Master download turned out to be a huge elaborate hoax, he knew they would toss him, and his feckless assistant, into a loony-bin somewhere where no one ever went, and they would smelt the key.

It was no more than he deserved.

He allowed his body to go limp as the big man dragged him along the darkened corridor.

'Holy FUCK,' Carl heard him shout.

He felt the hand holding him let go of the back of his t-shirt, and his face bounce off the carpet. It was the last thing that his poor, ruined features needed, but it woke him up to what was occurring.

'Jesus, Mary, and Joseph the Worker are you a facking ghost?' he heard the big man utter. 'Where the facking hell did you come from?'

Carl took this moment of freedom to make good his escape. With his head still spinning, he searched for the scissors. They were back where he'd come from, just outside the bay he had been hiding in.

'Holy Fuck. You stay away from me,' the big man shouted.

Carl had no idea what could be scaring the big man so much, and he didn't have the time to look; all he knew was he had seconds to get to the discarded scissors and secure this big guard in the service of The Master.

He didn't think he was going to be able to make it, as his hands and legs didn't want to work properly. He was crouched on all fours, crawling towards his freedom, each time he put his arm down, it felt like it was about to buckle underneath him.

From what felt like a hundred miles away, the guard was backing away from something that was spooking him good. Carl thought he could hear a female voice, one he recognised, but he put that thought away almost as quickly as it developed.

There's no way she's here at this hour.

Eventually, he reached the scissors. He wrapped his hands around the handle and gripped them tight. He watched as blood dripped from his wounded face, slicking their grip, but taking away none of the confidence he had in them doing their job, properly this time.

He sat down and turned himself around. The big man was backing up towards him, blocking his view of whatever it was scaring him.

Carl tried to stand, but his spinning head stopped the attempt. He felt like he was about to be sick. He filtered out the scared jabbering of the security guard; he didn't want to even think about what could be scaring him. It couldn't possibly be any scarier than some of the things he'd been seeing—and doing—over the past couple of days.

He gripped the scissors and fought the vertigo dancing around his brain. Battling against all odds, he stood.

When he did, he saw what was scaring the guard.

Stood before him was a wild looking woman. Blood was streaking down her face, looking a little like that woman, or girl, in that film he'd seen ages ago. The one whose dress was ruined by John Travolta, at prom night. He couldn't think of the name of it. It was just a single name, like Barry, or maybe Gary.

Either way, she was standing before what he recognised as a portal, but the security guard wouldn't have. Through the portal, Carl could see a darkened room filled with filthy brown-green water. In that water were hellish, demonic looking fish and a thick, vile tentacle that looked like something that belonged inside an organism rather than on the outside. *Or maybe it's Gerard's dick come to life!*

'Look, bitch,' the security guard pleaded as he backed away from Tasha. 'I've got no fight with you. I don't know from what Hell you have come, but I—'

He didn't finish his plea.

Carl buried the scissors deep within his back.

He needed to push with some force to get them deep enough to cause problems. It took all the effort he could muster, but he did it.

The big man reached behind him while turning at the same time. It was a strange contortion, and it threw him off balance. He fell backwards. His weight drove the scissors further into his fleshy back. It must have penetrated a major organ, as his face screwed up as if he was trying to release a large build-up of wind. He shuddered, released a deep, shaky sob, along with all the gas he had been trying to expel. He then lay still.

'What have you just done?' Tasha asked as the man expired before her.

'What I had to,' Carl replied, feeling good with his response. He thought it was something his character would have said in the film of his life, or a cheesy, cheap Lovecraftian novel, where the hero killed one of the bad guys who was trying to stop him from doing something noble.

Then a depressing thought occurred to him.

I'm the bad guy!

I'm the one who needs to be stopped.

He was the good guy. He was trying to stop me from bringing forth the fucking Master.

He stared at the vision of Tasha. Her face was covered in deep scratches, lesions that were bleeding, dripping down her face. Her hair was wild. Carl had used the term *looking like she had been dragged through a hedge backwards* many times in his life, but right then, Tasha actually did look like she had.

'What did you do, Carl?' she asked again, looking down at the body of the man on the floor.

A puddle of blood was spreading beneath him. Carl didn't know how he knew, probably because of all the murder programmes Amy made him watch over the years, but from the colour of the blood he knew the blades had pierced the man's kidney.

'He was trying to kill me! Look at my face,' his mouth flapped, spitting blood at her as his lips tried to form words. He didn't think she would mind, as she was already covered in her own.

'Why are you here?' she asked, not taking her wild eyes from him. 'How am I here?'

Carl looked at her.

'I think you need to sit down,' he offered.

She did as she was told, taking a seat in the bay where he'd been hiding minutes ago.

'There's something you need to know. There's things I found on Gerard Medley's laptop.' All his S's were coming out like hisses, and he thought he might have sound funny, if it wasn't all so tragic.

'I know about the laptop, Carl. I know about The Master. I know he wants us to reboot the users. I'm getting the same messages.'

Carl suddenly felt as if the weight of the word had been lifted from his shoulders. He had someone he could share all this madness with, other than the personification of madness himself, Gerald Medley. 'Have you seen the monsters out there? In the water?'

Tasha nodded.

'You're having exactly the same'— he paused; not knowing how to express the horrors he had been experiencing— 'experiences as me?' It was as good a word as any.

'It looks that way.'

Carl sat down next to her and laughed. It was a deep, humourless chuckle. 'Thank God for that. I thought I was going to be stuck with that old bastard, Medley for all eternity.'

'What do you mean, stuck with?' she asked.

'I mean I've been working with him all day. We're nearly done. I think when we hook this one up, we might only need one more and then we'll be at one hundred percent.'

Tasha shook her head. 'One hundred percent of what?' she asked.

Carl blinked at her. 'The Master 2.1 download. What did you think I was talking about?'

Her eyes widened. 'Tell me … Tell me you didn't.'

'Didn't what?' Carl asked, genuinely confused with her question.

'Turn them off.'

Carl didn't answer straight away.

Tasha seemed to understand the nature of his silence. She stood and backed away from him. Carl rose with her, not understanding the nature of her shock.

'Where are you going?' he asked. 'You've got to help me get this body to—'

'Server Room One,' they both said in unison, only Tasha's was a question.

Carl nodded, a ghost of a smile on his bruised and beaten face.

'What's happening in Server Room One?' Tasha asked. 'Is Jodi still in there?'

Carl nodded again. 'Yeah, she's helping.'

'Carl, what the fuck is she helping you with?' she asked, backing away even further. She was heading towards the window, blocking herself in from any quick exit she might need.

'Downloading The Master 2.1.'

'Did you …?' She swallowed. 'Turn her off?'

Carl nodded. 'Then I turned her on again. She's in there right now. You can see her; I just need help getting this guy in there. This is a big fella. I really think he'll get us a long way towards where we need to be. We're almost on eighty percent already.' He could hear the madness in his own voice, in the fact that he was speaking at least three octaves higher than his normal voice. 'You can help us!'

'I'm not helping you kill anyone else,' Tasha said, her voice barely a whisper.

Carl smiled—it felt uncomfortable to him, and not just because of his swollen lips. 'We're … we're not killing anyone! We're turning them off and turning them on again.'

'Listen to yourself,' she shouted, her raised voice louder than it should have been in the quiet of the empty office. 'Listen to what you're saying, Carl. Turning them off. You're killing them. Did you turn Jodi off?'

'She's …' He pointed towards the location of the server room.

'Don't.' Tasha stopped him, holding her hand up to whatever flow of drivel he was about to spout. 'The visions, the voices; did you succumb to them all?'

'They're not just visions. They're messages from The Master. We need to turn them all off,' Carl said as he advanced upon her. 'Help me with him I promise he'll be the last.'

'The last?' she asked, her face draining of colour. 'There's more of them?'

Carl nodded. 'Ten, maybe more. Not forgetting my Amy and her boyfriend! Oh, and Gerard's wife and the whore he took home with him.'

'Carl, listen to me. You need to get out of here. Whatever this portal is that's gotten me here, step though it with me. Come to mine; we'll get away from here. Far away. Let Medley take all the blame. He's mad anyway. People will believe he's working on his own. Come on.' She held out her hand. 'Please, Carl.'

He looked at the outstretched hand. He looked at the dead security guard on the floor, his lifeblood pooling out from underneath him. *Probably not worth anything to the network now, anyway,* he thought, looking at how big the blood spill was. He looked at the portal still hanging in the corridor, then finally looked at his hands. They were covered in blood. Some of it was his own, some was the security guard's, but the majority of it, the blood he couldn't see, belonged to the others, the good people of the company he worked for.

Even if they weren't his friends, they had been his colleagues.

'Please, Carl. Let's get away from all of this. We can go together.' Tasha was pleading now. The tears in her eyes were soaking her cheeks; her outstretched hand was shaking.

His eyes went to her.

Tasha.

He'd always liked her. Always thought she was funny in a shy, awkward way. He'd never, not even once, seen her as the woman who might save him.

His salvation.

His reclamation.

He held his hand out towards hers.

She smiled.

There was genuine warmth in that smile. Love, even.

Her fingers curled around his as the hands embraced.

He then pulled her towards him, taking her by surprise. She lost her footing and stumbled forwards. With perfect timing, he moved his head back before bringing it forwards again with great force. He headbutted her directly on the bridge of her nose.

The force of it made his already beaten face feel like it was caving in. He saw stars. Dark stars. Worlds and constellations different from those he knew about—other than the Big Dipper and Orion's Belt, he was pretty much lost anyway—flew through his vision. Millions, if not billions of lightyears away, other civilisations, other Gods.

When his vision returned, Tasha was crumpled on the floor. He allowed her to drop, letting go of her hand. 'Sorry, Tasha,' he whispered. 'If you're not going to help, then I'll have to do it myself. The Master isn't going to download himself, you know.'

He turned his attentions to the dead security guard. He bent at the knees, straightened his back, and picked up the man's thick legs. He thought about the server room, and they were instantly teleported to the security guard's final resting place.

29.

GERARD WAS JUMPING for joy at the sight of the big man appearing in the server room. Carl noticed that the blood at the front of his trousers had expanded. *He's losing too much blood,* he thought.

'Excellent … excellent. Get him hooked up, quick, before he loses any more blood.' The old man was almost singing in his excitement.

The two colleagues struggled, lugging the heavy guard onto the rail alongside the three cleaners who were already networked.

'You do the eyes, and I'll go and check the download,' Carl said.

'What happened to your face?' the old man asked while whittling holes into the head of the big man.

'He got the jump on me. I came at him with scissors but fell over a chair.'

Gerard laughed. 'That sounds like it would have been funny. I wish we could have filmed it.'

Carl shot him a glare. He hated the old pervert with a passion, but he had to admit he was good at his job—by that, he meant cutting holes into corpses' eyeballs and plugging network cables in. He logged on to the server and clicked on the command prompt, refreshing the programme.

'Are you ready?' he shouted over to Gerard, who was holding the end of a network cable in his hand, the other end lodged into a cleaner's eye.

'Born ready, my boy!' he replied with a chuckle.

He looked at the prompt. It read:

Download continued …
MASTER V2.1
PROGRESS 79% ………………

'Go on then. Put it in … now.'

The old man chuckled and wiggled the end of the ethernet cable, plunging it deep into the red, bloody hole.

Carl heard the satisfying click as the small plastic clip fit into place. That was his cue to refresh the programme again.

Download continued ...
MASTER V2.1 ...
PROGRESS 91% ....

'Fucking hell,' Carl shouted. The annoyance in his voice caught Gerard's attention from enjoying the view of the dead hanging in the cabinet.

'Are we there?' Gerard asked, his face akin to a child on Christmas morning, asking if 'he'd' been yet.

'We need another one. We're on ninety-one. So close!'

'Is there even anyone left in the building?' Gerard asked, biting his bottom lip and noisily sucking in air.

'I don't know. I only saw the ...' He stopped talking, his face falling, changing from anxious to expressionless. 'Tasha is out there. She's in one of the bays. She came in via a portal; she knows all about The Master.'

'Hmmm, if I can get her to come in here on the pretence of helping us, then we can get our last nine percent. The Master 2.1 will be downloaded, and we'll have ushered in the new era of ultimate pleasure.'

'I'll go and get her,' Carl said, heading toward the server room door.

'No, I'll go. You stay in here and make sure the connection is still working. This is far too important for anything to go wrong now.'

Carl looked at the old man. His hair was wild, and he was covered in blood, most of it his own. His clothes were ripped and grimy, but there was a smile on his face that made him look almost ten years younger.

Carl nodded. 'You're right. This is far too important. You go and get her. She's unconscious in one of the bays. She's only light, so you won't need me.'

The old man nodded but didn't look away. 'We've come a long way in such a small amount of time, haven't we?'

'We really have. Can you believe this is going to happen? We're finally going to bring The Master home.'

The old man lowered his head and grinned. 'Should we hug it out?' he asked, opening his arms towards Carl.

'Fuck no. I'm not going anywhere near you, you filthy bastard,' Carl snapped, looking the old man up and down. Even though Gerard had castrated himself, Carl still wondered where those hands had been. He did *not* want them anywhere near him. 'You go now. Get Tasha and let's bring this motherfucker home!'

~~~~

The girl was indeed in the bay where he'd said she was, and she was indeed unconscious. Gerard looked her up and down. He wanted to know if she was still breathing, even though he could see her chest rising and falling under her jumper.

He watched as her neck twitched.

She was still alive.

Maybe just a little touch, to see if she's really *breathing.*

He leaned over and lay his sweaty, bloody hands on her, as if gauging if she was asleep, but in reality, he was doing nothing more than copping a feel of the girl he was about to sacrifice to The Master.

Licking his lips, he looked up and down the corridor, making sure the lewd act he was about to perform on her would go unwitnessed, especially by *fucking Carl.*

This is my fantasy, he thought as he felt his old ticker thumping.

He slid his bloodied hand up her jumper and caressed her breasts, taking time on the nipple, while his other hand slid down, in between his legs to get himself hard.

That was when he remembered. He'd recently cut his penis off. The pain that coursed up and down his body from his own grope was enough to send flashing lights behind his eyes. His heart stopped thumping and upgraded itself to a wild thrash. It was thumping in his ears however, and the pins and needles in his lower arm scared him.

He fell back, gasping for breath, holding his numbing arm, flexing and unflexing his fingers. He closed his eyes, only to see the dancing coloured lights that were his eyes visual interpretation of pain still performing in the darkness.

He forced himself to breathe through his nostrils, slow, deep breaths, before releasing them from his mouth.

His crotch was aching, and there were searing throbs of agony wracking through his whole body. The agony he could live with, it was something he embraced. It was the shooting pains in his arm he was worried about.

After a few moments, they abated. He wiggled his fingers of the offending arm, and the pins and needles began to recede. *Thank you, Master,* he thought, taking a moment to rest before pushing his aching body into the sitting up position.

He looked down at his crotch. The bleeding was worse than it had been earlier. *Not long to go, then The Master will look after me. He will give me a new body, one fitting of the work he will want me to perform.*

Grabbing at the desk above, he pulled himself up, taking his time, as his head was still whirling from the suspected heart attack and the searing pain from where his penis used to be.

Something strange happened to him then—or stranger than everything else that had been happening recently. It wasn't an altogether unpleasant experience.

He had heard about the phenomenon of phantom itches, of people who had experienced amputations but still felt the missing limb itch.

Well, he felt like he had a phantom erection.

He looked at the girl, still asleep, her chest rising and falling.

He closed his eyes, and in his mind, he took his phantom dick in his hand and began to pleasure himself.

Is this a virtual wank? he thought as his hand moved faster and faster up and down his imagined shaft.

Soon, he came to an imagined—*or was it virtual*—fruition. His knees buckled, and his eyes rolled to the back of his head. There was pain, but there was also pleasure. Both of them in equal amounts.

'That is what it will be like when The Master returns,' the voice in his head spoke. The words were soft, comforting tones. 'Take her to the server room, turn her off, and then turn her on again!'

'Yes, Master,' Gerard whispered, still in the rapture of his orgasm.

He took in a deep breath, steadying himself, before lifting the girl's legs. He thought about the server room, but nothing happened. No portal appeared, so he pulled her along the carpet, leaving bloody tracks in his wake.

~~~~

As he opened the door to Server Room One, the first thing Gerard noticed was how cold it was and that the smell of shit and dirty water was still hanging in the air. He also noticed the water outside the window was disappearing, leaving behind it the view of the next-door building.

Carl was sitting on the stool at the server monitor.

'… yes, Master,' he said as the door opened. He turned his head rapidly to look at Gerard.

'Who were you speaking to then?' Gerard asked.

Carl shook his head. 'No one,' he said a little too fast for Gerard's likening, before he turned his attentions towards the girl lying on the floor, half in and half out of the room. 'So, you found her, then?' he asked, changing the subject.

'Right where you said she'd be,' Gerard replied, keeping his distance from Carl, who seemed to be doing the same to him. 'Is everything set on the server? Once we hook this one up, then we're done? The Master returns, and we sit at his right hand.'

'Both of us?' Carl asked.

Gerard looked at the younger man. Something was changed about him. Something was different in the air. He noticed the stench had gone now, replaced only by the ozone of the electrical circuits and the heavy hum of human waste. 'Are we going to do this, then?'

Carl smiled and stood up. 'We'd better start, then. The sooner it's done, the sooner he gets here.'

His smile was unnerving the older man, and he made sure to keep his distance from his partner. There was something happening here, something he felt he wasn't part of. He didn't like it. *I'm the fucking managing director, for Christ's sake. I should be privy to everything.*

'Do you think we need to talk to HP about this one? Seeing as she's the last one and all,' Carl offered.

Gerard eyed the IT engineer through squinting eyes. *What's he up to?* 'That's a good idea,' he replied slowly. 'But, what do we do with her? She's not dead yet.'

'Let's tie her up. Maybe The Master needs the last one still alive.'

'OK then. How do you want to go about it?' Gerard asked. He wasn't liking the look on the younger man's face. He'd lied when he said he hadn't been talking to anyone when he came in. *I could smell the filth of The Master,* Gerard thought.

'We should use the power cables and the plastic ties. No one will be able to get out of them binds.'

'You do it, then. I want to check the download progress.'

Carl smiled, and a strange chill rose through Gerard's back, bringing his body out in a rash of goosebumps.

Both men circled around Tasha's unconscious body, neither wanting to turn their back on the other. Gerard knew something had changed between them, and he was determined not to be the next body hanging in the server rack.

Still facing him, Carl bent and picked up Tasha's body. She was flopping about, but nowhere near as much as the other bodies. There was still an abundance of life in her. The younger man struggled getting her onto the stool that was set up for access to the servers.

'Throw me those cables, the ones behind you,' Carl gasped, pointing to the small rack behind him. Gerard turned to look, then snapped is head back double-speed when he realised he'd been duped into looking away.

'These ones?' he asked, holding a small box that was filled with black power cables.

Carl winked.

Gerard threw it.

Carl caught it.

He held the box in his hands as if he was weighing it. 'These should hold her until we can contact HP. We're so close, I can almost taste it.'

'Me too,' Gerard replied, still not trusting the younger man.

'What's that showing now?' Carl asked as he began to secure the young woman to the stool, using the plastic clip-ties to strap her hands and feet to the metal chassis.

Gerard braved a quick look at the screen. 'It's gone up to ninety-four,' he said.

'Right then. That should do it; she's not going anywhere soon,' Carl announced as he pulled on the binds holding Tasha. 'So, lets send a message and see how HP wants us to do this.' Carl walked over to the screen where Gerard was standing, and the old man jumped out of his way.

'What's the matter with you all of a sudden?' Carl laughed as Gerard nearly fell over himself to get out of his way.

The old man shrugged. 'Nothing,' he lied.

'Send the message then,' Carl replied, pointing to the screen. 'You're the one with the contacts. Send the message and we can finally get The Master down here. Maybe he'll grow you a new dick.'

'Huh?' Gerard asked. He then looked at the spreading stain on the front of his trousers and laughed a little. 'I never thought about that. I wonder if he can. I wouldn't mind it back.' He grinned as a fantasy flittered around his head. 'A mechanical one.'

'Well, the original is still over there,' Carl said, pointing to the purple mound of rotting meat languishing in the corner.

Gerard ignored him as he typed into the computer, finally clicking on the SEND button.

'The message is sent. What do we do now?'

'Now,' Carl said, folding his arms and sitting on the floor with his back to the wall. 'We wait.'

30.

'YOU DON'T NEED to do this! Carl, you know me! We've worked together for years.' Tasha was awake now. The cold of the server room and the stink of the bodies hanging in the server rack had roused her from a disturbing sleep where she was in a theme park in America, having a bizarre conversation with a huge bronze statue of a mouse. The mouse was telling her she was part of a bigger picture and she had to get back to help usher in a new regime.

She didn't want to leave the theme park, she had loved holidays like this, but it hadn't been her decision to make.

Slowly, pain overrode the euphoric feeling of watching families enjoying themselves as they walked past. The throb of her nose and the sting of her gouged face replaced the feel of the hot sun on her skin. The stink of decaying flesh and shit dissolved the gorgeous smell of hot buttered popcorn in the air.

When she opened her eyes and saw the two blood soaked maniacs sitting on either side of her, she knew where she really was.

Server Room One.

'Please, Carl, let me go. I won't tell anyone what you're doing here. It's got nothing to do with me.'

'Well, it kind of has now. Don't you think?' Gerard replied.

She dragged her face away from her friend and looked into the face of evil incarnate. Gerard Medley, the managing director of the company, was sitting next to her. His thinning hair was standing on end, and the colour of his skin made him look like he'd been dead himself for a long time now. The black rings around his eyes gave him a sinister edge, and the blood all over his clothes looked to be mostly his own, was spreading up from the more condensed area at his crotch.

'Mr Medley, please let me go. I have a family. They'll be worried sick about me,' she panted. Panic was radiating in her chest, affecting her ability to speak. Her eyes flicked from the two madmen to the butchery that had occurred in the server rack. Jodi was in there. There was a cable trailing from her eye socket into the server. Then there was Leanne; she had always liked Leanne. All the others she only kind of knew. The holes where their eyes should have been were fitted with network cables. The cables were covered in gore and clumps of flesh.

The whole thing was a nightmare of epic proportions.

She closed her eyes and wished herself back into the theme park of her dream. But she knew that was folly. *Even the fucking mouse knew I couldn't stay there,* she thought.

'You—you're going to add me to that rack, aren't you?' she stuttered. She was beginning to lose all the feeling in her hands where they had been tied, overly tight, to the stool she was sat on.

Medley smiled at her. It was a hideous sneer, and she found she couldn't look at it for long. Carl's grin wasn't much better. He looked like he'd recently gone a few rounds with a heavyweight boxer and lost every single one of them. She looked at the last man on the rack, the one wearing the security guard uniform, and recognised him as the one who must have inflicted the beating.

'Yes, young lady, we are. You should be honoured. You're the last one we need to add. You'll be the one to complete the download—'

'To The Master?' she interrupted Gerard's little speech.

She watched as the two men swapped a look.

'Yeah, The Master. I know you know about him, but it must be you who ushers in the—'

'New regime?' she interrupted again.

'Yeah,' Carl replied, sitting back against the wall.

'You don't need to do it. This is all a mass hallucination. I think we've been spiked with some bad shit or something. We could all just walk away from this, go home, pretend nothing happened.' Her speech was breathy and rushed. She knew that both of these men were far too involved to be able to get away with anything, but if she could stall them long enough, just enough time for her to make an escape … They both looked exhausted, tired, and weary.

Right then, she knew she would be able to take them both in a straight fight. She didn't want to die here, not in a fucking server room. She'd never really had many ambitions in life, but dying in a stinking, cold room filled with murder and madness fuelled by two lunatics who were holding her prisoner hadn't been one of them.

A tear formed in her eye.

~~~~~

The old man was looking cagey. He looked like he had a plan, one that didn't include him. *Or maybe it does.* Carl knew if he allowed this plan to come to fruition, *he* would never see the ascension of The Master. *That old bastard will slit my throat and fuck the wound with whatever he has left between his legs, without a moment's hesitation,* he thought.

His eyes were scanning the room for the trusty screwdriver he'd used on the victims in the server rack. It was on the floor, next to Tasha's stool. His eyes focused on it. He was willing it to hide from the old man's scrutiny, or to fly into his hands, when the server pinged from behind him.

Carl didn't move. The only part that gave away the fact he wasn't a statue was his eyes. They flicked from the screwdriver, to Tasha, then to Gerard.

Both of them were looking at him.

Slowly, he turned from their intense glares and looked at the screen.

It was a reply from HP.

The screen flashed white with black text in the centre.

He read the message.

His heart dropped to the pit of his stomach. He felt like he needed to go to the toilet.

He needed to hide the message from the others.

He just hoped that they hadn't been able to read it from where they were.

~~~~~

The ping from the server was louder than it should have been, and it snapped Gerard out of the haze he'd been falling into. He'd been daydreaming of a mechanical penis extension The Master was going to gift him. It would be able to flex into hundreds of different positions, and it came with different appendages he could mount on it.

It made him think about all the delicious things that he would be able to do to Tasha's dead body with his brand-new and improved robo-cock.

The ping brought him back to reality. The reality that The Master was almost here. The ping also informed him there had been a reply from HP regarding how he wanted the last sacrifice—or indeed offering—to be made.

He looked at Carl. Their eyes locked for a moment.

He then flicked his away from his partner to see the white screen containing the black text of the reply.

He read it.

Then Carl stepped in the way, blocking his view.

But he had read, and understood, every single word.

~~~~

Tasha didn't know what to expect. The two madmen on either side of her looked to be having a Mexican standoff. In her addled and highly stressed mind, it reminded her of the ending of a film she had watched when she was a little girl. Three cowboys, all of them facing each other, all of them with their fingers twitching over the butts of their guns.

I'm going to die here, she thought. *But before I do, I think these two are going to kill each other.*

The ping from the server distracted her thoughts, and she looked at Carl. She could read the madness in his eyes. As he moved away from her, she flicked her gaze towards the screen.

Carl was sat in the way.

Tasha was able to shift her head a little, allowing her to get a better look at the screen. It was only a fleeting glance, but it gave her more than enough time to read what it said before Carl moved back in the way, before he closed the screen down.

How had the message been for me? she thought.

~~~~

HP needs me to kill Carl and the girl. That's easily done, Gerard thought. *But he's seen the message. The impudent little bastard, reading messages that are for my eyes only.*

The old man looked around the room before his eyes fixated on the discarded screwdriver on the floor. It was covered in drying human goo, right next to Tasha's chair.

~~~~~

Why did they have to see that? Carl thought as he hurriedly clicked on the button, turning the screen off. *I knew Gerard was planning something. That's why he wanted me to go and get the next body. I bet he fucking sent that security guard after me. Well, not on my watch, buddy ...*

With effort he didn't think he had, he turned and sprang forth towards the screwdriver on the floor next to Tasha.

At the exact same time, Gerard screamed and launched himself at the exact same tool.

Both men met with a clash of heads at the foot of Tasha's stool. As they ricocheted off each other, they banged into her.

The stool began to rock.

It then began to tip.

Tasha, with her eyes wide open, seeing everything that was about to happen, squirmed in the seat, taking it over its tipping point, and she fell to the floor with a crash.

~~~~~

All three of them lay unmoving on the dirty metal floor of the server room.

D E McCluskey

31.

TASHA WAS STILL awake. She had fallen on her side, but the worst she'd endured was a blow to the head. Her eyesight was a little fuzzy, and she knew she would have the mother of all headaches tomorrow—*if there even is a tomorrow*—but other than that, she was fine.

She was still attached to the stool. The plastic clip-ties hadn't given way in the fall. The more she wriggled, the tighter they became.

A small moaning alerted her to one of the others waking up. From her position on the floor, she couldn't tell who it was. If she hadn't seen the madness in Carl's eyes, she would have wished it was him; but then, if it was Gerard, she thought that, out of the two of them, he would be the easiest to take down.

She closed her eyes and waited for one of them to make their move.

~~~~

Gerard opened one eye. It hurt him just to do that.

He had a thought of closing it again, wriggling into a comfortable position on the cold metal-tiled floor, and falling back asleep. Maybe never ever waking up again. *How good would that be?* he asked himself, his thought strangely lucid through the agonising throb of his crotch and the dull ache of his head.

His one open eye scanned the room, familiarising himself with where he was, and what was needed to do. The message from HP had been for him, and his eyes only. He had been given a mission, and he was damned sure he was going to carry it out.

As he lifted his head, a small moan escaped him before he could do anything about it. *Fuck,* he thought. *I didn't want Carl to know I was awake.*

The girl was on the floor; her eyes were closed, and she looked either asleep or dead. Either way, it didn't matter, as he was going to address that problem a little later. Right now, he had a whole different problem to sort.

His former partner, Carl Riggs.

Slowly, holding his breath—more to stop him from vomiting or passing out from the pain, but also to curb any more involuntary noises—he reached out to grab the screwdriver.

~~~~

Carl was wide awake. He didn't want to be, but he was. He was lying on his back, contemplating life, and a lot of death. He thought about his kids, about what they would be doing right now, as he lay on a cold floor in a murder room contemplating bringing home a Master he knew absolutely nothing about. All he knew was it was something he was compelled to do. *Maybe brainwashed,* he thought. *I'd give anything to be with the boys right now. Just chilling. Amy making the dinner while they played silly video games or built a fort out of cardboard boxes and pillows.* He stopped that train of thought for a moment. *I've* never *built a fort out of cardboard boxes and pillows with the boys. Shit, I hardly even played with them at all as they grew up.* This thought made him sadder than anything he'd done tonight.

Tonight, he was bringing forth a new order to the world. He was building a new church. *I can't even build a fort.*

Then he heard the groan.

Gerard was waking up. *Shit, will that man not just fucking die?*

As he heard him moving, he moved his head a little, remembering the screwdriver. It was within his reach. All he needed to do was reach out and grab it, then he could kill the old bastard, just like the message from HP instructed him to.

The decrepit, but seemingly indestructible old man reached out a shaking hand towards the weapon, but Carl was faster.

He grabbed it by the sticky handle.

His movement surprised the old man, and he moved his hand away. Carl was surprisingly fast, faster than he would have thought. He lifted the screwdriver up before bringing it down again, right through the centre of the old man's veiny hand.

Gerard screamed as the cold metal passed through his flesh, snapping tendons, and ruining the cartilage within.

'Got you, you fucking treacherous old bastard,' Carl hissed over the old man's lamenting at his new wound. 'HP told me you'd do this,' he laughed. 'Not on my watch, you perverted old scumbag.'

Carl got to his feet and kicked Gerard, catching him square on the jaw. The old man's head was thrown backwards, like a football as it made the back of the net bulge. It banged hard on the metal tiles.

He then leaned in toward Tasha who was still tied to the chair. She flinched at his proximity. 'It's OK,' he whispered. 'I'm going to kill him now. He's the last one that The Master needs. HP told me.'

As he cut Tasha's bonds, she fell from the chair and rolled away from her captor.

'It's OK, Tasha. It's OK. I'm going to kill him and hang him in the server, then we're done. We can go. We can leave this place and never come back. We'll be free as birds. We can go together if you want.'

'Carl, you can't kill him. Don't do it. You don't know what it's going to do to the world. From what little The Master has shown himself to me, the future looks like a bleak place. Not somewhere I would want to live.'

'I have to. I've come so far. Look.' He pointed at the bodies hanging in the server cabinet. 'I've killed all of these for The Master. It's gone too far for me to go without closure. I killed my wife, Tasha. I killed her, alongside her boyfriend.'

'What about your boys?' Tasha asked, her eyes wide.

'They're safe. They're with my mum,' he replied, hanging his head low.

'Do you think they'll be safe when The Master returns? Do you think any of us will be?'

Carl didn't answer.

'Don't do it. We can go to the police. We can say that he did all of this. Tell them he tried to kill us, but we escaped.' Tasha was standing up, rubbing her wrists, flexing her fingers. 'We overpowered him, tied him up, and ran to the police. They'll go to his home and find his wife and the whore you said was there.'

Carl was nodding small nods as Tasha spoke more and more sense. 'What about Amy? And her bloke?'

'We can say he killed them too. Or we can use the portal to bring them back here. Come on, Carl, you know we can't go ahead with this.'

He looked at the multiple dead bodies hanging in the cabinet. His gaze then drifted over to the powered-off computer screen. He flicked it back on. The readout was now showing ninety-six percent. Next, he took in the sight of the old man lying on the floor, fresh blood pouring from his hand and from his thickening lips. *I only need to put him in, and it's all done,* he thought.

As if someone could read his thoughts, the room went dark. The stink of old, dirty water and death were rife again. He looked at Tasha saw that she was seeing all of this too. *I'm not mad; and Gerard, he's not either. Well, either that or we* all *are.*

'What is this delay? Did you not receive your orders?' the voice asked from all around them.

'We … we did,' Carl answered, shooting a look to Tasha, who was now hugging the wall, looking like she was trying to escape the room.

'THEN FINISH IT …' the voice boomed as the smell dissipated, and the room lightened again.

Without looking at Tasha, Carl stepped up to the old man, who was writhing on the floor. He picked up the fire extinguisher and slammed it into his head.

Without another sound, Gerard flopped to the floor. All the fight in the old bastard disappeared as he succumbed to the blow.

Carl, still holding the makeshift weapon, dropped his arms. A thought occurred, and he remembered how wily this old man was, how much pain and torture he had taken, yet still managed to bounce back. He raised the extinguisher again.

'Carl, no,' Tasha whispered.

Ignoring her, he brought the extinguisher down one more time onto the old man's head. *There's no way he's survived that,* he thought with a smile. He then picked the old man up. 'Give me a hand,' he demanded the frightened woman with her back to the wall. She shook her head. 'Please,' he asked, but still she refused. 'Pretty fucking please!'

All she did was continue looking for the door out of this silly place.

He tutted and continued the struggle, lifting Gerard's limp body onto the rail of the dead.

'Did you kill them all?' Tasha asked; her voice was low, almost as if she didn't want anyone else to hear the question.

Carl looked over his shoulder as he wrapped a loop of wire around the old man's neck. 'Some of them. The old man did a few too.'

'How did you know to ... you know, put the cable through their eyes?'

He shrugged as his attention returned to the job at hand. 'I don't know. It was just an assumption. Something that occurred to me.'

'Was there any configuration that you needed to do, you know, for it to work?'

Carl shook his head. 'Nope. It was just plug and play. I plugged Jodi in, and away the download went,' he chuckled.

'And the cable fit?'

'Yeah. Once the eye is popped, there's something inside the socket that's compatible with the clip.'

Tasha stepped forwards once Gerard's body had been secured within the cabinet. Her head cocked to the side as she watched him pick up the filthy screwdriver.

'I just stick this in here,' he said, forcing the long blade into the old man's eye. 'A little bit of force and the eyeball pops, just like ... this!'

Tasha winced as the blade cut into the soft ball residing within Gerard's eye socket. There was indeed a popping noise, that was not at all unpleasant, and a clear fluid began to run as he forced the long blade in a little further.

'There's something that'll cause you a little bit of ...' With one final push, he sunk the screwdriver deeper into the socket. 'There you go.' More of the clear liquid, this time mixed with what was obvious to Tasha, as blood, began to flow from the hole. 'All you need to do now is give it a little bit of a ...' He began to round the hole out, scooping what was left of Gerard's organic matter. '...wiggle, and pretty much, you're good to go.'

He put the screwdriver down on the table, wiped his sticky hands on his trousers, and picked up the network cable next to it. 'It just goes in here.' He pushed the network cable in, having a little trouble with it bending, as it met some resistance. Then they both heard the familiar click of the clip setting itself in place. 'And he's all ready to be networked. You'll see that the security guard there has already been prepped, so all I have to do it stick this end in here.'

The other end of the cable was pushed into the big man's empty eye socket until the snap happened again. 'We've now networked Gerard. The dirty old bastard would have loved that experience. He was a fucking loathsome bast—'

'He's still alive,' Tasha yelped, pointing towards the cabinet, where the body of the managing director had begun to shake.

Carl jumped at this announcement, thinking the old man had somehow survived the beating, and the gouging. He smiled as he saw what she was referring to.

The bodies of Gerard and the security guard were shaking. Tremors ripped through both bodies as the flow of information passed between them. 'That's what I thought when I saw that for the first time. There's no way that old goat could have survived any of that, not even him. For some reason, this happens when they become connected. It's nothing to worry about.'

Tasha stepped closer; she didn't think she really wanted to, but her morbid curiosity compelled her. She stared into the expressionless face of Mr Medley as it twitched and flickered.

'Let's check the download. It's got to be almost complete now,' Carl shouted louder than he was expecting, but the excitement churning around within him was building. The Master would be here any moment. It was a momentous occasion. It was why they had been working so hard for the last two days.

In his excitement to log on to the sever, he got his password wrong three times. He knew one more wrong attempt would lock him out. He almost laughed at that scenario. *Can you imagine The Master being delayed because I had to go and unlock my own account?*

He took a deep breath, flexed his fingers, and slowly typed his password into the keyboard.

As he pressed the RETURN button, he held his breath and closed his eyes.

When he had built up the courage to open them again and saw the desktop of his profile and allowed himself to exhale.

He clicked on the DOWNLOAD icon on the toolbar and waited a seemingly endless second or two for the black command prompt box to reappear.

Download resumed ...
MASTER V2.1
PROGRESS 99% ....

'Oh, for fucks sake,' he shouted.

~~~~

Tasha's attention had been on the old man's face. She had only ever met this man once or twice in her past life—that was how she was beginning to think of yesterday was … her past life.

What she knew of him, he wasn't the nicest man in the world. He could be nasty, petty, and lecherous, all at the same time. In the few lunch times where she had met up—mostly accidentally—with Leanne, she'd mentioned wandering hands and lewd requests made in jest but had said there was more than that on the underneath of what he called his *games*.

She was glad he was dead.

Dead and gone.

All in service of The Master!

She turned and saw Carl with his back to her, typing into the keyboard of the server. From her view, she could tell he was getting frustrated at whatever he was trying to do. *Logging on,* she assumed.

She picked up the long-handled screwdriver that had not long ago been buried deep in the head of the loathsome old man hanging in the server cabinet. She held it for a moment, enjoying the feel, and the weight of it in her hand. She especially liked the stickiness and slick feeling of the gore adorning the handle.

The room darkened, and her own personal smell reappeared. She'd come to enjoy that sweet aroma of decay and depravity.

'Bring The Master home, Tasha,' the voice whispered. Somehow, she knew it was only talking to her.

'I will, Master,' she replied.

'Oh, for fuck's sake,' Carl shouted, still looking at the screen.

Tasha took a moment to look at the readout.

Ninety-nine percent, she thought with a grin. *That's about right.*

Gripping the screwdriver in her hand, she brought it up over her head, then hesitated.

Memories flashed through her head.

Her first day in the office. Carl had been the only one who had spoken to her, welcoming her to the team. The time when her boyfriend, the only one she'd ever had, broke up with her. It was Carl who took her out to the canteen and bought her a cup of tea and a chocolate bar. When her mother died, he was the only one from the whole department who came to the funeral.

Her hand faltered.

Then more visions flashed through her head.

A thick tentacle smashing against the window of her living room. Putrid water seeping through cracks in the windows of their office. Deformed, hideous fish eating the rotting flesh of a multitude of dead bodies trapped beneath the dank waves.

The smell of death enveloped her.

She breathed deep then smiled as the blade of the screwdriver drove down, deep into the back of Carl's neck.

A strange sound uttered from him. Tasha thought it sounded like a goose or maybe a duck, but she was leaning more towards a honk rather than a quack.

Carl's body buckled, and he fell, dragging the screwdriver out of her hand as it was lodged in the flesh and muscle at the nape of his neck. He crumpled to the floor. Shaky hands reached out behind him, grabbing at the protruding tool, the one he couldn't quite reach, but that didn't stop him from trying.

The blood began to flow.

'You have to stem the bleeding,' the voice spoke. It sounded different this time. Normally, it sounded as if she were in the cinema, surrounded by it, but now it was localised.

It was coming from behind her.

She looked at the server screen and saw the download was still stalled at ninety-nine percent.

As Carl had allowed her to watch him connecting Gerard to the network, she knew exactly what to do, she was a quick study. There was some grizzly, wet work to be done, but once it was complete, then she would be at one—

'With The Master,' she said aloud. Her voice sounded strange, even to her.

'Not quite ...' the voice from behind her croaked.

She turned on her heel, recognising the whisper. It wasn't HP, or whoever it was who had been instructing her since she clicked on that infernal icon on Gerard's laptop, and it wasn't The Master, as he was still not downloaded.

It was Gerard.

The old man was stood before her. Over one eye was a deep purple bruise in the shape of the base of fire extinguisher. The other eye had fresh dark blood pouring from it, where an ethernet cable hung limply. Thick fluids that might have been pus dripped down the plastic sheathing, trickling down his ruined face. His teeth were strikingly white in contrast to the dark blood covering the lower half of his features. The welt of red around his neck also stood stark against how pale the rest of his skin was.

This man should have been dead, but somehow, he wasn't.

'Hello, pretty,' he croaked, flashing her a bloodied smile.

Tasha didn't feel the hard drive crash into her head. She didn't experience the sensation of the metal rectangle slicing through her skin and splitting her skull.

She never noticed any of these things as three large shards of bone detached themselves from her bashed cranium and imbedded themselves directly into her brain.

These three shards, each of them about the same length as her little fingernail, killed her instantly. She was dead before her lifeless corpse hit the floor, falling on top of Carl.

Gerard, or what was left of him, leaned over the tangled heap of bodies on the floor and grinned. 'Either of you want to help an old man out here?' he laughed. 'Fair enough,' he cackled when there was no answer and began to pull Tasha towards the server cabinet. 'Sometimes if you want something done right, you need to do it yourself.'

32.

THE NEXT HALF hour was filled with him struggling to attach the remaining two sacrifices to the network. This was not an easy mission, as each of them was bigger than he was, and he only had one working eye to see with.

When he had gouged out Carl's eyes and attached the cables between him and Tasha, he allowed himself a moment of reflection, panting and throbbing but ultimately feeling good about himself, despite him only having one eye, a cracked skull, and no penis.

He eyed the full rack of bodies hanging next to each other, all of them doing their bit towards the common good.

'We did it, Brenda,' he whispered into the dark room. 'We actually, only went and did it.'

As the two new members of the club began to vibrate, Gerard grinned and glanced at the small black box on the screen.

Download completed ...
MASTER V2.1 Installing...

As the little hourglass on the screen began to spin, indicating the software was beginning to install, the room began to brighten.

All of the bodies in the rack began to shiver and shake. It was more than a little daunting to see all the lifeless corpses suddenly dancing. But it was also intoxicating, arousing.

He laughed and began to clap along with their dance, to a silent rhythm only he was privy to.

The holes where their eyes had once been began to glow. A white radiance spilled from them, pouring like waves lapping against the sand of a beautiful, never ending beach. Only it wasn't water; it looked like mist.

The smoky substance oozed down the sacrificed bodies and began to pool about their dangling feet.

Gerard tore his fixated gaze from what was happening to look at the screen. He was a little dismayed to see that it, too, was glowing white. The same substance flowing from the bodies was seeping from the edges of the computer screen. It was also billowing from the server itself. Every opening in the machine spewed forth the thick white mist. It rolled down the edges of the cabinet, towards the metal tiled floor, where it merged with the substance expelled from the dancing dead.

Gerard began to back away. With his one good eye, he scanned the room. He'd forgotten where the door was and was now panicking, longing for a quick getaway. The mist was spreading along the floor, heading towards him. It was a rolling, tumultuous cloud. Faster and faster, it filled up the space.

It was billowing around the knees of the bodies and was almost halfway up the server rack when Gerard decided the light in the room, and everything else happening was just too much for him and he needed to get out as soon as he could.

For some reason he couldn't fathom, he felt the need to get as far away from the rolling cloud of mist. He felt—no, he knew—that if that smog touched him, it would consume him. Either physically or mentally—*or probably both.*

He wasn't quite ready for either, just yet.

Scrabbling for the door, his blood-slimed hands couldn't grip the handle for him to gain any purchase on it and open the door to his freedom.

The smoke was nearly upon him, he could see it grasping, reaching, clawing at his feet. He could feel the hunger within it. It was almost a physical thing. It was also the ugliest thing he had ever thought in his whole, ugly, perverted life.

He made a final concerted effort, using both hands, and found the grip he needed. The handle turned, and the door opened into the corridor.

Gerard fell out of Server Room One.

If there had been any witnesses to his emergence, he might have looked like a strange animal being born into a new world, covered in blood, scared, and disorientated.

He backed away from the door, banging into the wall behind him, leaving a red stain roughly in the shape of a human, before pushing himself away, staggering off in the direction of the reception.

The white mist that rolled out of the server room followed him as it rapidly filled the area outside the door.

The churning, rolling death was spreading rapidly from the server room, filling up the whole of the corridor, consuming the floors, the ceilings, the walls. It lingered for a moment at it caressed the bloody imprint Gerard had left.

The unfeasibly bright light illuminated the misty substance as it continued on its course of destruction through the corridor. Its increasing mass spewed from the room as the light accompanying it grew brighter.

Gerard was having trouble running. His legs were not working as they should. Every step was agony with his decapitated groin, and the dizziness where his head had been cracked with the extinguisher made it difficult to stay on his feet. The worst part was his depth perception confusion from the loss of his eye. This made him crash into almost every obstacle he encountered. He wished he'd taken the stupid cable out of his eye socket before he ran, as it whipped his already ruined face with every stumble.

He stopped for a moment, bending over to catch his breath. He leaned against the wall, putting his hands on his hips, and breathed deeply. From the corner of his eye, he saw the mist following him around the corner, it was like a sentient animal, stalking him, chasing him, ready to eat him.

He ran towards the main entrance doors and pulled on them.

They were locked.

He searched his pockets for the small fob that would open them and allow him out into the lobby, away from the white death that was coming for him. The fob wasn't there. He pulled the door again as he watched the smoke rolling down the corridor; it looked like it was moving faster now.

He closed his one eye and banged his head against the glass of the door. He looked up at the electro-magnets holding it shut and cursed them. *If I could just turn you off,* he thought.

Then he remembered the girls on the reception. Every time they let someone out, they pressed a button on the desk.

He eyed the rapidly approaching mist before running back to the reception desk. It was strewn with papers and sweet wrappers and all kinds of other stuff that didn't interest him. *All I want is that fucking button,* he shouted in his already throbbing head.

In a rage, he swept the contents of the desk onto the floor, leaving behind a long, red swathe in its wake. It had the desired effect, though, as the little button appeared after being buried under mounds of rubbish. He quickly pressed it and heard the doors click.

Rushing out from behind the desk, he grabbed the doors just in time, as the mist was now rolling into the reception.

He flung the doors wide and charged into the lobby.

They were on the third floor, so he briefly considered the lifts situated just outside the stairwell. The lights indicated the carriages were both on the ground floor. He looked back into the office and saw the mist seeping through the office doors. He didn't have the time for elevator luxury.

He would have to take the stairs.

Making his way as fast as his decapitated crotch would allow him, and his one eye could deem safe, he staggered down the stairwell. As he reached the second floor, he peered towards the doors. To his horror, the mist had penetrated down here too.

This made him move faster.

He did the same on the first floor and wasn't at all surprised to see the mist rolling out into the lobby there too.

With not much left in his tank, his heart pounding in complete rhythm with the throbbing of his penis-less crotch, he couldn't run any more. He longed to see The Master, to usher in the new beginning. *I fucking deserve it,* he laughed as he made his was down the last flight of stairs.

As he stood in the main lobby of the building—a large, airy, dark glass affair with minimalistic tastes—he watched as the thick fluffy white mist followed him from the stairs. It seeped from each of the elevator shafts and from the doors to rooms unknown that were left and right of him. It looked as if the whole building was on fire, only the smoke was a pure brilliant white.

It gathered in the reception, filling the large room. It crept along the floor until it touched the walls and the black marble main reception desk. It continued to creep until it stroked the far walls, where it began to climb. Within moments, the room was filled with the undulating mist, and the illumination he'd first witnessed glowing from the eyeholes of the dead, followed it.

The whole area was now too bright for his one eye to process, and he knew if he didn't get out of this lobby, out into the street, it would blind him. *Then I'd miss the return of The Master,* he thought as he hobbled towards the long wall of glass doors. As he shuffled, the mist instantly filled the location where he'd been standing, and the thought occurred that it had been waiting for him to leave before it could claim his location as its own.

He pushed on the two large glass doors, and they opened.

He stepped out into the night.

The air was freezing on his wet skin. His cracked head, his eye, and his crotch all screamed at him at the same time, but he relished the pain and the agony. He invited it on. *If this is what The Master demands, then it's what The Master gets,* he laughed.

The hour was late, or maybe it was early; as this part of the city was not one frequented after hours by many people, it was difficult to gauge. There were a few pubs and restaurants, but they only usually catered for the business trade and were normally empty by eight o'clock through the week. The sky was dark and cloudless; Gerard guessed this was the reason it felt so cold.

There were stabs of light coming from behind the huge buildings that his building was but one of. It seemed that the dawn of a new day was coming, maybe to herald the ushering in of a whole new era too.

He hobbled across the street to the small pond area where people would sit and eat their lunch on nice days and gaze over at the beautiful skyline of the city. Ignoring the view, he turned and regarded his building. He was shocked to see every window in the large structure was illuminated. The light was not the sickly yellow flickering lights of fluorescent tubes he would have expected to see, but the pure, brilliant white of the mist that had chased him all the way from the third floor.

There was movement in the light.

Strange shapes cavorted back and forth within the sick light. They didn't look human to him, not from this far away. Part of him was relieved he'd escaped the madness of that building, and part of him, a larger part, wanted to be back inside, dancing, and frolicking with the strange, odd, deformed creatures that now had dominion in his building. Their dances looked wrong, but in an erotic, seductive manner, and he longed to swell with them. He wanted to fuck them, he longed to be fucked *by* them. The sirens of a dead sea were calling to him. He would have sworn the strange beings were beckoning him to join them.

He was just about to take his first step back towards the illuminated building, the one that was swelling with the white mist, when something strange happened in the sky directly above the building.

'Master,' he croaked as his eyes were drawn to the phenomenon.

Clouds were forming in the still night. Bizarre clouds, the kind he'd only ever seen in films, or on documentaries. They were whipping themselves into a frenzy, whirling around and around like a cyclone. It seemed to him that a tornado was building up there, only he couldn't feel any of the effects of such a weather formation. There was no wind, nor were there any disruptions around him.

Stranger still, the formation seemed to be localising over his building. All the other structures around the city, that he could see from his vantage point—and there were many—did not seem to be affected by what was happening.

A light began to glow from the rooftop. This light was brighter than the one that had chased him through the stairwell. It was brighter than anything Gerard had ever seen. Maybe even brighter than the sun. He knew he should turn away—he was in danger of burning out his only remaining eye—but he couldn't. It was just too beautiful.

It shot upwards into the sky like a beam and joined with the weather formation swirling above. The mist began to rise too. It began to lift from the top of the building, slithering its way up the beam of light to merge with the churning clouds.

Gerard gawped open-mouthed at the events unfolding before him.

He was witnessing the second coming. The arrival of the Old Gods. They were back to claim their rightful place within this world, to bring about a new—or was it old?—way.

Their way!

He had been a key component in that return. It had ultimately been him who was responsible for it.

The glass door of the building next to his crashed open, and a bedraggled man fell from it. He was covered in blood, and his clothes were torn. He looked like he had lost an arm somewhere along the way, as his crimson shirt sleeve dripped and flapped as he fell. His whole body was saturated in a deep, dark red.

The man struggled to stay on his feet. He looked in a hurry to get away from his building. Gerard then noticed that the same light that was pulsing from his building began to throb from this one.

He rubbed his one eye and blinked before looking into the windows and seeing the exact same oddities cavorting up there. They were fucking in the same light as in his. The same urges to join them coursed through him.

The man who had fallen from the building joined him on the grass. There was no communication between them, just a sense of knowing, an understanding of what was occurring.

Gerard's eye flicked towards the man's ear, where he saw a length of Ethernet cable hanging from it, swinging with his every movement.

The same weather phenomenon and light emerged from this building, with the same mist clinging to it, climbing towards the clouds.

As the mist and the clouds joined, the area of the sky illuminated too. It became a small patch of daytime in the night sky.

The two weather formations merged.

Another building in the background began to glow, followed by another, and then another. Pretty soon, most of the buildings in the city skyline were glowing, and the sky had become a huge, tumultuous maelstrom.

More people joined them on the grass, all looking like him. Roughly the same age, men and women, all sporting torn clothing, all covered in blood, missing various parts of their anatomy, with cables hanging out of various orifices, natural or unnatural.

One thing united them.

They were all looking up. All of them had smiles on their faces.

Gerard had found his congregation.

The sky was a frenzy of whipping clouds, climbing mist, and strange illumination. Every building in the whole of the business district was glowing.

I guess The Master needed a lot more power than just I could offer, Gerard thought as his gaze passed back to the frenzied sky.

An opening occurred in the centre of the storm. It reminded him of something he'd seen on TV once. It was a live birth. The clouds parted like the woman's vagina had done prior to the miracle that was about to occur, only this was on a grander scale.

A much grander scale

The same excitement was oozing from his colleagues. Even though there had not been one word uttered among them, he could sense a collective exhilaration. They were all part of the same team, cogs in a machine that was bigger than them all, possibly the biggest thing in the whole world.

Something emerged from the gaping vagina in the sky.

It was inhuman, it was horrible and wrong. It was also *old*, magnificent, and all encompassing.

Gerard felt two things happen at the same time.

The smell from the server room was back, only it was different this time. It was thicker. It stunk like the worst sewer he could ever imagine, like too much death and decay, like shit and rotted flesh had been fucking, and given birth to something that was the very definition of the word hideous.

He liked it.

He felt a twinge between his legs. That twinge became an itch. He wanted desperately to scratch it but knew he couldn't; the pain would be just too much for him to bear.

Looking around, he could see the others were also noticing this. The first man who had fallen out of the building next to his was holding his missing arm. There was something growing inside his shirt sleeve. Whatever it was, it wriggled and squirmed, moving in no way like any arm should ever move.

That's when the itch in his trousers became a movement.

It was just a tiny flick at first, but it grew. Something was alive down between his legs.

He opened his trousers and looked. In between the mixture of drying and fresh blood he saw it. There *was* something growing where his penis used to be. It was only small, yet he could feel its power within him, growing, becoming dominant.

The squirming felt … delightful!

His sore and bloody fingers made hard work of the relatively easy task, of removing his trousers. But before long, they were down, around his ankles. It felt exhilarating to be bottomless in the outside, in front of his building, with other people there. The squirming from between his legs had gotten faster, sending butterflies up and down his stomach. He needed to get naked; whatever it was growing down there needed to be set free.

He looked around him; everyone else who had lost appendages were all doing the same as him. Where they had once had arms, legs, eyes, other parts, they were all growing tentacles, and getting naked.

Long, thick, pink flexible growths were emerging from their bodies. He could feel the one between his legs stretching, expanding.

He noticed he was now able to see out of both his eyes too. Only, his new eye was showing him things that should have been impossible. He was seeing things that were happening behind him. That was when he realised a tentacle was growing from his eye socket, with an eyeball attached to the end of it.

With both hands, he reached down between his legs and caught the thrashing tail, attempting to control it. Once it was in his grip, he looked up to the gaping vagina in the sky and the unholy abomination spewing from it.

Great, vile legs, or they might have been skeletal fingers, were protruding from the opening. They thrashed obscenely as they forced their way through the birthing canal of whatever demon, or dimension it had been imprisoned in.

'GET ON YOUR KNEES,' a voice boomed.

Gerard couldn't tell if it was coming from the heavens or if it had been implanted into his brain, but at that moment, he didn't care. He just followed the instruction blindly.

Without even thinking, he dropped to his knees, averting his eyes from the unholy sacrilege occurring above him.

'CLOSE YOUR EYES … YOU ARE NOW THE SCUM OF THE OLD GODS, AND YOU WILL BE TREATED ACCORDINGLY!'

There had been many times in Gerard's life when he'd played the subservient to another's dominatrix, so he was used to being talked to in this manner, when it was a sex thing.

Before he closed his eyes, the eyeball on the end of the tentacle looked around him. He watched as the others, all the people like him, the scum of the Gods, did the same. He guessed they had all received the same email and also guessed the server rooms of their companies were lined with ex-employees, all of them dead and wired into their network in some manner.

All of them turned off and turned on again.

A smile creased his face, and he cowed his eyes, ready to take his reward for his part in the new dawn.

'YOU ARE ALL THE SLAVES OF THE OLD GODS. I AM YOUR ONE TRUE MASTER,' the voice continued to boom. 'YOU HAVE ALL SERVED ME WELL, BUT YOUR USEFULNESS IS AT AN END. RISE AND MEET YOUR GODS …'

Gerard didn't know what the voice was talking about. He'd been a good servant. He'd done everything he'd been asked to do, including murdering his wife, his friends, his colleagues. Now, to be told his usefulness was at an end, felt like a slap in the face.

He has given me a new penis, a new eye, and now tells me my usefulness is over. How can this be?

The old man stood, his trousers were still around his ankles and the tentacle between his legs was thrashing angrily. He wanted to shout, to scream his admonition, to voice his ire. As he opened his mouth to yell, something caught his attention. His flexible eyeball swivelled towards the building he'd emerged from not ten minutes prior.

The ungodly light emitting from the building was almost blinding him. He shielded his face from the glare and brought his tentacled eye back to rest in the shade his hand brought. No matter how much shade he offered, he couldn't block the light issuing from the buildings all around him.

The thing that had caught his eye was hiding within the glare of the light. It was just a silhouette, a shadow, but something about it frightened him. He pondered, just for a moment, about how after all he'd seen, all he'd done over the last day or two, something as innocuous as a shadow could scare him like this one did.

The outline, as that was all he could make out, was long, but something told him this wasn't just one being. It was made up of a number of different shadows. It wasn't a singularity.

He thought of all the obscene things writhing in the brilliant light, and he felt his tentacle twinge and grow.

They, or was it an it, was getting closer.

Rise and meet your Gods? he questioned. *Are these my Gods?* He had hoped there would be just one God. When he'd first seen the vicious probes hanging from the clouds, he'd had the idea there *was* just one God, and that was it being born into this world. But now, it appeared there was more than one.

There were indeed *Gods.*

He watched as the shadows approached. They hadn't only come forth from his building but were coming from all the buildings, everywhere. Everyone, all his peers on the grass verge, wore the same expression as he did. Their eyes were wide, their jaws slack.

They have been fed the same lies as me.

The shadows continued to advance. As they got closer, the definition became sharper. Details opened up to him. He could now tell that the shadows were human. *Or maybe had once been human,* he added as they moved closer. The way they shuffled told him they were something other, more than human, but he didn't want to dwell on this thought.

He began to step backwards. He wanted to get away. Far away. But he knew this was all of his own doing. He'd done his part, more than his part, in bringing this forth.

This abomination seemed unfair to him.

I want to be a God!

'DO NOT MOVE. YOU WILL KNOW IF YOU ARE TO BE SPARED. THE NEW AGE IS UPON YOU. THIS IS THE NEW REGIME!'

The shadows were now out of the glare of the buildings, and Gerard finally saw that they were indeed human. They had been human, either this morning, or yesterday at the earliest.

Leanne was in the forefront. She was followed by the girl from IT, the first one they'd done. Then came the big security guard. They were all shuffling purposefully towards him.

The holes where their eyes had been, were glowing with the same intense white that was emitting from the buildings. Gerard could see the white mist that had scared him so much, pouring from the holes.

The pain that shot up his arm was agonising. It made him dizzy, so woozy that he staggered backwards, clutching the appendage. No one, not one of his new colleagues on the lawn stopped to help him. None of them even looked at him; they were all trapped in their own personal Hell.

His chest was thrashing, and his breath was short, shallow. Sweat had built on his top lip, and it itched like a bastard.

The pain in his arm shifted; it was now in his chest. His eyes blurred as he fell back onto the grass.

The only saving grace from falling was that he could no longer see the reanimated faces of the people he'd killed, sacrificed, and hung in the server room. All he could see now were the lights of the tall buildings feeding into the storm above, the storm that looked like a vagina. The one that was giving birth to the twitching, thrashing fingers.

A shadow blocked out the light. He was momentarily thankful for the reprieve from the glare, until his eye on the tentacle shifted to see what, or who, it was shading him.

249

The face was a familiar one.

In fact, there were two of them, they were merged into one nightmarish vision of a Hell he would no longer be part of.

He knew both faces.

They had conspired to kill him before he'd killed them.

The being that was now the amalgamation of Tasha and Carl looked down at him as he lay on the grass. The strange light of this strange night was bathing him, offering him zero comfort. The mist pouring from their four, ruined eyes was reaching for him. It was beckoning him, calling him in, ordering him to embrace it.

'Hello, Gerard,' Tasha's side of the face said, her voice was different. It sounded like a thousand people all speaking at the same time.

'Remember us?' Carl's side asked, the grin on his half of the dead face stretching almost over to Tasha's side.

The scream building up in Gerard's sore throat would have been ear-splitting if the heart attack that had been bubbling just below the surface hadn't swallowed it up.

His arm spasmed and his jaw locked as his heart finally gave up on him. The last thing he, the Managing Director and CEO of Tunbridge Ltd, saw before the darkness enveloped him, collected him, was the walking dead. It was all the people of this once great city. They were now all hideous parodies of humanity. They were merged, halved, diced. Their flesh sluiced from their bodies; tentacles were there shouldn't be tentacles protruded from their obscene bodies. The white light and the mist was pouring from various holes. It gripping and tore at the others around him, the ones who had made it out of their buildings, the ones who should have been worthy, just like he was.

He was there to witness the dawn of this new age.

The last thing he felt were strong hands gripping him; that was before the ripping began.

Then as the darkness came to take him, and he felt there might have been a reprieve from these horrors, there were *things* in that darkness too. Powerful things. He could hear a laugh, coming from far away.

It sounded like HP.

~~~~

The new age Gerard Medley had facilitated arrived.

The great abomination from the sky descended. As its unearthly skeletal fingers wrapped themselves around the famous landmarks of the old city, time had run its course for humanity.

It had met its doom.

HE was back to usher in a new order to this world's chaos.

The Master had returned!

D E McCluskey

Reboot: A Cosmic Horror

Author's Notes

I WORKED IN IT for the best part of twenty-five years; actually, scrap that, it was not the *best part* of twenty-five years. It was actually the most infuriating, boring, degrading, mind-numbing part of twenty-five years.

Now, don't get me wrong, there are people out there who absolutely love IT, and they enjoy their careers within their chosen field, and I say *do what you love,* but it's not, and never will be, for me. I really did enjoy the people I worked with, and I loved the craic of working within a busy office, but I resented the structured of it all. Be in for nine, and you can't go home till five. Why have you been in the toilet for ten minutes? What do you mean you're sick? We're short staffed, you need to come in …

NOPE, NOPE, NOPE, NOPE, NOPE! That's not for me.

I always tried my best to find something alternative to do. Something to alleviate the mind-numbing boring monotony of it all.

So, because of my loathing for my job, my mind began to wander. Wild and wonderful scenarios would form in my head; weird stories would take shape in the foggy boredom of fixing emails for angry, ignorant, rude bellends who wanted to know why their phone wouldn't get emails while they were on holiday in the Balearics with their family!

Get a life … dickwads!

Anyway, this story is a bit of a homage to that life.

People who live for their work and are ignorant of the world crumbling around them. all they are bothered about is not being able to print.

Writing these strange tales in a format that people seem to like is cathartic, a way of me escaping my humdrum existence. It's my revenge for all the snotty emails and teeth gritting, having to be nice(ish) to people who have absolutely no intention of being nice to you.

If you see yourself in this story, or even in these short notes, then have a little think. Somewhere, you might just be getting killed in a horrific, gory, maybe even comedic manner by someone you've pissed off at work.

This is my time now to thank some people …

As always, my first thanks is to the ever-present shadow of Tony Higginson. He's not an editor, but he knows books. He shouts at me for using far too many exclamation points! he rages at me about using a timeline … which I have never done, yet his advice is golden.

Lauren Davies (my fiancé) lives through these books. The crazy fact of it all is she isn't even a huge horror fan. Before she met me, the nearest thing she'd read to horror was the Twilight Saga. Now she's proofreading Lovecraftian nightmares filled with gore and goo … For that, I thank you.

Lisa Lee Tone is a brilliant editor. Another one who shouts at me. She shouts mainly for my use of Americanisms (when the book is set in the USA). I'm from the UK, so a lot of the American way of life gets lost in my translation. That's why I set this book in Liverpool, just to do her head in again. Thanks, Lisa, you are brilliant.

Simon Green (RIP) came up with the original concept of the book cover after the travesty I put together. Although he did use my idea as the basis of the computer screens, the bloody hand was my idea! This guy is one of my oldest, truest friends. (#edit… Simon Passed away suddenly between edits of this book, and another book will be dedicated to him.)

My proofreaders, and my ARC readers from the various groups on Facebook. Without whose feedback I would be lost, are as follows:

Kelly Rickard is the FIRST, the LAST, and the EVERYTHING when it comes to proofreading. I would be in some mad danger of ridiculous typos and inconsistencies without her input. Fortunately for me, she actually likes my books and has read them all.

There are just TOO many friends and readers to mention, and if I start listing them I will undoubtedly miss someone out, THEN I'll be in trouble.

Lastly, but no means leastly, there's YOU, the reader. I love you in so many ways that I can't count (and you probably don't want to know about). Please keep reading, and (if the old and new Gods allow) I'll keep writing!

Dave McCluskey

Reboot: A Cosmic Horror

Liverpool
June 2020

9 781914 381096